"Entering a Paul Park universe means slipping into an eerily compelling plane where nearly palpable visions transform as disturbingly as the images in a sexually charged fever dream. . . . Park produces some beautiful writing here, as well as compelling insight into the nature of 'the world outside our blinkered range.'"
—*Publishers Weekly*

"Lurid. Violent. Melodramatic. Lewd and splendid. Filled with gratuitous sex, meaningless violence, erotic obsessions, tumescent monsters, and murder most carnal. The spellbound reader is drawn inexorably—kidnapped, as it were!—into the dark heart of the most profound inquiry into sexual and racial identity since Salman Rushdie's *Shame.* Paul Park at his inimitable best."
—Terry Bisson

"A brilliant and brutal exploration of what it means to be human, and what it means to be Other. *Celestis* mixes exhilaration and dread, memory and desire, into a postcolonial wasteland of guilt and insight, into sexuality, love, and slavery. Paul Park is one of the most important science fiction writers of the nineties."
—Michael Swanwick

Other books by Paul Park

Soldiers of Paradise
Sugar Rain
Cult of Loving Kindness

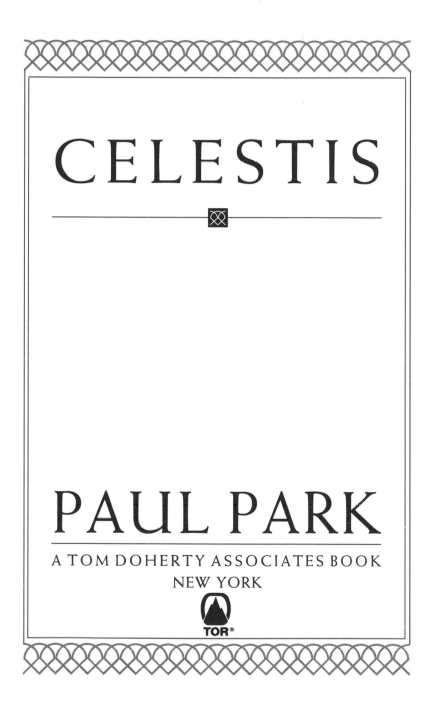

CELESTIS

PAUL PARK

A TOM DOHERTY ASSOCIATES BOOK
NEW YORK
TOR®

CELESTIS

Copyright © 1995 by Paul Park

This book is printed on acid-free paper.

A Tor Book
Published by Tom Doherty Associates, Inc.
175 Fifth Avenue
New York, NY 10010

Tor Books on the World Wide Web:
http://www.tor.com

Tor® is a registered trademark of Tom Doherty Associates, Inc.

Design by Lynn Newmark

Library of Congress Cataloging-in-Publication Data

Park, Paul.
    Celestis / Paul Park.
        p.   cm.
    "A Tom Doherty Associates Book."
    ISBN 0-312-86285-7 (pb)
    I. Title.
    PS3566.A6745C6   1995
    813'.54—dc20   95-4274
                                                        CIP

First hardcover edition: June 1995
First trade paperback edition: April 1997

Printed in the United States of America

0 9 8 7 6 5 4 3 2 1

This book is for

Terry Bisson
Dennis Boutsikaris
Ellen Datlow
David Eppel
Andrew Failes
Deborah Hedwall
Judy Jensen
Lisa Jose
Lynn Latson
Roger Lawrence
Shelley List
Martha Millard
Peter Murphy
Lisa Nowell
Jorge Pedraza
Rosemary Quinn
Stan Robinson
Carl Rubin
Audrey Thier

with love

CELESTIS

I

1a
Images from Home

She had been a guest of the family for a few days while she recuperated from a last round of treatments. She was fine. But in bed she was supposed to cover her mouth and throat with saturated gauze.

She had laid out the score for the sonata on the quilt. She sat cross-legged above it, trying to see some pattern in the clumps of notes, perhaps the hint of a landscape or a face. Something to help her; in her lap she had some postcards from England. Lake Windermere, Durham Cathedral, Trafalgar Square. Also a program—an actual program and not a photostat—from a John Bock performance of the *Emperor* Concerto at the Royal Albert Hall. A long time ago now; who could say how long? The date on it had no meaning. But surely Bock had died and gone to heaven.

Cries and laughter rose up from below the windows of

her room. They were playing an early game of croquet on the lawn. She sat rocking slightly on the quilt. She closed her eyes and raised the program to her lips, inhaling the faint fragrance of the world.

Another photograph lay on the sheet. She put the program down and stretched out her hand. She turned it over. It was a portrait of herself, taken a few years before. She was in makeup for a play at Ursuline, where she had gone to school.

She propped the photograph against a pillow. And then she began to strip away the gauze from her cheek, testing with a troubled hand the softness of her skin over her artificial jaw.

1b
The Consul

Well, in any case you'll have nice weather," said the consul from where he stood by the window. His tone seemed to suggest that it might rain.

Certain aphasics, unable to understand what is said to them, nevertheless can carry on whole conversations based on other clues. Simon, after eighteen months of practice, had developed part of the same sensitivity to gesture and to voice. Seated at his desk, fingering the red, white, and blue striped necktie he was already starting to regret, he thought about the little things.

The consul smiled. "I envy you," he said. "It sounds like a fun party." But the small waggle of his fingers seemed to indicate a different sentiment.

"Then why not take my place? Sir, the invitation is in your name. It's you they wanted all along—I barely know them."

The Fourth of July was a state holiday. The staff of the consulate had all stayed home. Simon's office had not been vacuumed since Friday; by Monday, a chalklike dust had covered all the surfaces. Now, on Tuesday, the consul's shoes brought up ridges of white dust as he walked across the carpet. "I'd love to," he said. "I'd really love to." Then he frowned. "But I have work to do." With his right toe he chafed the side of his left heel, leaving a small mark.

"Please, sir, I scarcely know them. If you'd really like to go, I think I can hold on here." Simon put his hand proprietarily on top of a stack of folders on his desk: purple, red, and orange, a spectrum of descending urgency.

The consul's face assumed a pained expression, as if it hurt him to be taken literally. Standing beside the desk, he reached his hand out for the orange folder. "No, no, my boy," he said. "You go. Please. Enjoy yourself. There'll be some . . . important people there."

Already distracted, he let his voice die away as he perused the first item in the folder. It was an oil lease that Simon was preparing for Extz (9) Petrolion, highly complex, but also highly futile. No one had heard from the company for more than two years.

As he read, the consul moved his lips. Simon turned his face away. "It's just that information on the offshore pipe," he said.

He watched the dust-cloth curtains stirring gently in the open window. The venetian blind threw strips of darkness back into the room, which faded as a cloud passed over the sun.

The ceiling fan above his head raised the corners of the papers on his desk. Simon got to his feet and walked over to the window. He peered through the slats of the blind down into the white street. Behind him, the consul had curled into an armchair with the folder in his hand, mouthing the words of the dead lease.

"I'd just as rather be excused," admitted Simon finally. "I don't get on with them at all, to tell the truth. They'll be at their worst on a day like this. They'll be dead drunk by three o'clock, and I'll be stuck between some fat engineer and some red-faced widow who'll be telling me how hard it is to find a proper cook."

"I see you checked the guest list," murmured the consul without looking up. "I know just whom you mean."

"I didn't have to. I was there last year. I don't have to go again; they dislike me already. They're racist, for a start. And then I had to go and admit that I didn't know their song, their 'Star-Spangled Banner' song. I'd never heard the tune."

"That's what we call 'expatriotism,'" said the consul, marking his place momentarily with his forefinger. "You must admit it must have irritated them to meet someone who had actually been to North America. It must have worried them. None of them has."

"I don't blame them. I was stupid to have brought it up. I just don't want to see them again."

A small wind rattled the slats of the venetian blind. Simon found the cord and pulled it sharply; the blind clattered upward and vanished into a slot at the top of the window frame. He pushed his hand out through the layers of white gauze until he touched the open air, and then he moved his arm to one side, clearing a two-foot gap. Unimpeded, the light beat down upon his cheeks and face, and thrust its way into the room. Behind him a stray paper left his desk and kited down onto the floor.

"Nevertheless," came the soft voice of the consul, "it is likely to be cooler in the hills."

The consulate stood in a neighborhood of flat-roofed

whitewashed houses not far from the port. Simon studied the expanse of rooftops, then looked down into the street. A man had come to the doorway of the house opposite, a stooped, attenuated form swathed in white robes. Hesitating, looking both ways, he stepped into the dust, dragging a small sledge down the ramp. Simon watched him labor up the street, his back bent, his head wrapped in strips of cloth.

"It's the way they treat them, that's what I can't stand," he said after a pause. "They work them to death in their mines and their damned fields, and all they talk about is how lazy they are, and how stupid, and how much they drink. I just can't stand it after a while."

He let go of the curtain and turned back into the room. "You exaggerate," replied the consul, raising his eyebrows without looking up from the folder. "Besides, there'll be some natives there. I think I read about it."

"Only their special pets. You'll see."

The consul had come to the end of the lease. He raised his head and studied Simon for a while without speaking. Then he shrugged. "Where is the invitation?" he asked. "Do I have it?"

"It's in there."

It was the fourth piece of paper in the folder. The consul held it up. "You're wrong," he said. "Junius Styreme will be attending, and his daughter. Weren't you telling me about her? She'll be performing a musical interlude—Beethoven's Piano Sonata no. 31, Opus 110. It seems a strange choice of music for a barbecue."

He lowered the invitation and looked at Simon over the top of it. "I've heard her play," he said. "She is not brilliant, except when you consider what she is. The amazing part is that she plays at all. Still, with all-new knucklebones . . ." He paused.

"It's the only reason I might go," conceded Simon, and the consul smiled.

He was a small, thin, arch, unmarried man. Expressions flitted quickly over his thin face: smiles without gladness, frowns without anger. "Don't think of it as a favor to me," he said, shifting in his chair. "Still less as a favor to yourself. You understand—nine-tenths of what we do here is for show. Especially now. The people in that sector are scared stiff. If sometimes they seem a bit intolerant, well, that's probably the reason."

"You mean the attack on Gundabook."

"Of course. Over the past few years twenty percent of the landowners in that area have sold their holdings and moved east. Jonathan Goldstone made a packet by buying up all that land for next to nothing, but that's not why he's doing it. He's doing it to demonstrate he's not afraid. That kind of courage deserves our support, regardless of what you or I might think of him personally. Or, I suppose, politically."

Simon listened for a while to the hum of the fan. "I suppose you're right," he sighed.

"Yes, and is it that much to ask, really, for one of us to drive up in the Rolls with the flags flying, and eat some fried chicken, and listen to a bit of Beethoven? It might give people the illusion of security. It's all we're really good for now that communications are so poor. This," he gestured toward the folder in his lap, "this is all nonsense."

It was impossible to tell, either from his tone or from the motion of his hand, if he was serious or not. Simon said, "If that's true, sir, wouldn't you want to take care of it yourself? I mean, if it's so important." But then he had to smile when his employer burst out laughing—a strange quick pantomime of mirth.

The consul's next face was a sadder one. Abstracted, furrow-browed, he sat staring at the medallion in the carpet, not looking up as Simon walked past him to sit down again behind his desk.

Many of the older colonists were drunks, and Simon often found himself sniffing the air around them as they spoke, as he tried to follow the false starts of their conversation. He suspected in his employer, however, a subtler, more private vice, a medication that didn't hinder precise speech or clear thinking, but attacked instead the will to move. Ever since Saturday, when the relay station had forwarded the video chip from New Manchester, the consul had not changed his clothes. He had slept on the couch in his office and eaten his meals at his desk. Yet during that time he had done no work, taken no calls. He had spent his time pacing the floor, or reading novels, or staring out the window. Calm moods succeeded anxious ones. In his office with the door closed, he had played the chip over and over.

"The car will be here at eleven," he said. He got to his feet. Standing in the middle of the carpet, he leafed through the orange folder to the end before replacing it on the desk. "There's one more thing," he said, touching the snowstorm paperweight on Simon's blotter. "You will be careful, won't you? I've given you a local driver, one who knows that area. He went to school up there. He's going to pass through Gundabook on the way, but don't get out. Don't stop. It's just to show the flag."

He was standing in front of Simon's desk, fiddling with the paperweight, flipping it idly in his hand. There was a dark stain upon the shoulder of his gray suit. Simon studied it. "What do you mean?" he asked. "What's the danger?"

The consul shrugged. The stain moved up a few inches and then subsided. "This is between us," he said. "Though some of it you know. Gundabook was burned by a group called the NLC, the National Liberation Coalition. But did you ever stop to think what *coalition* means?"

"Not really."

"No. Neither did I. But I received some information from the mayor's office. Someone claims to have seen demon tribesmen among the terrorists. Witnesses. What would you say to that?"

He held up the paperweight, so that snow fell softly over the Houses of Parliament. "What would you say?" he asked.

"I'd say I'd heard rumors. Then I'd say they'd been extinct for twenty years."

"Yes. Well, there is that." The consul smiled, then frowned. "And yet there's evidence. Photographic evidence." He paused. "You won't mention this at Goldstone, will you?"

"Of course not."

"You won't mention any of this. We've been abandoned—you understand that."

He spoke with uncharacteristic intensity, accompanied by a rare moment of eye contact. "You weren't born here. But I've seen things more trivial than this, and they had air force cruisers over Shreveport within six months standard time. Demons in the Territory—I told them about it. I described it."

He held up the paperweight. "Tell me," he said after a pause. "Does it ever really snow like this in London?"

Simon shook his head. "Not much."

The consul returned the paperweight to the desk, placing it on a corner of the blotter with exaggerated care. "You know what I'm talking about," he said.

"Sir, not entirely. I—" Distressed, Simon interrupted himself. The consul's face had closed momentarily into a pinched, aggrieved expression. In all the months that he had worked there, Simon had never seen it.

"There are five million Aboriginals under our jurisdiction here," said the consul. "Seventeen thousand of us. Morale is quite important."

"I see that."

"Anything that we could do, it would be helpful."

"Yes."

"I'm telling you so that you can see the urgency. So that you can act appropriately to reassure the people you meet this afternoon. Besides that, it's in confidence."

"I understand."

"You heard rumors. Perhaps I may have dropped a few hints myself."

"Yes, sir."

The consul fished in the baggy left-hand pocket of his suit and brought out a sealed envelope. "Take this to Jonathan Goldstone. Give it to him the moment you arrive. Don't tell him it's from me. Tell him we received it here."

He laid the envelope on the blotter. Then he took from the same pocket a piece of paper creased into quarters, crumpled and bent. Again, with exaggerated care, he laid it next to the envelope in front of Simon.

"It's Gundabook," he said. "Reverend Jamieson was taking pictures of a little league game directly before the attack. This was the last in the roll."

Simon unfolded the stiff paper and spread it out. He ran his fingernail along the row of hooded figures. They were facing toward the camera. Some had automatic weapons. Some had raised their fists.

"It's posed," he said.

"Of course. The camera was found abandoned at the scene."

In the photograph the Gundabook Youth Center was already on fire. Black smoke hid most of the facade. The terrorists had pulled out some of the bodies of their victims and arranged them on the lawn. Seven hooded Aboriginals stood in a row above and behind them, along the base of a pile of furniture which had been dragged out from the building. Two wore sweatshirts from the University of Shreveport.

"That one is Harriet Oimu," said the consul, indicating the central figure in the line. "All the others are still unidentified."

"What about the man?"

A human being stood apart on the top step. He was hooded like the others. He held the end of what might have been a chain in his right hand.

"Judas Iscariot," said the consul, his eyes glittering with abrupt moisture. "He has a cross on his lapel."

Even among the grains of the enlargement it was visible, pinned over the man's heart. The chain was less easy to make out. Perhaps the man had moved his hand. Or perhaps there was just a blemish in the print, and the mind required a clue to explain his connection to the demons. The adversaries. Seven feet tall at least, they rose from behind a debris of broken chairs. There were two of them, and one stood in front, showing its long, powerful naked legs. Its eloquent arms, its graceful hands were held out in a supplicating gesture.

Simon had studied the language at the Institute for Foreign Cultures at the Warburg. But he didn't recognize this paradigm.

"What does it say?" asked the consul.

"I don't know."

The consul sniffed. "I felt sure you'd tell me something. The governor said no one is supposed to see this. But I told him you had a right to know. Because you're going into danger. You have the right to be prepared."

"I don't recognize the shape. It's difficult in just a photograph."

The demon's face appeared in profile—earless, mouthless, sharp, unnatural. Its hairless and misshapen head was packed with alien brains. Just to see it, even in a picture, brought Simon a feeling of excitement, of inadequacy.

Of course the Aboriginals in the picture were alien too. But it was a long time since he had thought of them that way. The ones he knew, servants, and the prosperous folk he saw at parties and receptions, had been assimilated too completely. They were beaten down. Tamed. But this was the real thing, what he was looking for, perhaps, when he came out from Earth.

"Homo Celestis," he said.

All colonists, when pressed, had stories of their father's father's time, stories of the second expansion: how the demons had torched the farms and forced their native slaves against the barricades again and again, stinging their unaltered minds with violence and pain, not caring if they lived or died.

Simon had heard the consul's story before. Now he prepared for it again. He prepared his face. "When I was ten years old," the consul said, "my father's boys brought in the body of a little one, newborn. They had it hanging from a stick. And everyone was happy, because we thought it was the last we'd ever see. Its eyes were full of bugs. The boys had hacked it with their machetes. When my father came in through the curtain wall and got down from his jeep, they all fell onto their knees in the dust. The Aboriginals—they all were crying out with gratitude. The link was broken, they said. They said it was all done."

He shook his head and brought his fist up to his mouth. "By God, we were proud then. Proud of our own strength. We were the heroes then, with our therapies and drugs. Who could have predicted all this guiltiness?"

The fan went round and round. "Who could have predicted this?" he said. "Demon warriors in Gundabook. Everything we've done, and every choice we've made—look at them. Look at their guns, their clothes. Abos playing at rebellion after we've stuffed them full of Thomas Jefferson and Mao Tse-tung. Everything they are, they owe to us. It makes you sick."

1c
Katharine (i)

The first time she had seen the music she had known it was about the Virgin Mary. Beethoven was not even a Catholic, so far as she had heard. Still, she knew it must have been what he'd intended. When her father had managed to find a recording, a compact disk of Wilhelm Ganz, she had always listened to it starting with the second movement, not wanting to hear him play it differently.

The music already gave her an image that could not be altered. She felt the same way about other parts of the cycle. In Opus 81A, at times you could catch glimpses of another scene, the martyrdom of her name saint, Saint Catherine on the wheel, illuminated as if by lightning in the harsh cascades of notes. And the slow movement of Opus 13, she had relabeled on her score sheets "The Descent from the Cross." There too you could see the Virgin, particularly in the chords of the left hand—a hard, worn, solemn woman, her eyes dried out from crying.

But in the first movement of Opus 110, she was still young, and you could imagine a whole introductory passage full of a kind of ordered levity, a theme of the young virgin that Beethoven had never written down. Instead he had chosen to begin at the moment of the Annunciation, which was no angel in his version, but simply an A-flat-major triad, sudden, irrevocable, the first stirring of life in the girl's womb.

Katharine Styreme sat on her bed at Goldstone Lodge, studying the first page of the score. From that first chord the life of Christ flowed irretrievably away, and yet it was a small thing after all, intimate, mezzo piano, the first beat of a tiny fist, the first kick of His foot. And then a moment of calm doubt, of hope. My soul does magnify the Lord.

Katharine's wristwatch chimed the quarter hour, and she got up to take her pills. Her cosmetics case was lying open by the window seat; she fetched a glass of water and stood looking out the window to where some other guests played softball on the lawn. She fingered one of the brown capsules.

At this longitude the sun was less than halfway up the eastern sky. There was a gap cut in the oak trees, so it was visible from the house—it cast long shadows and a pleasant light through a ring of gathering clouds. She turned back into the room to admire its effect upon the wallpaper. This was the most luxurious guest room in Goldstone Lodge. The furniture, the glass was all imported. How many of her race, thought Katharine, had ever stayed here? Was she the first?

She swallowed the pills and drank most of the water. As she put the glass down on the window seat, there was a knock on the hall door. "Come in," she said and then waited, watching her father—it could only be he—rattle the knob for a full ten seconds before she crossed the carpet and pulled open the door.

He stood leaning on his cane. "I miss you," he said simply. "I came upstairs to take my medicine."

Katharine stepped aside to let him enter. He had changed into a new suit of clothes, beautifully cut and padded around his frail shoulders.

Yet even so, today he looked close to death. His hairpiece looked too big for him, and all the chemotherapy had left his skin unnaturally white, as if covered with dust. Out of breath, he took a few steps into the room, and for a moment Katharine imagined that she could hear the labor of his heart, so clotted and tumescent it could scarcely beat.

He reached out his left hand to her; she took it and led him over to the window. "My neck is stiff today," he complained. "Please come down and keep company. The concert is not for several hours." He peered around the room, his eyes enormous under his spectacles. "This is lovely," he said.

"Yes, Father, isn't it? It's nicer than my room last year."

"Last year Jonathan did not owe me so much money." Styreme reached out a brittle hand. He leaned forward so that he could peer out over the lawn. "Look at that cloud!" he said. "It is possible that it should rain."

--------- 1d ---------
Gundabook

A sour odor in the air, and Simon swallowed as he stepped into the car. To waste time, he made the driver go the long way round, by the esplanade and the embankment.

The port was silent that morning in honor of the holiday. Driving by the waterfront Simon could see five plump galleons in a line, wallowing in the roads. Out there the sea achieved a rich orange under the bright sky.

The sea was small and narrow: a lake, really, only a hundred miles long. The water was not deep. Close to shore its mineral content gradually increased, drawing the color of the water through a dozen lightening shades, merging finally with the dust-white shelf of the lagoon. Here and there cracks of pure water reached toward land, and these were full of boats. Simon could see activity out there: sticklike figures pulling sledges, stumbling across crusts of half-submerged alkali. And in the roads smaller boats passed back and forth among the anchored galleons, their dark sails mixing with the distance as they stood out from the land.

Eventually the Rolls turned from the waterfront and made its way back through the town. Near the purification plant they turned away from Lyndon Johnson Boulevard and passed through a shantytown of dockworkers' houses—a maze of iron rooftops and calcified mud walls. As Simon squirmed in the backseat, his driver gunned the engine through the narrow lanes, his finger on the horn. An old man leaped out of the way, and Simon leaned forward to object. He rapped his knuckles on the glass partition. But then already they were out, driving west on Frederick Douglass, up the ramp onto the causeway.

The lagoon stretched to the horizon on either side, a flat, unbroken plain. Here and there the wind had blown away the dust, revealing the hard black surface underneath, as slick and smooth as ice. Simon could see a lone boat heel upwind, precariously balanced on one blade.

Simon's driver hit the pedal and the great car shuddered forward. Recently cleared, the road ran fourteen miles without a bend until it found the white hills of the mainland. The car accelerated steadily, and soon it was surrounded by a roaring cloud of dust. Occasionally as it struck a patch of mineral accumulation it would fishtail ominously, until Simon reached for the speaking tube. "Please slow down," he directed. "Please don't wreck the car." And then as an afterthought: "Stop when you get to Gundabook."

They passed through the security checkpoint at the end of the causeway. The solitary policeman saluted as they drove by. Simon turned to watch him in the rearview mirror, a gaunt, gray, turbaned figure with a nightstick in his hand. Then he disappeared; the driver turned onto the expressway. Twenty miles to the south lay Shreveport, the American administrative center. East lay the melting desert under the changeless and unmoving sun. The car turned north and west, past Landfall.

Nine enormous domes stretched away perpendicular to the road, a line of silver prefabricated hills. They had been erected almost eighty years before, in hopes of a larger population, greater energy needs, back when the land reclamation project was still new and still successful. Two fission generators had been assembled; one was more than enough now. The rest of the domes were used to store equipment that had scarcely been unpacked, though some of it had been cannibalized for other projects.

Lately the domes had come under renewed demand as storage sheds, although the landing field was still quite distant. The car drove on past miles of transport company hangars and then past the railway depot. Its yard was filled with pyramids of molybdenite, each one covered with a tarpaulin and rubber tires; on the other side of the road, a mile or so off toward the sea, six petroleum storage tanks loomed up, again like topographical formations. In this landscape, among increasingly stupendous structures, it was as if the eye were being prepared for the last one, the sight of which could never actually be assimilated or understood—it was too huge. Landfall was the base of the elevator that led up to the station many hundreds of miles away.

Even its support structures were too big. The one nearest the road took five minutes to drive past: an undifferentiated mass of white concrete. The cable itself disappeared almost immediately up into the sky. Half an hour later Simon looked back and saw nothing. In the months after his arrival, from time to time he had glimpsed one of the counterbalancing freight cars, each a mile long. He had seen them catch the sun. Now of course the schedule was discontinued.

They left the shore and for an hour they climbed up through the hills, the colors changing around them as they protruded up into more temperate zones.

Here in this world the sun rose and set only for travelers. The colonists still talked about day and night and morning and evening, but it was out of a nostalgic habit, a collective memory. The words had no meaning under the inevitable sun. For Simon the slanted light, the long shadows in the strip of the planet where humans lived, suggested a perpetual afternoon. Now they drove west with the sun behind them toward the great meridian, the terminator line between the light and dark. After a while Simon switched off the air-conditioning and rolled down the windows. The air had lost its chemical taste.

Away from the shore the land acquired an unnatural beauty. When he first arrived in country Simon thought he'd never tire of it. He could not have anticipated a time when its strangeness did not fill him with hunger and contentment. Now as he leaned back against the leather seats, he tried to think about his change of heart.

Sometimes now he found himself nostalgic even for things he'd always hated, for the dreary, rainy streets of his childhood in Golders Green, for the concrete towers which stank of urine, of brussels sprouts and beer. He would never smell that smell again, and it was gone. Gone for good.

Perhaps, he thought as he stared out the window of the speeding car, it was just those words, something magical about those words that brought a tight feeling to his throat. There was nothing rational about it. There was nothing in his past to miss. Except the structure of the day, the proportions and rhythms of human life, there where the sun rose and set, where morning followed night, where summer followed spring.

When he had first arrived in country, he had been astonished by so many things—the richness and the waste, the enormous gasoline-powered cars, the stupefying variety of food. But above all by the constant daylight on the bright side of the world. For months it seemed to him that he would never get tired, when at three o'clock in the morning he found himself walking the streets of Shreveport under the yellow sky, snapping his fingers, humming to himself. Two hours of sleep were all he needed as his mind dried out under the immobile sun and his memory of the drizzling clouds of London broke and pulled away. Later he would park his bike along the roads and run out upon the white salt pan, invigorated by the lighter gravity, the caustic wind.

But now today as he leaned out the window, the air seemed to whistle through his lungs, bringing no nourishment. The hills seemed sterile, grim: a hundred miles without a blade of grass. And when they came out of the Zabrisky Tunnel and into Crystal Reef, even that gleaming landscape was depressing to him. The sight of it seemed burdensome. Few cars passed them, and he was aware of the thin road weaving through the vast formations, and himself upon that road, isolated, insignificant. The light cascaded from the quartzite slopes; it hurt his eyes; it dripped from the pinnacles of raw quartz; it was like water in this desiccated land.

They rose to the level of the plateau. The country underwent another change here. They passed through striations of white crystal and gray schist, mixed with bentonite and clay. A succession of unnatural shades: yellow, pink, orange, red, and then they were up on the plateau, and Simon could see mountains in the distance. Here he let his breath out in relief, for they were coming into places that human hands had at least touched. Touched and altered. They passed an abandoned pump station, and the road followed a ditch, long dry. Simon stared out the window. He listened to the pebbles rattle off the fender of the car.

They passed a thorn tree, then a row of cottonwoods. It had been an enormous project to make soil here on a world without photosynthesis. And even though desert reclamation was one of the half-dozen or so human sciences for which necessity had proved to be the mother of invention over the past two hundred years, still the work had been full of failures and defeats. In other places the bacteria had held on longer, combined more fruitfully with sand and clay. Even when they passed the irrigation line, it remained a harsh landscape. Though now there were occasional trees, and fields of dry weeds on either side of the road.

Harsh. And boring, also. They were still ninety miles from Goldstone Lodge. Simon rolled the window up and laid his cheek against it. In time he fell asleep and he could feel the car bound forward, as if partially released from the burden of his consciousness.

When he woke, it was swerving wildly. He sat up and looked forward through the glass partition in time to see the driver glance back at him in the rearview mirror. Sweat trembled on the driver's lips.

They came up over a rise and found themselves suddenly among a clump of houses. Shadows flickered on the roadway up ahead. Simon saw the driver's fingers hover over the horn, saw him glance again into the rearview mirror. Then there was movement on the road, a streak of black on the right-hand side. The driver hit the horn, twisted the wheel, but not in time: there was a concussion off the right side of the fender before he stomped down on the brake.

The car slid to a halt amid a shower of grit. Simon listened to the sound of gravel pinging off the roof. He had struck his head against the door handle. Raising himself up, rubbing his eye, he was surprised to see his driver sitting motionless in the front seat, his head bowed down below the level of the windscreen, almost to the center of the wheel.

For an instant Simon thought the fellow had been hurt. "Ah," he said, opening the door on his left side and stepping out into the road. He reached for the driver's door and pulled it open; the man was trembling. His head was bowed and his lips were moving. He was examining the center of the steering wheel, his eyes closed into slits.

Simon felt light-headed. He straightened up and looked over the roof, and it was not until then that he heard a whimper coming from the other side of the car.

They had hit a black dog, a Labrador shorthair mix. It lay with a broken spine ten feet beyond the right front wheel, its tongue hanging in the dust. Simon walked over to it; he squatted down and lifted up its heavy head. The creature growled and tried to bite him. "Get the gun," called Simon, and when he looked around again, he saw his driver standing by the open door. He had fetched the Aurox machine pistol from behind the seat. Immediately Simon ducked behind the fender, but the man just stood there with the gun over his arm.

"Christ, no!" shouted Simon. "Not that one. There's a twenty-two in the glove compartment. No, never mind." The dog started suddenly, opened its mouth as if to vomit, and lay still.

"Gundabook," whispered the driver.

For the first time, Simon looked around.

The car had come to rest near the center of a small square, surrounded on three sides with two-story brick buildings. Several of these had been burned and stripped by vandals: a bank, a dispensary, a feed store, a church. Their rough facades were dark with soot and daubed with white graffiti—KILL A PIG; FREE THEODORE OIMU; even, Simon noted with surprise, YANKEE GO HOME.

In the center of the square stood a twelve-foot replica of the Statue of Liberty, painted over with slogans of the NLC. Her head had been struck off, and it had rolled into a litter of broken bottles and burnt cans, extending out from the entrance to the store.

Simon stood up. The shadow from the decapitated statue slanted deep and black almost to the corpse at his feet. The sun loaded him down with a burdensome glow; there was no wind. The little flags on either side of the hood hung limply from their staves—the Union Jack, the Stars and Stripes. Symbols of countries that no longer existed except here, in people's minds.

"We should find the owner of the dog," he said.

"Dog, no owner."

A cluster of low buildings, round huts of a typical Aboriginal design, stood behind them along the fourth side of the square. A man squatted on his hams near the entrance to one of these, his shirttails out, his face obscured by a pair of sunglasses.

"No," said Simon. "Put that gun away. There's no one here." He rubbed his hands together and then wiped them with his handkerchief. Lu (4) Slut, in Camden Town, had kept a Labrador.

He stuffed the handkerchief into the side pocket of his jacket and walked the few steps back toward the car. The driver didn't move. He just stood there shaking his head, his white face twisted up, his painted lips trembling. "Primitive," he said at last, his mouth contorted with the effort of speech. He pointed toward the gutted church and then crossed himself expertly, right to left, left to right.

What did he mean? What did they ever mean? The driver was an altered Aboriginal, which meant he took his choice of one of twelve chemical compounds. Developed to break the link between the demons and their Aboriginal slaves in the old days, they had since been refined to give pleasure, to regulate mood, to block up neural passages, to smooth unnatural fluctuations in the patterns of the brain, to reproduce, as far as it was possible in alien creatures, the experience of human thought.

But did they work? Simon always asked himself. How could you know? The driver could never have afforded the more complicated, personally coded medications that allowed high functioning—not like the Styremes or, Simon supposed, most of the NLC. The man's jaw hung slack. Was he afraid? There had been a demon in this place. Perhaps he sensed it.

Simon looked at his watch. It was so quiet here. The human town was abandoned. Simon turned and walked away toward the native lines, toward where the man had squatted with his sunglasses. The driver protested: "Sir, please, sir." But Simon ignored him. He walked back through the square—empty now.

He moved through the huts of the service community. It was not large. The real Aboriginal town lay behind it on the other side of the embankment.

Clouds were forming near the sun. Happy to be outside after two hours in the car, he climbed to the top of the gravel ridge and crossed the railway tracks, which curved away into the distance toward Deseret. The Aboriginal encampment lay beneath his feet, as he expected. It was built along a refuse dump. Compared with the gutted town behind him, it was full of life.

No civic codes were enforced here. The encampment spread at random over half a mile, streetless, without water, without power. Tarpaulin houses. Metal, plywood shacks. People lived in junked cars, in hundred-gallon drums. Many of the houses seemed only a few feet high; men crawled in and out of them on their hands and knees. Others had put down sheets of cardboard over the ground, and they lay on them under black umbrellas. It was a fine, cool day.

Simon turned to the left and walked along the tracks, away from the station. People knelt beneath him, relieving themselves, vomiting up their excretions in a way that never failed to disgust him.

There were no trains anymore; down below, people lived in holes dug into the slope and lined with plastic. Concrete culverts held whole families.

He heard a noise on the gravel behind him and turned around. An Aboriginal stood there about ten feet away.

He was less than five feet tall. Smaller than Simon's driver, and different, too. Aboriginal servants in Shreveport and the Territory usually underwent some surgery, paid for by their families or their employers, to make their faces tolerable. Something to give expression to their blank features. Just pieces of plastic bone under the skin, hints of brow lines and noses and cheekbones and chins, and they would learn to move them in vague approximations of smiles and frowns. Otherwise communication was too difficult, too disconcerting.

But this man on the railroad track was untouched, raw. He stood hunched over, his back and shoulders round, his arms long, his hands practically fingerless—thick and clumsy. Yet he was the shape of a human being, and for that reason he was difficult, almost painful, to look at closely. Simon's eyes seemed to want to change him, to fill in details, stretch him up straight, straighten his limbs, put his small bald head into proportion. Automatically they did so, and it was only through a conscious effort of will that Simon could look at him clearly, examine him as the man came closer, for he was approaching on his short legs with graceful, mincing steps. His face was meaningless, that's all—pale and un-formed, full of small wrinkles and ridges that went nowhere and made no pattern. And in the middle of it a lipless hole. A toothless mouth, and above it, two amber-colored eyes.

There was nothing threatening about him. He was not strong or fast. His movements seemed tentative, unsure. Yet Simon stepped backward along the railway track and put his hand up as the Aboriginal got close, as if to ward off an at-tack.

Two holes near the juncture of its neck: its ears. It clamped its padded palms over them and squatted down, and turned away its face back toward the town. Was it respond-ing to him? Or perhaps to something else, and Simon turned his head also, half expecting to hear from that direction a loud and painful voice.

1e
Demons (i)

IN OUR MINDS WE ARE ALONE. HERE IN THIS DARK. O SLAVE O SLAVE O MAN. DO NOT HURT. DO NOT TAKE US UP. INTO THIS SUN. NO MORE. NOT AGAIN. NO.

The Party

But he heard nothing. Simon looked back over the roofs of the deserted houses toward where his car stood in the middle of the square. And it occurred to him suddenly that the NLC might still be here, hidden in some vacated building. That they might have sneaked back to the site of their most conspicuous success, to be within striking distance of a number of rich and isolated targets. The thought came borne to him as if upon a tiny wind, that Harriet Oimu might think of this town as a kind of home. Perhaps that was why the consul had asked him to pass through.

These ideas occupied him as he walked back toward the car, and for the rest of the drive. They colored his mood, darkened it as the weather darkened, as a storm built slowly out of nothing.

At one o'clock the sun was hidden by a nimbus of bright clouds, the only clouds in all the sky. The air seemed heavy, and as Simon drove the last few miles, the clouds spread out from that single source, forming in complicated lines, undisturbed by any breath of wind until they covered the whole sky. And then the rain came, a sudden cloudburst.

The land from Gundabook was fertilized and irrigated. It changed around him as he drove: its essential differences gradually submerged under layers of civilization. The salt cliffs, the orange, white, and yellow mineral formations disappeared, replaced instead by dirt and fields of grass. With the rain new smells came to him, smells of home. Once his school had made a trip into the country. It had taken hours to get there, through miles of semi-abandoned suburbs. Once they finally arrived, it had been wet and green.

Here greenness was still rare even after generations of effort. The road ran straight toward the mountains, through fields and fences on both sides. Rain spattered the windscreen. Each drop liberated a new smell.

At the signpost he turned east off the main road. He passed through a security check—two men in denim shirts. Their red armbands were each marked with a crude stick figure like something drawn by a child. They saluted his car as he came through, although they were not soldiers.

He passed a pair of wrought iron gates decorated with the Goldstone coat of arms—oil derricks on a yellow field. Outside of them the grass was crisp and sere. This rain was a rare occurrence. But once he was inside the walls, the pelting drops seemed more appropriate. Sixty years of irrigation had turned the park into a jungle. Palmettos, jacarandas, and magnolias, imported at miraculous expense, had grown up into tangled thickets, while along the drive the oak trees were already fifty feet high. Through them Simon caught intermittent glimpses of the Lodge, a rectangular mansion modeled on the White House in Washington. Jonathan Goldstone's grandfather, so the story went, had given his builder a Xerox copy of a fifty-dollar bill and told him to do his best.

The car drove over a stone bridge a half mile from the house. A small stream choked with cattails curled away on either side. It marked the boundary of the undergrowth; from the far bank the grass swept up over a long slope, up to the porch of the main house, where it broke on shoals of ornamental flowers. Here and there under the trees slow fountains of spray swept back and forth, redundant in the rain.

Simon parked on the grass under a large tulip poplar at the end of a long line of cars that wound down from the house. He sat drumming his fingers on the steering wheel, waiting for the rain to stop. Then he turned and looked through the partition into the rear seat. The driver lay on his back, snoring through his nose.

At Gundabook, when Simon returned to his car, he had found the driver drunk already. The man had taken a bottle from the passenger's bar and guzzled a whole mouthful. Simon had been gone for hardly twenty minutes, but the fellow was already incapable of driving. Simon loaded him into the back, where he had immediately lost consciousness. A new record, Simon thought a little bitterly, leaning his elbows over the partition. He picked up the flask of bourbon from its rack.

Someone was knocking on the glass above the driver's head. Simon reached over and opened the door, revealing Ronald Starker in the gap, holding an umbrella. He started in at once: "Mayaram, old chap, thought you might need some shelter."

He peered into the car, puzzled by the sight of the driver in the backseat. "I say," he continued as Simon replaced the flask upon its shelf, "you didn't give him whiskey, did you?"

Simon eyed him with dislike. He had met Starker several times at official gatherings in Shreveport, and he was always the same—his suit immaculate, his manners idiotic. He was a character out of musical comedy, a parody of a Englishman, and Simon suspected that the role had been assumed for his benefit. Even now, when he was clearly distressed, there was a hint of mockery in Starker's tone. "You mustn't give them whiskey. That's the first rule out here. Never give them whiskey. They don't have the head for it."

Starker himself looked far from sober. Simon shrugged. "We had an accident," he said, getting out of the car. Under the tree the rain had almost stopped.

"We can't just leave him," said Starker. "Not with these bottles here. He'll kill himself." He handed Simon the umbrella and leaned into the car, pulling out the liquor from the rack. "We'll lock them in the trunk," he said, taking the car keys from Simon's hand.

His accent had flagged while he was speaking, but once he had safely stowed away the liquor, it came back. "An accident, you say?"

"At Gundabook. We hit a dog."

"Bad show."

Simon retrieved his keys, and they walked in silence toward the house under the pattering umbrella.

Ronald Starker was a delicate man with yellow hair and a sly, foolish face. But his moustache was robust; it curled aggressively over his thin cheeks. Simon examined the man's upper lip for evidence of glue. "But what's the point?" he asked himself, angry in a bored sort of way. He resisted the impulse to reach out and snatch the moustache from the fellow's face. What if it was real? Serve him right—no one had used the phrase *bad show* in legitimate conversation since 1936.

On the lawn they passed remnants of a dismantled softball game. Servants moved over the grass, picking up bats and leather mitts while players and spectators on the porch rubbed themselves with towels. One or two waved at their approach.

Starker smiled and raised his left hand above his head. "Be thankful you've missed playing their ridiculous game," he said. "Not like cricket, eh?"

"I hate cricket," Simon answered untruthfully, for he had never played. But the man was gone. He had pulled up the lapels of his jacket and sprinted the last few yards to the porch. A pretty girl came down to meet him, carrying two glasses of champagne.

Simon shook his head. Above him the clouds presented a hard, roof-like surface, and it had gotten dark.

He stooped to pick up a first baseman's mitt lying in the grass near his feet. When he straightened up, he saw his hostess waiting to greet him. She stood away from the others, alone on the lowest step, holding out her hand.

"I'm so happy you could come," she said in the sweet southern drawl she had inherited from her mother. "It's Mr. Mayaram, isn't that right? You'll have to excuse us—we were expecting your consul, Mr. Clare."

A steward bent to light a hurricane lantern on the flight of steps behind her, and it shone down on her cloud of soft white hair. Though a small woman, Naomi Goldstone gave an impression of serenity and power. She stood erect, her big head carefully balanced at the end of her long neck, her hand stretched out in front of her. She wore a simple dress of Chinese silk.

"I'm afraid he couldn't come," said Simon. "He had a reception at the governor's." Lowering the umbrella so that he could hold the baseball glove under his armpit, he reached out to touch her fingers.

"We sent Ronnie Starker down to see if you were all right. I hope he made you feel at home?"

"Not exactly," Simon confessed. Mrs. Goldstone laughed and stepped onto the grass. She was barefoot.

She took the mitt from underneath his elbow and slipped her right hand in where it had been. She turned him away from the house and walked him a few steps back out onto the lawn, while he held the umbrella over them both. "Well, yes," she said. "I suppose he must be irritating to a real Britisher."

"A little. He can't really talk like that. I mean all the time."

"Why, no, of course not. His parents were Australian. He just does it to make fun of you."

"Yes," said Simon. "I'm surprised he thinks I'm worth the trouble."

"Well, yes, it is surprising, isn't it?" Mrs. Goldstone burst out laughing, and then she hushed herself by raising the baseball mitt up to her lips. "Oh, dear," she said. "Mr. Mayaram, you don't mind if we tease you? The most interesting single man left in the Territory—you don't mind if Ronnie's jealous?"

They were standing near the center of the lawn, looking back toward the house. The rain hit the umbrella with fat, resonating drops. Twenty or thirty people gathered around a covered table on the porch where the steward was serving champagne. Some of the men were dressed in black tie, some in uniforms or blazers, and some wore shorts and T-shirts. Among the women there was a similar range of style. Most wore long gowns, but some had on blue jeans, and six or seven were in bathing suits. They had come up from the pool when it had started to rain.

"That's my daughter," said Mrs. Goldstone, indicating a young woman in a net bikini. Then she turned back toward him. "Tell me, Mr. Mayaram," she said, squeezing his arm, "you don't happen to own a dog, by any chance? No? Well, then maybe you'd better go wash up. You must be tired after your long drive."

Simon let his smile solidify as he escorted her back toward the steps. Two elderly women came down to greet them, and Simon stayed long enough to be introduced. He held up the umbrella for a while, but at the first break in the weather he abandoned his post. When the first crack opened in the solid surface of the clouds, he made his excuses and ran up the steps onto the porch. Consigning the umbrella to the depths of an ornamental urn, he passed into the house through the glass doors, looking for a bathroom.

"Is it racism?" he asked himself as he walked down the hall. "Is that all it is? Is that why they're like that?" The bathroom door seemed to be stuck and he forced it open, revealing a native houseboy sitting on the floor. The space was cramped and narrow and the man seemed to take up most of it. His legs were crossed, his hands folded on his breast in the five bugs position.

His eyes were closed, "turned inward," as his people said. His right hand was trembling slightly. A small vibration seemed to emanate from it, seemed to produce a small hum. Ordinarily Simon would have shut the door and gone. But he was angry. Or half angry and half curious—he stood knocking his fingers on the jamb until he heard a noise behind him. A woman was there; she stepped past him into the room, and with the string of her apron she hit the man across the face. "Lazy," she said, her native accent weird and harsh, "lazy, lazy boy." Her spine was twisted, whether from surgery or some natural deformity, so it was hard for her to hit the man with any strength. Nevertheless, he brought his hands up to protect his face. The humming noise shifted in pitch, and Simon closed the door.

Opposite, a little farther down, another door was labeled WOMEN on a thumbtacked piece of paper. Simon left it open while he washed his face and hands. Leaning forward on the sink, he examined himself in the heart-shaped mirror. The water beaded on his dark cheeks, dripped from his dark chin.

These people's parents and grandparents and great-grandparents had landed on an astonishing new world. From Goldstone Lodge, five days' drive over the terminator, and you were at Shackleton Station on the ice. From there in the freezing darkness, you could actually see into the center of the galaxy. With your naked eyes you could see into the black hole that was the galaxy's black heart. You could see stars break apart. But here they were playing baseball and beating their servants; not one of them, Simon was sure, had made that trip.

Someone was playing a piano on the other side of the wall. Or rather, someone was playing one chord over and over. Someone was banging the piano like a gong, yet each time the sound was different. Each time there was some small difference in force, volume, clarity. The sound stopped for a moment and then started again.

Simon wiped his hands and combed his hair. He flushed the toilet even though he hadn't used it, and walked out into the hall. He followed the sound of the piano through four empty drawing rooms until he found one with some people in it.

As suddenly as it had started, the storm had cracked apart. Simon squinted at the new sunlight pouring in along a wall of high French windows. Rents and fissures had broken the black clouds; patches of shadow and reflected light complicated the tiled pattern of the floor. Simon hesitated at the doorway. Junius Styreme stood on a gleaming square of marble in a corner of the room. His daughter sat next to him at the bench of a grand piano.

Styreme stood leaning on his cane, nodding to himself. Simon guessed that his suit had cost a thousand dollars; still it did nothing to hide the old man's essential difference or his proximity to death. A lifetime of psychotropic medication had turned his bones to brittle sticks. Anticollagen, the aging fluid, had made a cancer blossom in his heart. It had frozen his joints, knotted his fingers into claws.

By contrast Katharine Styreme was a miracle of art: her glossy black-red hair, her beautifully sculpted face. Her head was bent almost to the keys. As Simon approached over the gray and white stone tiles, she turned her head toward him and then stood up in confusion as the last chord died away.

Yet she had changed even since Simon had last seen her at the banker's reception in the capital. Surely then her waist had not been so narrow. Or perhaps then her dress had not been so tight. She wore a golden crucifix around her neck, attached to a small chain.

"I'm sorry to disturb you," he said. Styreme's eyes had vanished underneath his spectacles. They had closed down into slits. But Simon thought he sensed a flicker of warmth in the smile on Katharine's face. Perhaps it was just politeness, but perhaps she recognized him—at the reception they had been introduced. She had asked about the acoustics in the Royal Albert Hall.

But before he could verify what kind of smile it was, it disappeared. The loathsome Ronnie Starker had materialized in another doorway and was calling out to them. His shoes skittered over the floor.

"Don't mean to interrupt, old chap," he said, winking as he sidled past. "Naomi's orders. Guests of honor, what?" And then to Junius Styreme: "I've been sent to find you. There's champagne being served on the porch."

"We do not drink." The old man's eyes were scarcely visible.

"No, of course not. But there's real apollinaris. Last you'll ever see."

More voices. From the doorway behind Simon, two men came into the room, dressed in Stetsons and string ties. They were drinking beer out of plastic cups. One was Simon's age, the other ten years older. The young one had a bad complexion. He put his hand on his companion's arm. "Oh, Christ," he said.

The young man wore a sharkskin coat, the older man a yellow shirt with pockets and pearl buttons. A miner named John Grant, he had been at the party last year. He too frowned when he saw Styreme, but then his brow cleared, and he came toward Simon with his hand out. "Well, if it ain't Karl Marx," he said. "What happened to you this year, boy? We were dying out there. Twelve to five before the game was called."

He had a lump of platinum in his belt buckle the size and shape of a toad. "Simon Mayaram," said Simon, shaking his hand.

"Yes, I remember. You're with the consulate."

Ronald Starker was pulling the Styremes away, out the other door. The old man was leaning on his daughter's arm.

Something about they way she looked, something about the sheer planes of her face seemed to suggest a crust over immeasurable depths. Her heavy lips, her long and narrow jaw—she was so different from the wives and daughters of the colonists. There was even, thought Simon, something exotic in the way she smelled. "God damn it," said the younger man, "they sure do stink. No matter how they hide it. You can always tell when they've been in a room."

John Grant shrugged. "She's all right, I guess."

"From the outside. That's a million dollars' worth of split genes you're looking at. Plastic surgery. Real seductive till you get up close."

"What do you mean?"

"No vagina. Old man wouldn't spend the extra twenty grand. Because they're Roman Catholics. Marry her, he just might throw it in. Sweeten the deal."

John Grant shook his head. "I won't ask you how you know," he said.

"Don't ask." The younger man thrust out his hand. "Spike Laudenberg," he said.

"Simon Mayaram."

"Listen," said Spike Laudenberg. "No, wait—you need a beer." He clamped his fingers under Simon's elbow. "They've tapped a couple of kegs out on the grass. Coors all right?"

He led them back through the doorway and a series of L-shaped corridors out onto a side veranda and down onto the lawn. An old servant was dispensing beer around the corner from the porch, under the shade of a rhododendron tree. He had a wide, fat face and a gap between the ceramic ridges of his teeth.

"Coors all right?" asked Laudenberg again. Simon shrugged. Suddenly thirsty, he took a big swallow from the plastic cup that had been thrust into his hands. Yet the girth of the cup was so tremendous, the level of the beer scarcely seemed to recede no matter how hard he sucked at it; finally, out of breath, he lowered the rim and stared out over the wet grass, glinting in the sudden sun. The consul had been right. It was a beautiful day.

In the distance the storm pulled back over a line of charcoal-colored hills. Above him a warbler was singing in the rhododendron tree, an imported bird that was quickly dying out after having destroyed most of the local insect life. A sweet sound nevertheless.

"Listen," said Spike Laudenberg. "I wondered if you could tell us any news."

Simon took another swallow. Then he shook his head. "I'll tell you what I know. The consul has sent four messages to New Manchester, at two month intervals. Since then the situation has deteriorated, of course."

"That's all anybody knows," said Laudenberg. "But you were there. Fuck New Manchester—you were on Earth. You were there more recently than anyone."

Simon had arrived in country about two years before, on the last ship to have carried passengers. Except for him, they had all been scientists headed for Shackleton Station on the planet's dark half. He was the only one who had stayed in Shreveport.

He nodded. "My news—that kind of news—is forty years out of date. More than forty years. It doesn't mean anything."

"Well, tell me," the man persisted. "Whatever you know. Was there a revolution? A war?"

Simon shook his head. "I can't give you the answer that you need. These words, they don't mean what you think. Not anymore. Not when I was there. God knows what they mean now."

There was a pause. Then John Grant continued as if Simon had said nothing: "Doesn't make any sense. If there's a war, I've got a thousand tons of aionium super-heavy just decomposing on the siding. They could have it cheap."

Six or seven other men had come up from the beer kegs. They were dressed in cowboy boots and western shirts, the ubiquitous uniform of west-country miners. Like John Grant they were tough, burned, anxious men; the last year had been hard on them. The breakdown in communications, on which their livelihood depended, was not unprecedented in the colony. But this one had corresponded with a seismic murmur of civil discontent.

"No joke," said one. "I've got six months' worth of work just rotting in the shed. The only reason it's not more is because of that Jewish lawyer from the C.L.U. No offense," he said, looking around at nobody. "My boys have been out for nineteen weeks, which saves me paying them. But if I see that son of a bitch on my property again, I'll shoot him without fail. What if this had been a normal year?"

Long hours at official receptions had drained Simon's capacity for outrage. At least it was a beautiful day. While preserving an outward look of rapt absorption, he allowed his attention to expand. Fifteen feet beyond the miner's head, a greasybug slid through the air, emitting its slow drone. Nodding thoughtfully, Simon watched the warbler leave its perch.

"Nothing like that," he said. "Local troubles, that's all. They have murders now. Riots. Suicides instead of war. There's not a lot to fight for."

Spike Laudenberg was watching him. "That never stopped anyone before. What about disease?"

Uncomfortable, Simon looked down. Yet still he felt the pressure of the miner's stare upon his cheek. He could feel the man assessing him, weighing him, finding him wanting, and at that moment the pressure was relaxed. Laudenberg grunted and turned away.

"I get a bad feel from this," he said to Grant. "Really bad. It's an environmental thing, I'm sure of it."

He took a stick of gum from the pocket of his suit. His eyes were clear and blue.

The older miner shook his head. "It's so darn frustrating. Six years ago I had a chance to diversify, but everyone was making so much money, it just didn't make sense. Now it's too late."

Simon frowned. He made a little clucking noise of sympathy with his tongue, and then took another swallow of beer. The beer was definitely a help. He wondered now why he so rarely took the precaution of drinking to excess. All those sober moments—now they seemed like such a waste.

"You got that right," said another man. "I'm just sitting on my hands. Domestic market, damn it all to hell. Christianman . . ."—here he named a native businessman—"Christianman has sewed that shit up tight."

"Domestic market," repeated Simon, nodding sagely. He

thought: mere drunkenness is not enough. Not unless it leads directly to unconsciousness. The miner kept on talking, explaining the iniquities of the Christianman cartel— how, by cunning manipulation of the quotas set aside for Aboriginals, they had established several important and unfair monopolies. Simon studied the man's lips and tried to estimate how much he would have to drink before unconsciousness might intervene. He pictured himself sliding to the turf, a blissful smile on his face, while John Grant fanned him with a towel. Too late he realized how astute his driver had been. The man had seen his opportunity and had jumped on it.

"That Abo son of a bitch," continued the miner. "He won't be satisfied until we're dead."

An immaculate new world, thought Simon, and on it they had resurrected all of the most shameful and most boring aspects of the bad old days. How had they managed it? Out of bad books and bad films—nothing like this had existed on Earth for hundreds of years.

"Never satisfied," he said. He took another gulp of beer. He seemed as far from the bottom of the cup as ever.

"Whoa there," said a low voice by his side. "You'll never last till dinner at that rate."

Simon lowered his cup. Beside him stood his hostess's daughter, the girl whom Naomi Goldstone had pointed out to him before. She had changed from her bikini and was wearing what appeared to be a man's dress shirt and nothing else.

She put her fingers on his arm. "Natasha Goldstone. My mother sent me out to look for you. She said you had nice eyebrows."

The miner had taken his hat off, and Natasha smiled. "Let's get away from here," she whispered, pulling Simon by the arm. "There's more people to talk to than this bunch." Nevertheless she nodded to Spike Laudenberg, and then they had turned around and were walking toward the house. She laughed. "I'm not positive about the eyebrows, but Mother was sure right about the rest. Those guys are the biggest assholes here. No wonder you're half sloshed."

They walked along a gravel pathway flanked on either side by tiny bushes. "No wonder," agreed Simon companionably. His heart, which had sunk into his stomach during the past few minutes, now surged importantly inside his chest. He examined Natasha with appreciation. Her black hair was wild around her face and shoulders, an unbrushed mass of curls. Her features were irregular; Simon imagined that someone seeing her in profile from the right side and the left might think that he was looking at two different women, or perhaps the same woman in different moods. Her nose and mouth protruded forcefully. She had long, naked legs.

"So what's the verdict?" asked Natasha. Embarrassed, Simon turned away. But she was pulling on his arm and laughing. "Anyway, it's not me you should be looking at. I'm more of a go-between for the guest of honor."

"Mr. Styreme?"

"God, you are a dunce. I mean his daughter, though I warn you, it'll be hard to tell. But I was helping her with her nail polish and I mentioned your name. She said she had met you at a reception for her father and that you were interesting—that's a direct quote. A first for her. She's never said that about any man before, so I assumed the rest. She'd be furious if she knew."

Simon heard the small chug of a walnut beetle somewhere over to his left. His face felt hot and strange. "So you might be mistaken."

Natasha shrugged her shoulders. "Of course I might. In

fact, I probably am. But if you have better things to do—God, I'm sorry to have dragged you from your friends."

"You're right. I'm sorry. I'm just surprised you spoke about me. How did you guess I was coming?"

Natasha laughed. "I had a bet with my mom. We were speculating, because Dad said that his invitation was a test, that if the consul came himself, it would mean at least one person in the administration was on his side. But if they sent a flunky, that meant they'd abandoned him. But of course Mom and I had our fingers crossed, because we figured that the flunky they'd send would probably be you, and at least you're good-looking. And well-traveled, to say the least."

They had reached the corner of the house. Natasha Goldstone seemed to have a lot of cuts and scratches on her right shin. Simon studied them, and then he raised his head. "Do you know her well?" he asked.

"Who?"

"Katharine Styreme."

"We used to go to summer camp on Lake Meninjau. Before that we were in school together, only I couldn't tolerate the nuns."

"So you're friends."

"That's the idea. God, Momma told me you were hopeless, but she never said you were a moron. She said you could speak five languages."

Simon dumped his beer out on the grass and looked into the bottom of his cup. "I'm sorry," he said. "And I'm grateful that you rescued me back there. But Katharine Styreme, it's just that, well, she's lovely, isn't she?"

Natasha gaped at him and then she laughed. "You poor jerk," she said. "It's all right—I forgot where you were from."

She seized him by the hand again and pulled him over the lawn. "And get rid of that stupid cup," she said as they climbed the steps onto the porch. "They're drinking real champagne in there. Like from France or someplace."

Simon could hear a string quartet warming up somewhere. A crowd of people gathered around the double doors which led into the house. Simon deposited his plastic cup into the same ornamental urn that held Starker's umbrella as they joined the crush around the door. "I found him, Momma," he heard Natasha say. "He was getting wasted with the what-do-you-call-it. With the Clu Clucks Clan."

The covered table where servants had been dispensing drinks was now abandoned. Inside the door, the rumor went, a crate of newer, better liquor had been opened up, and people thronged around with glasses in their hands. The ballroom, which had been empty twenty minutes before when Simon had passed through looking for a toilet, was now crowded. On a dais at the west end, four elderly men were tuning their instruments and glowering at their sheet music with dismal and embarrassed faces. The glass roof had been opened, and the columns that supported it were covered with larkspur and morning glory. Simon stared upward with his mouth open.

"I'm glad it only rained that little bit," said a voice beside him. "In March we had a hailstorm that broke most of those windows. It started around ten o'clock at night, and by twelve o'clock the sun was out again."

Lowering his eyes, Simon recognized his host, a burly man with a gray beard. His bald head shone in the filtered light, the result, Simon decided, of some artificial polish. He was taller than Simon and immensely wide; his shirtfront was as broad as an expanse of polar tundra. A diamond earring sparkled in one ear.

"Jonathan Goldstone," he said as Simon's hand disappeared into the middle of his fist. "I was hoping Mr. Clare could come."

"That seems to be a fairly general wish."

Mr. Goldstone released Simon's hand undamaged. "It must be. When you're hanging from the cliff by your fingernails, you can't help but wonder."

"Yes, of course. But I'm sure if Mr. Clare was aware of any change, he would have wanted to come tell you himself."

Goldstone looked over Simon's head into the crowd. "Well, that lets you off the hook," he said. "Where's Natasha? She was supposed to bring you some champagne."

The musicians on the dais had started up, playing an arrhythmic, atonal version of the Blue Danube. Goldstone listened for a moment and then shook his head. "Jesus Christ."

Simon turned toward the music. A servant had materialized next to his elbow, bearing a tray of hors d'oeuvres. As he reached out to take one, he looked for a moment into the man's clear, mournful eyes before he smiled his thanks. "Don't judge them too harshly, sir," he said. "Music and dance are our concepts, not theirs."

"*One*-two-three, *one*-two-three—it's a waltz, for Christ's sake," said Jonathan Goldstone. "Besides, you're wrong; they told me they could play. If they had come to me and said, 'I'm sorry, Mr. Goldstone, music and dance are your concepts, not ours' "—here he mimicked the local accent so precisely that Simon might have laughed, had he not been studying at that moment the old servant's reproachful face—"I wouldn't have hired them. Fine, no hard feelings. But they advertised."

Simon shrugged. "There's a demand."

Mr. Goldstone selected several canapés, placing them in a row along his broad left palm. Then he waved his fingers and the servant vanished.

The makeshift bar where they were dispensing drinks was behind Simon, so once again it took him by surprise when Natasha suddenly emerged out of the ambient noise, standing beside him carrying three glasses of champagne, and accompanied by Mr. Styreme and his daughter. The old man was out of breath. He leaned upon his cane, spreading his feet and poking it out in front of him with both hands on the crook. Its sensible rubber end made a small mark on the floorboards.

"What do you think?" asked Mr. Goldstone. "Mayaram here says I can't expect too much of these musicians, considering they are native to the Territory. Thank you," he continued, removing the apex of Natasha's carefully balanced triangle of glasses.

"That's not what I meant," cried Simon. But Natasha was holding out a glass to him and giggling. In the moment when he took it, the time for explanations passed and was replaced by a cold silence.

"The young man does no favor to condescend," said Junius Styreme. He allowed his bifocals to sink an inch along his nose, and then raised his head to stare at Simon through the lower half. Then he turned his head, as if to listen to the music better. "Strauss, is it?" he asked. "Richard Strauss," he added, giving his r's a fine German roll.

"Johann, Papa," murmured Katharine.

"Yes, of course. Johann Strauss the younger, is it not?"

"That's right, sir," confirmed Simon abjectly. "And I didn't mean—"

But Katharine interrupted him. "Music is the language of the soul," she said.

Her voice was queer in her restructured throat, a little hoarse, but pleasing nonetheless. "That's what I said," contended Goldstone, the sun shining on his scalp. "But Mayaram seems to think it's something more genetic." He drank a sip of champagne and rolled it appreciatively on his tongue. "What do you think?" he said, looking across at Simon. "It's a Pol Roger '97—almost the last good prewar year."

Simon swirled the wine in a circle without drinking it. He gazed at Katharine Styreme, willing her to look at him. When finally she did so, turning her beautiful head, he spoke as if to her alone. "I feel that I can talk about these things," he said, "because for many years my own race was a subject one, conquered and colonized by what you call the Europeans. If we managed for a long time to survive as a culture and a race, it was by not letting go of our own traditions while we assimilated all we could. So, for example, even in zone seven, my schoolmasters insisted we receive instruction in our style of music while they taught us Vedic scriptures and the Upanishads . . ."

This was a lie. Traditions of that sort no longer existed anywhere in London. He had said it for effect, and the effect was a bad one. Too late he realized the trap that he had opened for himself. Katharine Styreme blinked at him, a solitary blink. "You're not a Christian?"

Simon managed a smile.

"You are not. Yet you are named for Simon Zelotes, one of the Twelve."

"Well, exactly. My father . . ."

Jonathan Goldstone grinned and scratched his beard while the old man continued to examine Simon through the bottoms of his bifocals. Natasha giggled, sipping her champagne. As for Katharine, there was a molten fierceness in her eye that put Simon in mind of the goddess Kali, in whom anger is combined with a beguiling sensuality.

Her eyes themselves were a remarkable color, a dark, tawny orange mixed with streaks of gold. She stared at him and then she turned away. "How strange it is," she said to Natasha. "In the almost two hundred years since you first came here, you have brought us two enormous gifts. One is this gift of European music, and the other is the news of Jesus Christ. And yet so many of you have no appreciation of either of these things. You carry with you a treasure which you cannot understand, at the same time you are debasing and enslaving our people and polluting and ravaging our land."

"We are the unworthy vessels of a higher power," suggested Goldstone, still grinning until Katharine turned to him.

"I believe that is correct," she said.

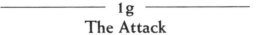

1g
The Attack

Natasha Goldstone couldn't have been more than nineteen. After supper she gave him a tour of the house, and they made love in an upstairs bedroom.

Accordion music drifted through the window, mixed with voices from the east lawn, where guests still gathered around the barbecue pits. The sun threw a soft white light over the drop cloths that covered all the furniture. "I swear to God," she said. "You should have gone after Katharine. Though maybe she couldn't promise you this."

"She doesn't like me."

"No, that's just her way. Besides, she's one to talk. Debased and enslaved—her father was in textiles, for God's sake."

"Even so."

"How could she not like you? You've probably actually been inside the Vatican. Maybe even Carnegie Hall."

Simon reached down beside the bed to pick up the bottle of wine. He propped himself up on his elbow to drink, then bent down to transfer some of the warm liquid into Natasha's mouth. They had not taken off their clothes. Or rather they had retained their shirts; his jacket and pants, her denim shorts lay tangled at the bottom of the bed.

"Be quiet about her," he said, and she was giggling. He pushed her down among the pillows and kissed her underneath her ear. Her long white shirt was unbuttoned down the front; he replaced the bottle of champagne upon the floor, and then he ran his hand under her collarbone and down the length of her body. Everywhere the sun had touched her it had burned her brown, which made the softness of her breast doubly fine, the whiteness of her skin there and lower. Doubly white, in contrast with his own. Her hair grew thick in her armpits and in a circle around each nipple; he kissed and licked her gently there and then moved lower, running his tongue along the bottom of her rib cage, across her sunken stomach. And in the meantime, his right hand reached still lower, picking at the thick hair around her groin, combing it between his fingers, touching the skin lightly underneath. His left hand slid under her back, and then he moved it down along the length of her spine, kneading the muscles of her lower back until she arched away from the mattress and then settled back and sat upon his palm. He reached his fingers up along the crease of her buttocks, spreading her apart but not touching her yet, because although she still retained some of his wetness, she didn't yet have any of her own until he reached up to his mouth with his right hand and licked his fingers one by one and secreted some spit inside his palm. Accordion music drifted up from down below. Someone walked slowly down the outside hall, continuing past their closed door.

"Ooh, baby," sighed Natasha, and then he was touching her, rubbing his fingers into her, gently and then hard. He felt calm. Happy yet detached, though he did have an erection in a modest sort of way; it looked so wizened and so strange.

He opened her up with his left hand, and then he pushed his right thumb into her, reaching back until he fit his nail under a ball of flesh—what was that, her cervix, perhaps? It was shallower in her than in some women. He rotated his thumb. She was arching her back, thrusting up against him. And then her moisture seemed to change consistency—it seemed thicker, he could feel more friction, her muscles were tight and she was drying out, sensitive to his smallest movement, and so he pulled his fingers out of her, afraid of hurting her. His mind was moving slowly, and as sometimes happened, it seemed to concentrate on single images: snow on the Houses of Parliament. The paperweight in the consul's hand. The Aboriginal policeman in his brown uniform and his turban, seen through the back window of the Rolls. Single images that took the place of thought: he was squatting in the dust at Gundabook, the dead dog in his hands.

He slid his left hand out from underneath her, and he moved between her legs. He licked her once, experimentally, letting the taste of her mix with the barbecue sauce in the back of his throat. Then he raised himself up to look at her, admiring the pleasure on her freckled face, admiring the swell of her small breasts, her black hair tangled on the pillow. Her eyes were closed.

With his right hand he brushed the hair back from her pubic mound, and then he bent down to take her lips between his lips, and slowly and carefully he kissed her to what he guessed was orgasm, because she relaxed and shuddered and lay still.

His fingers were cramped where she had squeezed them between hers, and he had cut the underside of his tongue against his bottom incisors.

Then she sat up and she was smiling. She folded her legs under her, so that she was sitting up and he was lying with his head upon her lap. He rested his head on her brown thigh and wiped his lips with the back of his hand and picked a piece of hair out of his mouth. She put her hands on his head.

"Tell me about Earth," she asked, as they all did.

But he was sure she didn't want to know. Instead he told her a little bit about the voyage in the ship. How he had come with the astronomers who had gone on to Shackleton. "Have you ever been there? It's not far away, over the line. They're looking for neutrinos in the ice. It's a black hole. Have you seen it?"

"I've seen pictures."

He lay with his head on her brown thigh. He was aware of a small sense of irritation. "No, of course not." Then: "I killed a dog today."

A crease appeared between her brows as she assimilated this. She shook her head, and he continued: "My driver hit a dog. It was some kind of Labrador."

"Today?"

"As we drove up. At Gundabook. It must have been abandoned in the town."

They had opened the window to ventilate the room. White gauze curtains had hung listless in the still air; now they stirred slightly. Natasha turned her head. A cool wind blew across her face, and Simon could see the sweat drying on her cheek. No sound reached them from the open window, and there was silence through the corridors of the house. The music had stopped.

Simon reached down beside the bed and picked up the bottle of champagne. He drank a little sip, almost the last. And then he took a larger gulp and held it in his mouth and pushed her back down upon the bed. "No," she said and tried to twist away. But he was insistent; he pushed her down and spread her legs apart, and he could feel the champagne popping on his tongue. He bent into her again and licked her, and then she was shuddering and crying out, her fingers locked into his hair. Then everything was still, and at that moment Simon heard the sound of the piano down below, the opening of the sonata, soft and yet distinct, coming from the ballroom two floors down—the first chord and then the first high trill of notes, and in his mind he held an image of Katharine Styreme bent low over the keys. Her face was flushed, her eyes were full of some response. Some feeling—something.

Ashamed, uncomfortable, he turned his face into Natasha's stomach. She was stroking his head, and then he felt a shudder in her diaphragm. But he was listening to the music. So beautiful, it was.

"What's wrong?" he asked, raising his head. She turned over on her side, sobbing quietly. Her black hair was spread out over the pillow. He reached up to touch her face.

"What's wrong?" he asked again. But she was shaking her head, crying softly into her fists. He sat up on the bed and stared out the window past her shoulder.

From somewhere in the park there came a sound like the crack of a stick, a bough torn off a tree. And then another sound that shook the glass. A soft concussion on his face. The music stopped again.

Natasha didn't notice. "How can you?" she said. "How can you be so—" Cruel? Stupid? Calm? She turned her face into her hands so that he couldn't hear.

Drunk and unsteady, he stood up. He went to the window and saw nothing except the lawn sloping away. But there was gunfire from outside and a commotion in the house. Doors slammed. People shouted.

When he looked back into the room, he noticed a corner of an envelope protruding from inside his jacket on the bed. It was the letter from the consul that he was to have delivered. Now suddenly he felt he must search for Jonathan Goldstone and press it into his big hands.

Or better maybe to stay here and wait for the noise to go away. He went to the bed again and put his hand onto Natasha's shoulder. She twisted away from him. The shirt fell open on her pretty breasts.

Gunfire and the smell of smoke. "Just go away," she said. "Do you think that's all it is?" Then she went on and on as if she couldn't hear. Her tears had dried and she was angry now. But instead he was putting on his pants. He was listening to the crashing sounds, the cries and footsteps. Someone running down the hall. And maybe they would have passed by except for the sound of Natasha's voice. "What is it?" she said. "What's going on?"

1h

Demons (ii)

Always they were taken to see hatred in this world of light. The car had taken them out of the dark. Out of the dark house. They were locked for the long way, touching with their hands, but then came the explosion, and the car had shuddered, stopped and shuddered, and then stopped. The doors opened and the light came in. There was a big house. People had guns and cans of gasoline. Others came out. Some had run away against the grass.

A man had a big gun, and he was holding it before they shot him on the stairs. The light was coming down from the tall sky, and it was showing all the faces with the lips pulled back against the teeth, the tongues against the teeth, the mouths open, the arms flailing in the hurtful light. Like the other time, it had already begun when the dark car opened, and they were spilled out into the middle of the hatred with no warning, just the explosion, and the shuddering and stopping of the car. Flames were already jumping up. They hid their faces in their hands, the center of a circle and then the two foci of an ellipse, for they had pulled her away, and they had pulled her down. He would have gone with her except for the sharp chains. But in his mind he had his arms around her, and she had her arms around him, and her face was against his face. "AH," she said, "AH, AH, AH, AH," which meant one thing only, for he could feel the shooting and the fire, and in the separate dark where he and she always embraced it was as if she had released him, had taken five steps away. They had hurt her with the burning pain. Shackled and bound he was, shackled by the miserable slaves, and he was weak, so weak, so weak.

II

2a
John Clare's Dream

As usual after he had taken his painkillers, the consul found it difficult to sleep. At nine o'clock he had heard a report, half anticipated, of an assault on Goldstone Lodge. He had shut himself up in his office. His back and sinuses had required medication at nine-thirty and again at ten. In between and afterwards, he tried to work, tried to read. He paced the carpet with quick light steps, clapping his hands. He closed the blinds and drew the curtains, but still the sun leaked in, the constant sun.

Toward midnight he took to watching the video from New Manchester. He watched it many times. Sitting in his armchair with his feet pulled up, finally he achieved a kind of rest, a waking stupor. But at least his mind no longer moved over the face of his kidnapped assistant, touching it obsessively the way he had sometimes imagined touching it with his bare fingers. Or rather it was not the same, because always before in his imagination Mayaram had been asleep when he had touched him, sunk in happy sleep. But now his eyes were open and his face was worried, apprehensive, and perhaps a little tense, perhaps a little reproachful also as he looked at the consul—unjustifiably, of course. These events had been a terrible shock.

A waking stupor. But his mind was silent for moments at a time. Sitting in his armchair, he stared at the monitor on the far wall, watching the video chip over and over. He played it backward, forward, controlling it with the remote. He turned it off, then on again, freezing the final image of the sun over the lake, the blue hills of Africa, a couple of stray birds.

What was this picture? It didn't exist anymore. It hadn't existed for two hundred years or more. He brought the video back to its beginning for what he promised to himself was one final time. He meant to study it one final time, to see if there was some detail that he might possibly have missed. But when he started the video forward he found himself miming the voices and providing a commentary, as if he were sitting here with someone, Mayaram perhaps. He should have shown it to Mayaram before he left.

"Look at this excruciating color," he said. "We do better work than this."

For fifteen seconds he watched the new flag of what he supposed was the #3 Nordsee Federacion, arrayed against the State Department seal. "Three cheers for the orange, pink, and lime green," he muttered.

Then he put in Mayaram's voice, reasonable and compassionate: "It makes you understand how poor they are."

The flag, lit apparently by strobe, flickered away. "You'd think they'd need us more than we need them," muttered the consul to himself. "This imbecile probably lived her whole life under a dome. She probably goes to work in some electric bus at seven miles per hour."

In fact John Clare knew little about what life was like on New Manchester, except for what he had inferred from their import lists. He had never been there. New Manchester was spread across a string of asteroids, the closest more than six light-years away, or five months for an unmanned cargo ship. New Manchester had been their trading partner, the closest relay point by far. Because it had originally been a British outpost, all communication with it passed through him. Yet it was frightening how ignorant he'd kept himself, he thought now, miserably, too late.

He touched the remote, and the video progressed another couple of frames. A face appeared on the screen, trisected by lines of static. Careworn, green, it drifted several feet above the shoulders of a torso seated at a desk. Then it descended as gently as an Exxon shuttle.

The official was dressed in a semi-transparent quilted suit made of some unrecognizable material. Something to protect her skin, perhaps. Her green skin: apart from that, she looked Chinese. Her lips opened, and she talked silently for a while until the sound came on. "The flamingos," she said, "which once waded this proud marshland in their thousands, are now almost extinct. M'boko says that when the last bird is gone, his family, too, will have to leave the lake."

"This is my favorite part," murmured the consul to himself. He touched a button on the remote. Beneath the image of the face upon the screen a secondary image suddenly came clear: a boy squatting in a bright landscape. He raised his hand and waved.

"Let's say there was a revolution," said Clare. "I'd put this rubbish on every channel."

"Their staple, an aquatic member of the taro family, grows well in this marshy soil. But it depends on guano for its cultivation. . . ." The voice of the announcer faded into static, replaced gradually by the voice of the official at his desk. For a moment it appeared to issue from the mouth of the squatting boy, who smiled as he held up a large root.

"It's too perfect not to be deliberate." Clare froze the image for a few seconds and then thumbed it backward a few frames, forcing the gestures of the boy into a jerky dance.

Somehow the transmission from New Manchester had gotten mixed up with something else, a wisp of a broadcast lost among the unimaginable distances from Earth itself, perhaps, a third of the way across the galaxy. Yet whoever sent it and whenever they did, it must already have been hundreds of years old. Perhaps it had formed part of an historical archive, part of a vision of a shared heritage, a shared language which no longer existed. To watch it was to look backward into time.

The landscape faded, the boy disappeared. The official sat at her desk. "O.R.M.," she said. "No positive, 998 no change, John Clare. D.B. (#4) Short end cargo limit total. Pay schedule reflect, toto. Quick shit vite, no reason. Emergency is permanent, X.L.L. Hablamos Nyet. Fuck u (2) two. 20 hour here. No authority (101010xp6.). No request until this end, you no. Adio good-bye. Thirty seconds up."

Clare touched the button. The image of the official's face trembled on the screen. Underneath it, superseding it momentarily in clarity, was an outline map of Africa from the late twentieth century, perhaps. The flamingo's habitat was marked in red.

John Clare thumbed the image forward a few frames. Now a landscape stretched away, the color suddenly perfect, suddenly real: the blue lake pink with birds, the blue sky and the blue hills. "That's it," he said. "It's gone. They've cut us off."

When finally he did fall asleep, still sitting, still with his feet curled up, he dreamed he was naked, and his bare skin stuck to the leather of the armchair as he tossed and turned, and from time to time he sat up and rubbed his face. He dreamed that the automatic shutters were closed, the room was dark. Yet still the bulky furniture loomed about him, the desk, the chairs; this was not sleep. Only weariness had sharpened his anxieties, that was all. Only darkness had disorganized his thoughts and wrapped each one in camouflaging images. Mayaram, he thought, and in his dream he sat up to watch the video chip, and he saw a car bump down over ridges of sand, down toward the water. With his finger on the remote, he increased the magnification, and he saw the young man's face at the window of the Rolls as it drove along the blue shore of the lake.

Flamingos scattered from the bumpers. But there were demons on that lakeshore too, though he couldn't see them. Earth was no more than a dream to him, a picture on a screen. Even as he watched, he saw another image rise to the surface of his thoughts, another sun which was burning through that soft, bright sun, and now the Rolls was bumping through the fringes, through the toxic runoff of another lake—more real in memory, less real in dreams—where John Clare had been a child. There the red sun hung on the horizon, there it spilled out night and day across the long salt flat, there the air seemed thin even to those who had breathed it all their lives. There demons had persisted in the dark hills behind Lake McElroy, and in his dream John Clare remembered, and he could see it by the lakeshore as the Rolls bumped down—a circle of Aboriginals around the body. Its wrists were tied together and its ankles too, and they had slipped a stick under the knots and carried it down from the hills with its head hanging down backward, its bulbous head mouthless and earless. Its eyes were dry and full of bugs, its secret and coercive mind was silent, and its skin was punctured in a hundred places.

John Clare was five years old. Because he was a child, he could recognize a child. He had started to cry. He had not stopped when his father took him up and held him in his arms; had not stopped when his father slapped him; had not stopped mourning in his own way for that little creature whose world, after all, this was.

The Rolls bumped along the lakeshore toward the fringes, toward the dark. Where was Simon now?

The car bumped down along the lakeside through the blood-red shadows. It came to a slow stop, up to its hubcaps in the bitter water. The girl, also, was inside.

2b

Captives

Simon was asleep. His dreams were full of images that had pulled him deep below the surface of the world. And he had to let go of them to rise toward waking, and when he woke up they had sunk away, irretrievable.

Simon woke up in the dark. So rare in that country; for a moment he was confused enough to imagine himself back in the bedroom of his cubicle in Golders Green, immeasurably far away.

It was cold, too. He rolled over onto his back, onto the foam rubber camping mat which he had lost during the night. Had it really been night? Now it was dawn, it felt like dawn, and there was a damp chill in the air that felt like dawn in London.

Concentrating, he brought some focus to his eyes. There

was light above him, streaks of light upon the stucco wall. Weak, muted, still it was yellow, red, that false shade which made all life here seem false. He raised his arms up to his face; they were handcuffed together at the wrist.

He was in a small room with no furniture and one window high up near the ceiling. Coke bottles and Styrofoam fast-food containers scattered the floor, amid muddy footprints. Katharine Styreme was with him, sitting with her back up to the wall. He saw her mouth, saw that it was moving, and heard words. He had not been aware of them before. "Hail Mary, full of grace," she said. "Blessed art thou among women, and blessed be the fruit of thy womb, Jesus."

The familiar words, submerged in her queer voice, made an effect like the false light, and for a moment she seemed alien to him, utterly alien. The closer the similarity, the more grotesque the trick, because in another sense she was just like a woman, just like a woman sitting in the dark with her dark hair, her face puffy from tears. She sat with one knee raised, her head back against the cement wall.

She had on a university sweatshirt and a pair of jeans. Simon still lay in the clothes he had been wearing when he was captured; they stank.

"Virgin of all virgins best," she said. "Listen to my fond request."

He was lost among them now, and the more he could appreciate how human they appeared, the more frightened he felt. When he had first arrived in country, it had seemed reassuring how close they were to human beings, how familiar in appearance, language, customs. At least the ones he had to deal with: after more than a hundred years of occupation, drugs and surgery and time had broken every link back to their past.

"Hail Mary," she said. "Wounded with his every wound, steep my soul till it hath swooned, in his very blood away."

He shuddered. Yet how beautiful she was. And surely at that moment she was close to him in her mind. Surely they felt the same helplessness, the same isolation, the same fear. Her wrists were cuffed together in her lap. Her skin was bruised where they had hit her.

"Where are we?" he asked.

"Hail Mary," she said, and then she bit her lip. She turned her head slowly to the side, so that he could see her profile against the lighter wall. Above her the red light—"We're in the fringes," she said. "Today they take us over the rim."

"What time is it?" he asked, a stupid question, and she shook her head. He brought his hands up to touch his eyes; then he sat up slowly. "What happened?"

"You were out. They gave you an injection."

Like others of her medicated class, she pronounced the word with a certain satisfaction. Her lips closed over it primly while he sat up and tried to reconstitute his thoughts. He remembered the first part of their voyage, blindfolded in the covered flatbed of a truck, always aware of her body next to his. Others had been with them, stepping over them when the truck stopped.

"What did they say?"

"They asked me to write a letter to my father." She pushed her cheek against the wall. "You'll see."

He tried to smile. "How are you feeling?"

"They left my pills."

His face was tight. He opened his mouth wide to stretch it. "Perhaps they'll bring some later," he said without thinking.

"But I need mine. They left them at the Lodge." Then: "They did it on purpose. To torture me."

"Oh," he said. "Oh, I don't think so." And then: "How do you feel?"

She turned to face him, and he could see the ridge of her eyebrows, her dark mouth. "I don't know."

He smiled and she smiled too, and then her face was full of tears. "There's something here. I can feel it waiting to get in."

For an instant he looked over toward the door, and she shook her head. "In my mind."

"What can I do?" he said, and she was just like a woman, just like a human being with some pain caught in her throat—she shook her head. "I don't know. I don't know what."

He got up to his knees and put his hands out toward her. For an instant she leaned forward so that her forehead touched his fists, and then pulled back. "Ah, God," she said. "They'll take us down."

She didn't do anything else, and in a little while he lay back. He stretched out on the mat with his hands clasped above his head, listening to some tiny noises: the scurry of a roach behind the wall, and some interior motion of his own, perhaps. He looked up at the red smear of light slanting diagonally on the white stucco above him. There was a smell of grease and plaster and then something else, something of her smell too as she lay down beside him. She was clumsy with her handcuffs; she kept her hands down, her elbows straight, which made her shoulders curl up off the mat. "Don't be frightened," he said, a flimsy consolation, because he could feel in the stiffness of her body a distress much deeper than fright. But even so, with a bravery that touched him she did not refuse to be comforted, but she turned onto her side and rolled close to him as far as her handcuffs would allow.

Or was it comfort? So easy to be sympathetic, to think you knew what someone else was feeling. So weak a connection, even in the best of times. But this? Who could tell even whether those drugs worked? They seemed to allow behavior, that was all—a pharmacological breakthrough that allowed results, that shut down certain parts of her. Together with more drugs that made her age, and yet who knew? Who knew what she was feeling now? She was trembling slightly, and perhaps that was the beginning of a physical withdrawal which would kill her. She had taken this medication every day she'd been alive. He imagined her standing alone in the house she grew up in, and she was holding in her hand a ring of fifty keys to doors that had never been unlocked.

"The Lord is my shepherd, therefore I shall lack nothing," she said. And then her voice sank to a murmur, but he followed the old words—one of the few Christian prayers he knew.

She finished the psalm, was silent a few minutes, and then started it again from the beginning. Simon rolled over onto his stomach. The litter of crushed paper on the floor contained some photographs, some snapshots taken with a Polaroid camera.

It was easier to see now in the room. Clouds had broken from the sun outside the small window, making an illusion of morning. Simon propped himself up on his elbows and reached his hands out for one of the pictures, idly curious at first. But when he held it up and looked at it, the words of Katharine's prayer took on a sudden meaning.

It was a photograph of Goldstone Lodge. It was a photograph of the east steps, where the keg of beer had been. He could see it on its side in the corner. On the steps a line of hooded figures, as at Gundabook.

Once again they had arranged the bodies of their victims on the grass. Jonathan Goldstone lay on his back. His shirtfront was smudged and bloody, his mouth was open, his eyes closed.

Next to him, her white hair covering her face, lay his wife. Simon recognized the pattern of her Chinese gown.

Away from the steps, closer to the camera, Natasha Goldstone was curled up on her side. She was naked except for her unbuttoned shirt.

She had been standing by the window when they burst into the room. Braver than he, she had cried out. He was putting on his pants and they had shot her—no. Simon listened to the murmur of Katharine's queer, hoarse voice behind him. He put his hand over the picture, looked at the light on the wall, and then looked down again.

As at Gundabook, the terrorists had dragged some furniture out onto the lawn. The demon was there. The demon stood in a wreck of broken furniture, looking back over its shoulder. Its long fingers made a shape out of the air.

"They're going to kill us," said Katharine in a tone that did not sound displeased enough.

"No. God, no, we're hostages. We're only valuable to them alive."

"They'll feed us to the monster. He'll kill us with his mind."

"It's not like that," he told her, taking a relieved refuge in pedantry. He laid the picture down on the floor between them. Awkward in his handcuffs, he held his palm over the image of Natasha Goldstone, whom they had shot in the stomach and the face. Through the eye, although you couldn't see it in the picture. They must have arranged her body carefully—no. He concentrated instead on the demon, on the minute pattern of its fingers. He had studied the language at the Warburg.

"It's not like that," he said again. "It's a prisoner as much as us. They've chained it—look."

He ran his fingernail over the demon's hands. "Pain in its ankles," he went on. "Pain and a great deal of fear. And look at this—it's saying, 'Where are you?' Turning back over its shoulder—you can see something's hidden underneath that table where the boy is crouching."

"There's another one," said Katharine without expression.

"There must be another one," agreed Simon, talking without thinking. "Perhaps a lover or a wife—you see that crook in the fourth finger. That's a diminutive, I think. And it's afraid, you see. Perhaps there's another one and it's been hurt."

She didn't say anything, so Simon went on, speaking more and more rapidly. "Look at this. The picture, the way it all was staged, it's meant to frighten us. It looks like something we know about, you see—superficially, at least. A demon warrior and its band of slaves. Two demons, perhaps. I think it's the other way round. Perhaps it's a mutant or retarded—anyway, they've got this poor brute captive. After all, the NLC, they've got to be on medication. Students, most of them. People one knows. They're not susceptible to any of that mind control. Not anymore. And I'm not. And you're not. Or at least . . ." He stopped, aware that he could not console her in this way, in this direction.

There was a rattling at the door and it banged open. Simon and Katharine struggled to sit up. Two masked figures stood in the shadow of the hall, one carrying a machine pistol. The other advanced into the room—a woman. She was wearing a Sorbonne T-shirt. It was baggy over her white arms.

These lucky few—the rich, the educated, the ones who could afford the surgery, they were like Americans in old movies with their chewing gum, their guns. Without a word she reached down for the chain of Simon's handcuffs and yanked him to his feet; he was eager to help, not to resist, for the skin on his wrists was sore. He shuffled out into the hall, bewildered by the dark, the quickness of rising; he stumbled. The man in the doorway led him down the hall, but then two more men rushed past him to the room, and they dragged Katharine out.

He heard her struggling behind him, but they moved him swiftly out into the light. They moved out through a broken wall; the house was a new one, but broken and abandoned, a farmhouse in the fringes, and outside the gold grass stretched away. The wind was in his face. Some trucks and vans were pulled up in a muddy rut; this was grazing land, abandoned now. The grass marched to the horizon and the sun was low, hanging in eternal sunset over the east hills.

Behind him they were hitting her, and he turned around quick enough to see her pull away and stagger out into the grass, out toward a low wire fence. One of the guns went off, an insincere popping noise. A woman in a beret fired once, high, and Katharine turned back with the grass around her knees, blood on her wrists. Her lips were moving but no sound came. Simon thought that she was praying until he heard the words. "Cock," she said. "Cock suck," and then a few more bits of hesitant obscenity that sounded so strange in her hoarse voice. "You can suck my shit," she said almost conversationally, and then started to cry.

"She needs her pills," he said, and the man beside him nodded. He looked frightened, shocked. No one moved, and they were holding their guns pointed at the ground. How young they seemed, suddenly. Simon left them behind and walked out toward her, kicking through the grass. Deflated, she watched him come, beautiful, deflated, in tears.

Aboriginal

After the assault, when he was well enough to talk, Junius Styreme met with the governor, the British consul, and the Board of Estimate. Later he drove back to Fair Haven, which was the name of his house in Shreveport, in the native lines. His chauffeur opened the car door for him, and then the guards he had hired took him up the walk. They abandoned him on the front step. Rather than put up with the incompetence of his own kind, Styreme had always hired human servants, who were forbidden by law from living in. Therefore that afternoon the house was both immaculate and empty. The cleaners had come when he was away, had vacuumed and dusted and put out his dinner near the microwave.

For a wistful moment he thought he might be hungry, but that wasn't it. He picked up a pork chop wrapped in plastic and knocked it twice upon the edge of the kitchen counter. Then he went out through the double doors into the dining room and stood with his hand on the back of a chair. He was seized and shaken by a sudden vertigo; he bowed his head, and when he raised it again, the room seemed to stretch out before him into a dispiriting infinity of couches and glass-topped tables. A decorator had furnished this place. There were only a few chairs stiff enough for him to sit on.

The carpets under his cane lacked solidity, and so he walked carefully down the long strip of wood that ran next to the fireplace and the bookshelves. He passed through the French doors into the music room. Katharine's piano was there, and the desk with her music and research. Sometimes late at night he had stood just here by the curtain, just inside the door. He had watched her work with the sun from the skylight in her hair, her reading glasses on her nose, and he had stood for several minutes without speaking sometimes— not because she would have been angry or dissatisfied to be interrupted (indeed that was a joy also, to see her tight-lipped smile when she became aware of him), but just for the pleasure of watching her expression. It was her expression as she pored over the pages of sheet music and text that made him think he'd succeeded in accomplishing the most difficult of all tasks among a people who had surrendered or lost everything—to pass on the knowledge that life was worth living. Even among the devices of the conqueror there was a material for happiness, and maybe that was the only place that it existed now in these sad days.

These terrorists at Goldstone, what was that except despair? They had not found it. In the interstices between their lives and human life, they had not found it. He limped over to the piano bench and lowered himself down onto it. He stared at the way the creases in his trousers fell over his sharp knees, and then he raised his head. Set onto the music stand was a letter.

A letter in an envelope without inscription; he took it down and turned it over in his hands. He knew that he would open it at last. Why else was he sitting here? But still he turned it over a few more times. There was something inside, not just a piece of paper. He held it up toward the skylight. It was hair, he decided, a lock of Katharine's hair.

Slowly, carefully, he rose to his feet. He limped across the floor. Katharine had fitted a bed into a side room, and he stared at it through the open door. "It suits me better than upstairs," she had told him; she was right. A small white space—he stood in the door with the envelope still in his hand. A small shrine to the Virgin in the otherwise empty fireplace, and where everything else in the room was spare and neat, the shrine was complicated and disorganized: a litter of old flowers, old candle stubs, matchbooks, incense dust, and crumpled sheets of music, all piled around the feet of a black figurine. It was the Virgin carved in ebony, with fat breasts and fat buttocks and a fat child giving suck. It was from Ghana, collected by a missionary there in 1910. It had been a Christmas gift from him.

Nearby, in contrast, the clean surface of her medication table—the prescription bottles lined up in a row. In front of them, four syringes in a velvet case. An open book of poetry. Last, an electrically cooled vial of anticollagen, the aging fluid without which human experience could not successfully be duplicated. He should know. The stuff was killing him.

After the attack at Goldstone, after the fire was put out, he had sent firemen into what remained of Katharine's room to see if they could find her medication kit. But who could locate anything in that saturated mess? He was afraid. As he had told the governor, he could not even remember the moment of parting, when the gun had fired during the sonata. His eyes had been closed. She had been gone before he knew.

"Ah, God," he said. "Ah, God." He pulled open the envelope. It was unsealed. A lock of hair, a color he had chosen. The single page said: $100,000. THEODORE OIMU. MAKE A SIGN.

There was to be no rescue attempt, no investigation, no ransom. The governor had said so. "I know I can trust you," he had said, "because your interests are the same as ours."

Before humans beings had come into the world, his people had abandoned their children without difficulty. They did not have this love. Now he felt his heart would burst. It was a mental state, he knew—an illusion. What could be done? Nothing, he thought, and found some comfort in the word.

He held the note up above his head and threw it down onto the tabletop. Breathless, stifled, he fled the house as quickly as his brittle legs could manage. He unlocked the back door and left it open. He moved down toward his property line. The sun was strong and he stood for a moment leaning on his cane, his thoughts in confusion. But then slowly his spectacles adjusted to the light; the world appeared progressively more tolerable as he set off down the walk and out the gate. He moved along the street.

There was a line of gold-leafed ginkgo trees on either side of the concrete walkway. He limped between them, passing the mansions and bungalows of prosperous Aboriginal families. These did not cover a large area even in Shreveport, even in the capital of the American Territory; in a little while he reached the radial canal. The shore was guarded and policed on the near side, the curb lined with motorcars. But on the far side of the canal the water was choked with refuse, and people lived in little shacks down there.

An iron footbridge crossed over: concrete steps and then an iron path. The footing was difficult for Junius Styreme. Halfway across, he leaned with his hand on the chain railing, catching his breath, looking down. Some local men were on the far bank. As he watched, they stepped down into the mud. They stepped out into the water and just stood there with the water around their legs. They didn't talk; they didn't look up.

The shantytown began on the far side. This was a different administrative district, not part of the city itself, although it housed most of the people who worked there. Nevertheless, on the maps of the city this was all vacant land.

Junius Styreme, his heart full of a pain that relieved all other pain, that was spreading like a drug through his dry capillaries, that enabled him to gather strength in a new way, wandered in this shantytown for several hours. Turned inward to himself, he made little significance out of what he saw. As he moved through the tar-paper houses and cardboard shacks, the same scenes repeated themselves endlessly. Yet each one appeared new to him, a new image, forgotten as soon as it was perceived. Many of the houses scarcely came up to his chest, and sometimes through the empty doorways he could glimpse people lying asleep, though it was the middle of the day. Others sat on the ground or lay down on strips of tin, and nobody had anything to do. And liquor was everywhere; people lay insensate in the mud or nodded drowsily with bottles in their hands.

He turned left at the embankment and wandered down toward the landfill. This was in some ways the center of the town, and supported the densest concentration of inhabitants. From there came the raw materials out of which all the rest was constructed: the car wrecks, the scrap metal, the broken wood. As Styreme limped down toward it, flocks of birds revolved above him, and his nose was assaulted by the stench. In some places the piles of garbage rose twenty feet high.

Only a small portion of the landfill contained household garbage. The rest was industrial waste of various kinds. There was a pool of blue liquid near where Styreme stood. On the other side of it rose a pyramid of plastic barrels. Each was stenciled with the logo of a Santander petrochemical company, in which Styreme owned stock.

People lived in houses built of bags of garbage, houses that were constantly collapsing, constantly rebuilt. And the crowds were thicker here: trailing long bags, men sifted through the piles of refuse, searching, searching.

In time more people gathered round. And it took him a long while to realize they were watching him. They were looking for some kind of interaction, though no one had said anything yet. But they were gathering close, and it seemed as if all he had to do was notice. All he had to do was to feel threatened, and then they were moving up against him, jostling and bumping him and plucking at his hands. Suddenly he was aware of the smell of their packed bodies. They were not glad to see him. They were whispering to him in a language he no longer knew, using words that tugged on his memory importunately, as the men were tugging on his sleeves. He opened his mouth and nothing came. "Please," he said finally, in English, a word that seemed to infuriate them more. Though still there was no hint of violence, there was something menacing in the way they closed in around him, buzzing and chattering in their famished voices. Styreme clutched the lapels of his jacket together. Then he reached into his inside pocket and drew out some currency, some Shreveport dollars. But as soon as they saw the money, the crowd knotted closer, redoubled its insistent pressure. Styreme bowed his head, shuffling with his cane, suddenly afraid that he might lose his footing on the garbage and the uneven mud. He tried to struggle forward to a flatter piece of ground, but no one budged.

He stared at the feet and legs of a man standing directly in front of him. After a moment, hesitant, abashed, he raised his head; the man was exactly his height. He stood with a dollar clutched in his thin claw—an unreconstructed Aboriginal. Or rather he had been inoculated only once, as the law required of the destitute, with the single cheap injection that had broken the demon link, broken his soul. But no plastic or genetic surgeon had ever touched him; Styreme stared at his face, amazed at how alien he seemed. A man of his own kind, yet so much stranger and more frightening than the human beings with whom he associated every day— their faces were transparent compared with this one. Hairless, flat, pale, the nose a tiny concavity, the mouth lipless and toothless, a tiny hole.

Incomprehensible sounds issued from him, issued from similar mouths all around. Then through those sounds Styreme heard another just as querulous, but with an inorganic confidence—a motor, in fact. A Jeep pulled around the corner of a pile of sand. It was loaded with empty barrels and driven by a human being.

Styreme felt a surge of relief. The Jeep altered its course and came toward them. The driver drove with his windscreen down, and he came fast over the ridges of mud, so that the barrels in the back jumped and clattered. He came straight toward the crowd, not slowing down. He picked up something from the seat beside him, an electric cattle prod. It glittered in the light.

Styreme felt a new uncertainty around him in the crowd, too slow, too aimless to be called panic. But people drifted away; by the time the jeep pulled up beside him, he was almost alone. The driver stood up in his seat, brandishing the prod. "Yah!" he shouted, and at the sound the men who had remained scattered away. They moved with great speed for a short distance, then stopped. Some squatted down to stare, others took up their tasks again among the garbage.

Styreme limped over toward the Jeep. "Yah!" the man said again, holding up his prod. "Get away," he said. But then the effect of Styreme's clothes started to penetrate and he lowered his hand, uncertain now.

"Officer," began Styreme. Then stopped; the man jumped down onto the ground with the prod held out. Styreme lifted up his hands.

"Drop it," said the man, and Styreme let his cane fall to the mud. He still clutched in his hand a few stray dollars. The man moved toward him with his back and knees bent; he was dressed in heavy workclothes with a plastic name tag pinned over his heart. STEWART, it read.

"Turn around and put your hands on the car."

Styreme debated the wisdom of calling the man by his first name. Then decided against it and smiled. He opened his fingers and let the dollars drift away, then turned and did as he was told. The man came up behind him and patted down his body, looking for weapons. Suddenly exhausted, Styreme bowed his head.

"Where's your pass?" asked the man, but then he found it. It was an impressive object, signed by the governor. Now he felt the effect of it; the cattle prod, which the man had been holding behind his ear, receded.

———— 2d ————
The Dark Line

Simon leaned forward, his handcuffs chained to a ring in the dash. The road was a dirt track and occasionally they drove overland. Then the car bumped over the ruts and the cuffs gnawed at his wrists no matter how hard he pushed his feet against the floor. It was getting dark.

All day the light had cut across the fields. Now the sun, clothed in a gorgeous layer of dust, was actually sinking in the east behind them, setting in a dark range of hills. It was a terrifying sight in this country. Simon's driver, a young man, also seemed to find it terrifying. He swallowed often, licking his dry lips.

Most of the NLC had given up wearing their masks after the first few hours. This man was named Frank, or at least

one of the others had called him that. He had a long, nervous face, much humanized. But after a few hours of watching him, Simon decided that he had never been far out of the
range of human variation. Some of the Aboriginals were like
that, and there was something in Frank's personality—trucu-
lence masking a painful insecurity—that seemed to cross all
boundaries. At university Simon had seen many like him;
this man looked like a recent dropout, a few years younger
than Simon himself, if such a comparison could ever mean
anything.

Now Frank's insecurity was uppermost. He had been a
witness to what Katharine had said when she was standing in
the grass by the fence, and perhaps it had shaken him. Perhaps also he was shaken by their progress toward the planet's
shadow; he was following the taillights of the car in front.
His own headlights barely illuminated anything. They were
a vestigial piece of car design, useful only during mist or rain,
and of extremely low wattage.

This was the first time that they had allowed Simon to sit
up, to ride outside of the closed truck, and he wondered
whether Katharine's outbreak had been responsible for that
too. Perhaps they felt it was important now to keep their two
hostages separate. Perhaps they felt—who knew? For whatever reason, Simon sensed a vulnerability in his driver. Frank
peered out through the windshield, muttering to himself,
and the cab was full of the stink from his sweat. There was a
pen in the breast pocket of his short-sleeved shirt.

They jolted on into the dusk, past abandoned farms.
Once they drove through a small village, its doors open to
the dark. Twenty-five years ago people had lived here, but
now there was not enough light to grow anything. The
shadow of the planet's terminator line was creeping over the
fields.

"Where are you taking us?" asked Simon.

Frank made an exasperated motion with his head. "You see? it tried to say. "You see?" The dark was gathering around them; the hills had touched the rim of the dull sun. And Simon felt a sudden goad of fright. Perhaps they didn't care whether he knew, perhaps they didn't care whether he looked out of the window now, because they were going to kill him. Perhaps now they could talk to him, because it didn't matter. He didn't want to know what they might tell him and not care. His curiosity fled away.

They were on a road now, one of the old demon roads leading straight into the dark. He leaned backward as far as his handcuffs would allow and closed his eyes; it was intolerable. Here in this new world it was intolerable. In another place, another time, he had spent hours and days staring at his own death, in love with the thought of it. But he had lost the knack. Here it was intolerable to do more than just glance at it sidelong for a few moments at a time. He opened his eyes again. "Have you heard from my government?" he asked.

Again that fleet, erratic gesture. Simon knew the answer. Clare would abandon him, he knew, and would be right to do so. The conviction of something happening that was right and correct gave him strength; he stared up ahead into the shadow, along the old stone road.

Frank swallowed, a slow movement that seemed to progress down the length of his throat until it was lost under his shirt. A plastic container capped with a baffle and a straw stood on the seat beside him. He picked it up and sipped at it. It was empty. He dropped it to the floor.

"You have a demon here?" asked Simon.

Frank looked at him. He drove too quickly over a crack in the roadway, and the cuffs cut into Simon's hands. They were following a white van; perhaps the demons were inside. Where was Katharine?

As if in answer, Frank reached into his breast pocket and produced a pill, which he attempted to swallow dry. It stuck in his throat, and finally he had to chew it down. "What will happen to her?" asked Simon.

Frank shook his head. His expression did not suggest anger or impatience with the fact of the question, but rather a response. He didn't know. He was not, however, taking any chances with his own medication; he pushed his finger back behind his gums, searching for more of the elusive powder to choke down.

They were following the lights of the car in front, and other cars in front of that. Now they shone brighter as the world guttered down. The sun was a strip of color over the black hills behind them. It no longer touched the ghosts of trees, the walls of the abandoned buildings they drove past. It no longer had an effect. Now it was just a thickening of the light, a thickening of the shadow, and the shadow would thicken now until it was opaque.

They stopped for gas. An Aboriginal with a jerry can came back from one of the trucks and filled the tank. Frank turned off the engine and got out to stand next to the bonnet. Simon let his head sink toward the dash. The lights were out now, and he looked up through the top of the windscreen. No stars.

The car at the front of the line started up again; its taillights flickered on. Watching, Simon saw a glimpse of his own death again, and again he could not look. The window beside him was open a crack; he wished he could close it. A cold wind was blowing from the west, from the dividing line, from the ice pack on the other side of the world. From the black hole they called the drain. He was hungry, tired, cold, irritated, and he could not believe, suddenly, that this caravan was not visible from the air. Or from the ground—the mining town of Ludlow was not far. He had to believe that the police in Shreveport could track it if they tried. But perhaps they didn't care. Perhaps it wasn't worth the risk. Or perhaps this was all part of some larger, hidden plan. The consul had been so anxious to send Simon to Goldstone in his place.

Frank got into the car and started the engine. The door was still open and the cabin light came on, and in the windshield Simon saw a flicker of Clare's face, his mirthless smile, in the reflection of his own. Or perhaps in the bleaching light he caught a glimpse of the common structure of all human faces; he looked over at the glass in front of Frank and saw nothing, just the shadow of a movement as the man brought a cigarette up to his lips for a last puff and then threw the end away. He closed the door. The light went off.

----------- 2e -----------
Katharine (ii)

The darkness came in over a range of hills eleven hundred miles west of Goldstone. At different seasons of the year the dark line would advance and retreat, the result of a small eccentricity in the world's orbit. But there was a larger pattern as well, slower and inexorable. The shadow moved forward little by little from west to east, perhaps a mile every year, and it had swallowed up villages and farms. This was the result of its enormous slow rotation, one turn for every nineteen thousand years, scarcely noticeable except in the fringes where the sun glowered on the horizon all day and the dead trees cast long shadows. Near Ludlow cattle grazed in what had once been wheatfields.

The demon road ran along the bank of a dry river and then turned into the hills. Katharine Styreme sat in the front seat of the white van. A draft was coming up from somewhere near her feet. The air was chilly. She could appreciate that without feeling it, for her skin was wet and hot. There was a distant ringing in her ears.

"Holy Mary, Mother of God," she prayed. She moved her lips, but no sound came. "Have mercy on me, a sinner. Pray for me now and at the hour of my death."

Moment by moment she examined her symptoms. She could not tell whether she felt normal or not. Surely the pressure of her concentration made it impossible to tell. Surely it was not so odd under the circumstances to feel feverish. To hear a distant sound in the bottom of your ear, like that ringing rush of silence which comes at the conclusion of a piece of music. She had not eaten that day, and her insides felt greasy and knotted.

Only she was aware of small sensations. The seat covering beneath her legs was made of two varieties of cloth, one of which made her itch. All around her she could hear a myriad of small noises—the rush of the wind and the bumping of the road, but also half a dozen separate engine noises, some constant, some intermittent. Also many creaks and rattles from inside the car. Insects throbbing in the grass outside— was it normal to hear so many? Or could anyone who concentrated hear them all? Her throat was dry.

The sun was down below the hills. The sky had crusted over above them. It seemed as solid as the roof of a cavern, and it was lit with all the bruised colors of sunset—murk purple, gray, and dirty yellow. Clouds hung like stalactites, damp and solid.

She had an itch near her navel, and she ran her fingers down under the waist of her pants, over the bare skin. "Ah, God," she breathed, and pulled her fingers back.

She saw herself on the first step of a stair, and it descended into a universe, a hell of new sensation. A first step toward punishment and dissolution. She thought of the words of Saint John Chrysostom: "It is then that our eyes shall be opened and the veil drawn back."

A stench was rising through the vent. She leaned the top of her head against the partition behind her and closed her eyes. She concentrated for a minute, listening to the sounds of the engine, the breath of the driver. The itch went away.

They drove on and on into the dark. She dozed. When she opened up her eyes again, there was a wall beside the road, a rough stone wall. And then they came in under a stone gate, and the noise of the wheels was different on the new pavement. What was it behind her head? She could feel a thumping in the closed compartment of the van.

"Holy Mary, Mother of God," she prayed. "Have mercy on me, a sinner."

They turned a corner and the ground fell away. A long, straight road led down into a small valley ringed with hills, and she could see on the floor of it a congeries of buildings. Light shone from the windows and doors of some rectangular stone structures. Nothing had ever looked less welcoming.

The van paused at the crest of the hill. It pulled off onto the margin and let some of the cars behind them pass. Katharine turned her face to look out of the side window, and she was listening to the sound from the other side of the temporary partition.

2f
Demons (iii)

I AND I. IN MY MIND I KNOW. IN THAT WOUND OF HER I KNOW. NOW THE DARK DREAM SPILLING OUT FROM ME. I AM CUT, CUT OFF, CUT DOWN AND NOTHING NO.

III

⊗

Penultimate

All around him in the darkness stood the broken ruins. This valley in the old days, before the light had fled, before the humans came, had been a city. Slaves lived in the buildings now, rebel slaves who had broken the law, broken the link, broken the bond, and left the world helpless.

He limped a few steps forward. Chained, he stood among the rubble in the open air, under the dark sky. Here, scarcely a stone left standing. Behind him, the only part of the building still intact, the single room where his sister lay. It was the mark of how weak he was, that the slaves could let him stand here without watching him; he closed his eyes. Anything to escape them—a tiny tremor in his mind, and then he moved into the dead world. Slaves could not make that motion anymore, and human beings never could, and now he was alone in dead time with the roof over his head.

He felt a seizure of vertigo, and he sat down on the flat stones and sat hugging his knees. In a little while he raised his head, and he was sitting in the great lyceum.

All was in darkness, yet in his mind, separate from the perception of his eyes, he could see vague shapes and images: a row of stone chairs along one wall. In the middle of the floor, the dais and the throne. The cold table of Amat III and her sarcophagus. His father had told him, had shown him the way and made it real, and in the memory that his father shared with him he could spatter this hall with intermittent light, hold up an intermittent candle to the painted friezes that ran the length of each wall, the long processions of portraits, the decaying colors.

He was dressed in a coat that Martin had made out of a blanket. It was a long, itchy garment, comfortable only when he was sitting down. As now. Now it was held away from his skin by its own stiffness, and he could curl up inside of it and pull his arms out of the sleeves and wrap them around his bony chest. AH, AH, he thought, TO LIVE LIKE THIS. PULLED BACK.

He got up from the floor and limped out into open space. His ankles were joined by a three-foot chain. His feet were cold on the cold stone.

He limped along the row of chairs. Images appeared to him, combinations of his father's memory and some other sense which was not sight. Sight found no purchase in that pristine darkness. Instead he listened to vibrations in his body. Having no ears, no hearing to distract him, he was supremely sensitive to these vibrations, and he felt them move across his fingers, into his chest, into his belly. This movement mixed with fluctuations in intensity, and it let him know the location, the mass, the speed of approach of all the objects around him, even in some sense their shape. Shapes blundered out of the darkness. He put out his long hand to reach the face of a statue, and at the final instant when his fingers grazed its cold skull, his perception combined suddenly with his sense of touch, and with his father's memory, and with his sight also. Because now that he had moved, in fact there was some tiny light in that dark hall. It seeped down through a crack in a distant door. He turned and limped toward it, and as he did so he was alerted also to another rhythm in his body, which he had always been aware of at the limit of his consciousness, but which was now growing in intensity as he approached the door. A harsh rhythm of breathing and a beating heart, erratic in the breast of the only other creature like himself, and he could feel it in his body as he limped up toward that light, reaching his hands out as he did so to touch the faces of the statues, for he was passing through a double row of statues.

The walls came toward him and he turned a corner. The light was stronger here and more direct. This was the hall of spirits, the room of the dead, and he limped up through the tall sarcophagi. Here the great men and women of his race had been laid out in death, sealed up in stone. The light from the distant doorway filtered over the long shapes, and he could see the outlines of the death scenes painted on their sides. Scenes from the invasion time. When the murderers came. How many had perished from their bullets and their hideous diseases?

He passed the tomb of Amat II and let his fingers slide over the painted image of her vomiting up blood.

But in a sense even all this—this hall, these kings and queens—had been a human creation. Before the invaders came, his people had not built like this. They had not needed this. No, they had borrowed from their murderers, and they had changed, and then they had all died, and sweet darkness had filled up the valley little by little. It was sweet black water leaking through the bottom of a boat until it foundered.

The light was stronger now, and he was at the door. Light came through the long vertical crack next to the stone frame; the door was open a few inches. He put his hand on the carved wooden surface next to the bolt, admiring the play of the light on his pale fingers, hesitating before he pushed back the door. He hesitated, and then put strength behind his hand, a long, slow push and then the light was spilling out at him, piercing through the widening crack, hurting his eyes. It was as if the light were resisting him, and he pushed harder until finally the door gave way, pushed open, and he was standing in the real world in the light.

Now he could feel throughout his body his sister's heartbeat and her breath. She was lying on a low bed in the small room. There was heat here too, from a cylindrical kerosene burner near her head.

She lay on her side, doubled up around her wound. During the attack on the white house she had been shot in the stomach, and now she lay asleep. Reverend Martin sat by her. "No change," he signaled with his awkward hands.

By contrast the demon's hands seemed perfectly articulate, even to himself. He concentrated on the movements he was making. He molded the heat and light in the small room between his fingers, making patterns in the air that had an abstract beauty as well as many kinds of meaning. Small, fluttering motions of his fingertips meant, "Ah, ah, I can't stand it." A subsidiary part of a larger pattern—he made a cupping motion with his palm. It meant, "Can I do anything?" Also: "What happened?" Also: "What will become of me?" And at the same time he was reaching out with his mind toward his sister, trying to find some entry to the fortress of groggy pain that she had built around herself. I AM HERE, he told her, but there was no reassuring tremor in the air, no sympathetic movement in the synapses of his brain, no indication to show that she heard or understood or even cared. Or not quite. Because he could still feel her inside her clumsy walls, her mind burning like a white-hot flame, becoming more intense as it contracted and relaxed. And it was as if there were a figure in the heart of the flame, a fire lizard that cried out: DON'T LEAVE ME. Also: I MUST GO.

"I don't see more I do," signaled Reverend Martin with short, crisp gestures. "Wound infect and no here. No medicine. I be fake to you. No very hope." He got to his feet so that the demon could sit down.

She was resting on a pallet of straw laid down on a narrow stone couch. The demon sat on it and reached out his hand. He cupped his fingers around her small shoulder where it protruded from the blanket. He could feel the fire burning under her skin. He could feel her wound, a gnawing pain deep in his guts where the pellets ran in.

With his other hand he made a sudden movement. "Can you say why this happened?"

Reverend Martin shrugged, a human gesture, and the demon turned to look. "Man at white house. He gun. Secret gun in cloth. Later we kill him."

"Please, I said why. I mean why." Then in a little while, "I was there."

Speaking with his left hand only, the demon concentrated on simple meaning. His right hand, with which he would have added his emotions, his ambivalences, was silent and receptive on his sister's shoulder. I AM HERE, he said, and then he listened with his touch.

"Sorry I not see," stammered the priest. He spoke loudly, in big, heavy gestures, though the demon was close by.

"Woman Oimu husband man is in a prisoner. Shreve Port. He giant strong. Gov fighter. She catch prisoner to change. Two prisoner. Also money—she lusts."

The gestures were so big, so crude, the demon didn't have to look. He could feel the vibrations in his body. But he was looking at his sister's face, his older sister, and he was remembering all the times that he had seen it lit with meaning, with delicate articulation, with the laughter that had always seemed to burn under her skin, mocking but not cruel, an utterly distinctive shade of white. "Laugh anger," he had called it. Sometimes he had seen it burning all around her when she raged at him. All gone now. The color was deep red. Down deep and dry. It had pulled back from her face.

She lay curled up on her side, covered with blankets. Her face was in the crook of her elbow and her hands were still. Her eyes were closed sometimes and sometimes open, but she never looked at him.

He listened to the motion of Reverend Martin's hands. Because he wasn't watching, he could make them smoother. "I'm sorry," they said. "I didn't know it would be like this. This is my fault."

It was Martin who had found them in the cave when their mother died. He had cared for them, had learned their language. "Don't blame yourself," the demon said. He moved his feet, and the chain between his ankles rustled on the cold floor.

"I didn't know that this would happen. I didn't think that they would use you."

"Don't blame yourself. We would be dead except for you. We would have starved to death."

"They promised me that they would treat you well. Otherwise I never would have . . ."

The demon raised three fingers of his hand. "They hate

us," he said simply. AND WE HAVE NO STRENGTH OVER THEM, he added in his mind.

"I thought it could be a real coalition," continued Reverend Martin. "I thought it'd be a good thing for the world. I thought that they could love you as I love you if they took the time."

The demon let go of his sister's shoulder, partly to talk more clearly, partly because of the wound in his belly when he was touching her. It was suddenly intolerable. "Hatred never goes away," he said. And then because he couldn't stand it, he tried to concentrate on other things. "But tell me what is happening now." He turned back to the priest, reducing the man's speech to half speech once again.

Reverend Martin, who had bowed his head, now raised it. "I no see," he said. "No plan they. No fight. Men is ready now. Too strong. We catch prisoner in Gold Stone. Female Oimu waits in husband maybe here. Wait for people spin. Spin around."

The same, perhaps, in every language: revolution. "And me?"

"Male Oimu doctor that I see."

"He won't touch her."

"No. Yes. He good man. He help sist may be."

"No, he won't." He turned back to her and pulled the blanket up around her cheek. Her skin was pale and all the talking lines around her eyes were quiet now. "And me?" he said, not looking back.

"I don't know. I don't know what they'll do to you. I thought there was a place for you with them—they promised. But Dr. Oimu—maybe they have plans. Maybe they can save her life."

"They have no use for us."

The heater needed more kerosene. Its flame was burning

down. His sister was curled toward it. Now she moved a little bit, shifting, rocking, rocking in pain, and he put his hand out to share it. He touched her again on her bare shoulder. I AM HERE, he said. Then she opened up her mind to him and he went in, and it was like walking into a hot storm of fear, and the sensation was so strong it took away his thoughts.

3b
Progress

Our religion is about death," said Katharine Styreme. "Death and redemption. That's why it is such a comfort at times like this."

They lay in a nest of blankets in another small stone room close by. Behind the site of the obliterated demon palace, numerous one-room buildings were arranged in groups of four, divided by muddy lanes. They were made of stone with corrugated iron roofs, many of which had fallen in. But several of the buildings still had doors that shut and locked; Simon and Katharine lay in one of these. Light came from a kerosene lantern on the floor.

"I know you know about these things, but it's important that you believe in them," she said. "Martyrdom is not the worst alternative. It is the best, as long as you have faith in Jesus Christ. Many of the most important figures of our church were men and women who were tortured quite literally to death."

Her tone of voice contained among many other things a small degree of satisfaction. Her lips closed over the words. Simon shook his head. "Please stop talking about it," he said. She had talked of nothing else for hours. But in a strange way: her words were urgent, but her voice was not. As if what she was saying were so obvious, it wasn't even interesting anymore. Or as if she was really thinking about something else.

Earlier she had quoted from what he assumed was the Bible—lists of catastrophes and strange apocalyptic images recited in a faraway monotone. Somehow the voice had given the images more power, as if she were describing something abstractly true. Something that had happened to her long ago. He had thought letting her talk would calm her, and perhaps it had. But now whores and kings and seven-headed beasts chased each other across a gray, tormented landscape in his mind. He had never heard anybody talk about these things. There were very few Christians left in Golders Green, in London.

"Did you see the devil?" she asked suddenly.

"What?"

"The demon in the picture—did you see him? They have him here."

Her voice had a new quickness, an edge. "It's not a demon," he said unsteadily. "They just call it that. It's another race of Aboriginals, like you. A person."

"You don't know anything about it. They hurt us and they made us slaves."

"That was a long time ago."

"It doesn't matter. The world has a dark half and a light half, and they are from the dark. They are Satan's creatures, and they ruled us with our sins until you came."

He sat up to look at her. She had relapsed to her remorseless monotone, but she was trembling. She was lying on her side. Her eyes were open, and she was staring at the lantern flame.

"You brought the knowledge of Jesus Christ," she said.

He lifted up his face and looked into the corners of the room. "Perhaps," he said. "But it was the drugs that did it. Barivase 9-12, and then the rest."

Her breath was slow and soft. "Maybe," she whispered, "maybe in the absence of the drugs, faith is enough."

He let his head sink to look at her. Her proud nose. Her dirty hair. "I'm sorry," he said.

Her pupil had closed down in the light. Her golden eye, preternaturally full, preternaturally clear, shone with the lantern flame. Her beautiful long lash, golden also, seemed to catch small fragments of the light. At this distance when she blinked, Simon could see the small incision on her lid where it had been inserted.

"They were full of sin," she said. "Everybody said so. They fornicated and went naked and committed incest. They broke every commandment. They lived for their sensations—everybody said so. Their sensations were . . . acute."

The light made her skin golden, too—a rich, tawny shade. She had pulled up the sleeve of her sweatshirt, and he could see the hair on her golden arm, each one meticulously placed. Her trembling had stopped. She lay quiet; now she turned over onto her stomach. He could see her breasts settle underneath her shirt.

She closed her eyes, then opened them. "I pray my father's safe," she said. And then: "Tell me about London."

In his mind, an image of Goldstone Lodge barely had time to form before it was supplanted by the dome of St. Paul's. Emotions came with each: fear and regret and unformed guilt gave way before a certain merciful nostalgia.

"London is a beautiful city," he said reflexively. "There are many beautiful buildings left over from the old days. It's on the seashore, at the mouth of a river called the Thames, and there are many bridges. They've got a zoo and a botanical garden, and theaters in the West End."

"Is it very large?"

"Oh, it's very large. Almost a million people from all over the world. They have a lot of things there that you can't find many other places. There's an English-language university, and it's good. Old-fashioned."

"Like here."

"Not like here."

She lay staring at the lantern flame. "I can picture the old buildings," she said. "I'd love to go. You know I've seen movies and photographs, and it looks so beautiful. So green."

Simon rolled over onto his back. He clasped his hands behind his head. "It's not like that. Not anymore. Perhaps two hundred years ago it was like that. Three hundred years ago: like a garden. It's more desert now."

She said, "I've got slides of all the concert houses. La Scala and the Salle Pleyel. It would be so amazing just to be there, just to be inside. Westminster Abbey—have you been there?"

"Yes."

"The Tower of London and the Louvre. And Notre-Dame. Just to see the buildings where the great events of history took place. Where the great men and women of our history actually stood, actually lived their lives. The stage where Sarah Bernhardt played Hamlet."

"You'd be disappointed." Simon looked up at the black cold ceiling. "It's still there, but it's not like that. People are poor. They die young, especially the women. No one lives long enough to make it work. Most of my first circle—you know, what you'd call my parents. They were dead from cancer when I was five years old. My little sister, she died too."

"Cancer. But I have cancer now. I feel it in my chest—just the beginning. But it's worth it, you know. It's worth it to be part of it."

"People are poor there," Simon repeated in his own

monotone. This was his Bible: "You don't understand. All the things you take for granted here. Hot water. Good food. Nice clothes. Free time. To eat something beside soybean paste. To drive a private car. To stand outside and look at the sun on a bright day without your goggles on. Nothing like that has existed there for a long time. Not for the general population. I tell you, when I first got here, I thought I had died and gone to heaven."

She looked at him then, a harsh, fierce look. "Is that what heaven means to you? Hot water? No, God's house is on Earth. He made it in seven days. This place—He was never here."

She put her cheek down on the blanket.

"It was beautiful," said Simon. "But they used it up and now it's gone. Everyone was expecting some new idea to take the place of all the things they wasted. But no one thought of anything."

With her forefinger, she drew a pattern on the blanket near her eye. "Someone had a new idea," she said after a pause. "It's why you're here."

"Of course. I'm not saying there's no progress. Transport and the space program, they were forced to make it a priority. Or at least it was."

3c
Katharine (iii)

Later he fell asleep. She lay beside him, aware of him. His smell. His breath. The noise from his smallest movement. "Mother of God," she prayed. "Be to me, oh Virgin, nigh. Lest in flames I burn and die . . . ah, God," for she could feel it now. She could feel the prickling on her skin. How long had she waited—five days? More? Waited for it to begin, and now it was beginning. Now all the shock, the hardship, and the power of anticipation could be dismissed. It could not account for this prickling on her skin, this desire to touch. Nothing could account for it.

She had been playing the sonata. She had been playing the first movement and had reached the part where the baby kicked inside the Virgin's womb. And as they dragged her down the steps to the car she could see the red flames going up. Where was her father now? But maybe already he could never recognize her. She could not recognize herself. Earlier they had given her cold hamburgers to eat and taken her out to the latrine. Now she lay on her back and lifted her feet up off the floor. Her rectum felt as if a greased hot bottle was being shoved into her guts. Her nipples were hard. Her mouth was filling with saliva so that she had to keep on swallowing it down; the blanket near her head was wet with it.

"Holy Mother, pierce me through," she whispered. "In my heart each wound renew." Tears leaked from her eyes, spit from her lips. She turned over, turned back to the kerosene lamp and watched an intricate tracery of light spread from the flame. It cast its pattern on the wall, thin lines of light, and when she looked closely she could see it separate into the component colors of the spectrum. She was conscious suddenly of her tongue in her mouth, a wad of muscle that was moving, moving. She could feel her own sweat leaking down her rib cage. The room was cold and she was burning; she threw off the blanket that was scratching her skin. Every time she exhaled, she could see crystals in the mist of her breath.

Simon Mayaram lay beside her, asleep. He was close by, and much of his body was uncovered now. She raised herself up on one elbow and studied him, especially the front of his dirty pants.

"Ah, God," she said, putting her hands over her ears,

aware that the sound she was hearing, which seemed intolerable, as threatening as an argument of beasts, was Simon's light snoring as he slept. She knew the sound. She had heard it several times in the last days and nights. But why did it roar now in her ears, why was she trembling, why did she spread her knees apart against the floor? She pulled the blanket up over Simon and arranged it by his head. Then she lay down again upon her side. She pushed her hands into her crotch and clamped her thighs down over them.

"Talk to me," she said through clenched teeth.

"Talk to me," she said louder, and she listened to the rumble of his snores suddenly cease. And it was as if he had stopped breathing; she heard nothing from him, nothing at all for moment after moment—was there something the matter with her sense of time? Yet she didn't want to touch him; how mortifying it was just to have him here with his intrusive male noises, his intrusive smells. How disgusting to have him lie with her, no doubt assuming intimacies that did not exist, could not exist. "Ah, Mother, protect me," she murmured, squeezing her hands between her thighs.

Yet she needed him. By herself, without him, she would lose her mind. She would be naked before the demon, and which was worse? Yes, she would touch him, she would wake him, she would start him breathing. She would not be alone; she couldn't stand it. She wouldn't lie alone in the darkness, measuring these incremental changes. She would not lie burning and itching in the darkness, wondering if his dreams had made him hard.

Why was he so still? She reached out to touch him, to shake him by the shoulder, and she would shake him roughly, violently, so that he wouldn't make any mistakes. Wouldn't confuse it with tenderness. She took hold of his shoulder and listened to his long, burbling sigh.

She held him by the shoulder, feeling with intolerable clarity the grain of his shirt, the ball of his muscle underneath it. Intolerable—she jolted him awake, withdrew her hand, heard with satisfaction how he caught his breath, watched with satisfaction as he pulled himself up out of sleep, swallowed, grunted, and sat up.

"O.T.O.T. (9) pissstiff," he said. Then he swallowed, shook his head. "What is it?"

"You were disturbing me. Your snores."

"Oh."

He lay down again in the nest of blankets. She curled away from him, her knees held to her chest, and he lay down next to her, also on his side. "Don't touch me," she whispered, but he only grunted and lay still.

"What was it like to come here?"

For a moment she was afraid that he had gone to sleep again. But then he started to talk, slowly and softly. She could hear the sleep in his voice. Normally precise and clear, his words were slurred now, mauled by tiredness. Words and phrases were spaced in strange ways, sometimes running together, sometimes separated by long silences unconnected to the sense. And it was as if she were listening to him with her brain divided in two, and with one half she was registering meaning and allowing his words to make pictures in the air. With the other she was listening to the sound of the words, and she was alive to the sound of the words in a new way, the knotted consonants, the slippery vowels. More than that: it was as if there were another meaning in each word which was made up of the significance of the sound itself. Inside every sentence was another sentence, because every sound, whether harsh or smooth, soft or wet, seemed to carry in it a small emotional consequence. And when he spoke, she felt with half her mind that she was wandering in a chaotic landscape of words, and each successive word was as complex in its own way, as requiring of response, as a different natural phenomenon. "I don't remember most of it," he said, slurring the sounds, so that the "remember most" was like a dark line of remote hills, holding among them the possibility, the presage both of pretty valleys and hard peaks. The "I" was an enormous tree that burst out of the ground in front of her and seemed to promise shelter overhead, for the sky was changeable. The "don't" was like some small wet litter of cans or bottles, some garbage in the path. Because there was definitely a path made up of the direction of his sentences, and sometimes it seemed a straight road, and sometimes it turned back upon itself, and sometimes she lost it altogether.

"I don't remember most of it. It's rare, you know. That kind of travel. Because the trip takes over forty years.

"No one wants to go," he said. "Because you have to give up everything. It's like dying. You leave everything behind forever," he said, and the "leave" was like a leafy hedge that ran beside the path, and "everything" squatted behind it, a furtive beast that was forever there, forever hidden.

"For what? A place where they speak a dead language. I learned it. Huge words, each one with its meaning. Not like home. In Golders Green it's disposable. The thing we could afford to throw away.

"And we've made progress. We've gone forward. Perhaps because of it. Freedom. Disposable thinking. Not many people want to give that up. Not for this rubbish. Not to go backward. Not to go back to a twentieth century that never was. Wreck this world as it wrecked ours."

The path had widened to a roadway as he spoke, and it was full of silent motorcars with the tops down, and each one held a family inside it that was smiling, laughing. And they were driving down a straight road toward the setting sun, and perhaps there were pressures in the long drive that caused their faces gradually to change. There were arguments breaking out, and frowns and long faces as the gauges sunk toward empty. As the people drove, they were throwing rubbish from their cars: crumpled-up newspapers and cigarette packages and even glass bottles, which shattered on the concrete breakdown lane. And it was getting dark with menacing rapidity because Simon was quiet now, and Katharine was afraid that he had gone to sleep again.

"And you?" she asked. Her own words had no significance.

"Besides, it's difficult. Terrifying. People have died. The ships are not for passengers. Not for human beings. Faster than light. They kill you and then wake you up. You're in a place. Dark and small. A coffin. Nothing—who would do it? You'd have to be crazy."

He paused for a long time, then went on. "I had gone to doctors. It was common. Twice before, I'd tried to hurt myself. When I was working in the foreign language office.

"They wanted to send someone. There was a scientific expedition. So I came. I'm a linguist," he said, and even with her eyes closed, she could see his gleaming tongue. "They were going to Shackleton, but I wanted to see the discovery. Homo Celestis, before they were all gone. A long, dark, quiet place. It was a death. Perhaps something at the end of it. Heaven, perhaps. Hell."

"How did you . . . ?" she asked. The words were empty husks dropping out of the cloudless sky, rocking downward with the same rhythm of her body, for she was rocking her shoulders slightly, her hand pressed to her crotch.

"Hurt myself? Once I walked out by myself into Silver Flat. It was the place of an old accident. I climbed over the wire."

"Once," he said, "I cut myself."

Again the tree was there. But it was different now: still straight, its bark was wounded, dripping sap. And it grew out of a pool, a flat, limpid pool like a mirror. And the road seemed to end there, seemed to come to an end at the round shore, stopped, perhaps, by the *t* sound in the word *cut*. There seemed no way forward. She stood on the shore of the small pool, looking down into its mirrored surface, admiring the sight of the black tree with its wounded bark, its leafless twigs and branches held beseechingly to the gray sky.

And when he started to snore again, it was a murmur in the clouds.

3d

Contact in the Flesh

She lay on her side on the stone slab, curled into the curve of his body, her long back pressed against his rib cage. Reverend Martin had fired up the heater before he left. It was hot in the little room.

The demon had changed the dressing on her stomach. He could no longer take her shirt off without hurting her. So he had torn it to strips and now lay close to her under the raw blankets, holding her, feeling her wet skin against his skin. He tried to keep her from moving. Even the smallest movement sent spiked jolts of pain through her and he could feel them. Out of her control, her body shook and spasmed sometimes; he held her close to stop it, and to feel also the cascade of naked and hallucinatory images that flowed out of her flesh and into his.

She was leaving him. Her skin was burning against his. Distorted by pain, by delirium, by rage, the images unwound from her at an intolerable and ever-increasing speed—her memories and his, for since his birth they had spent scarcely an hour apart. New memories inhabited his body, intolerably clear, and he felt inside of him a wrenching pain as old images from his past twisted themselves to correspond with them. He saw the steps of the white house and what had happened there—a chaos without cause or effect in his own memory—made suddenly new, suddenly clear. He saw his sister pull him down, saw her understand the gun in the hands of the fat man on the step, saw her pull him down and take the blast. And then regret it. LITTLE THING, she raged. LITTLE THING (and this was what she'd always called him), LITTLE THING (the buckshot thought hitting his body now), AH LITTLE MISERABLE THING YOU OWE YOUR LIFE TO ME. YOUR LITTLE LIFE I SAVED YOUR LITTLE LIFE.

She was his sister, his protector. In his deepest mind he thought of her that way. The deepest library of his mind held books of pictures, and she was there in all of them. But now he found himself assaulted by new images, new memories forced down over his own. Potent, brightly colored, irresistible, and merciless—the cave they had lived in, in the dark. The cave with the small entrance that went back and back. The soft bed where they all slept. When their mother didn't come, she had gone to find her. He had waited, shivering with fear. But now he saw her crouched over their mother's body in the black rocks. Crouched over the decapitated body. Moved her hand over the gunshot wound in their mother's chest. The back of her ribs visible in the big wound. The severed neck. Looking back toward the cave and thinking, AH LITTLE THING I'LL LEAVE YOU NOW. BETTER TO STARVE YOU. She had picked along the rocks for a long way. Then she had gone back.

Now she regretted it. Here, now, in his arms. She should

have gone. She should have run away. Yet she had . . . AH AH AH I TOOK YOU LITTLE THING. ALONE AND I WAS WHOLE AND STRONG. YOU ARE THE LITTLE THING THAT BROKE ME DOWN.

He felt her heartbeat knocking in his body. And another thump too. Reverend Martin was there. He had come out of the door. Now he stood in the small chamber, half turned away. He bent down to adjust the stove.

I SHOULD HAVE KILLED THE PRIEST— The demon pulled away, sat up. Contact was broken. He sat still for a moment, quiet, and then raised his hands. "What?"

"Nothing."

The priest fiddled with the gauge and then stood up. His coarse, crude gestures: "No thing. Wait."

"She is dying."

"We wait hope. We wait letter Theodore Oimu. He come. Not come bad. Doctor and fat man. I know help is only help." He took a few steps across the chamber. "Wait now. Pillow."

The demon sat up out of bed. The chain swung down onto the floor, hurting his ankles. Contact was broken. He leaned back against the stone wall and closed his eyes. In this way he eliminated everything but his sensations. They chased and fretted over his body without clarity or speech.

<hr>

3e
Theodore Oimu Dies in Shreveport Jail

It seemed only moments since he had fallen asleep, and then they woke him. They woke him with a match lit near his eye.

Theodore Oimu, M.D., spokesman for his race, ninth Aboriginal graduate from Shreveport University, six-time winner of the Governor's Prize for Social Fitness, former member of the faculty at Custis Medical College, prominent inventor and lecturer in genetics, founder of the National Liberation Coalition, lay fully dressed on the cot of his cell in Shreveport jail. He lay on his side in the windowless black room, his big head pillowed on his arm, and as he came awake he blinked and squinted at the flickering light so close to his face. He could smell it, feel its little heat.

And instantly he knew he was in trouble. He reached his hand out for his glasses on the bedside table. They weren't there.

In prison any disruption of routine is cause for fear. During the past few months he had been questioned often. Daily, sometimes twice daily in the past week—long sessions during which he had confessed to several things. But these interrogations had taken place in other parts of the building. The guards had come during his waking hours, and they had knocked on the door.

The flame burned out and it was dark again. Oimu heard a scratching sound and then the flame reappeared farther away. Someone nursed it between their fingers and then moved it close against his face again. But in the interval Oimu managed to look beyond the light into the eyes of the man who held it. The man was squatting on the floor next to the cot. He was dressed in black. He had a red armband marked with a crude sign. He was wearing a mask, a white piece of cloth knotted around the upper part of his face. Rough eyeholes were cut out of it.

Oimu groaned, and turned over onto his back.

Always before his guards had worn blue tunics or the insignia of the Shreveport police. This was something new, and he had heard of it. Jonathan Goldstone's Brotherhood of Man.

His cell door opened a crack, and against the light in the

corridor he could see two more men slip into the room, both dressed in black, both masked. The second one closed the door again and there was darkness as the second match burned out.

One of the new men lit a pencil flashlight. "Here," he said, and Oimu recognized the voice, for his memory was capacious and his ears were sharp. Recognized, and yet could not identify it.

The second man came forward and held out the light. The first man, still squatting, took it. He pointed it toward Oimu. Lying on his back, the doctor felt it play upon his face. In the dark room, he was reminded of an ophthalmologist's examination.

"Wake up," said the first man unnecessarily. Again Oimu recognized the voice. Again he failed to place it.

"Who are you?" he asked.

"It doesn't matter," said the voice. "Just a concerned citizen. Just a concerned *human* citizen."

Oimu flinched and raised his hand to block the light. "Please don't shine that in my eyes," he said.

"What do you want?" he said.

"Just some information."

"But I've told you everything. Please . . ." He attempted to get up on his elbow, holding his splayed hand out against the light. But the man took him by the throat. Without rising, without moving the light, which he held delicately in his left hand, the man reached out and took him by the throat, squeezing it closed. His hand was very big, very strong.

"Stop the shit," he said softly.

"Don't fuck with us," he said. "We're not the police. Not the fucking collaborationist police.

"We're not on your side."

Abruptly, Oimu's wristwatch made a pinging sound. The man expelled his breath. It was a soft, pungent wind in Oimu's face, and then the man released him. "Time to take your pill."

Oimu sat up. The man stayed where he was, his head on a level with Oimu's hand as he reached automatically for his pillbox on the table. The man's head was lower than Oimu's own, which made him more menacing somehow, not less.

"Where are my glasses?" Oimu asked.

"Could I have a drink of water?" he asked.

He choked the pill down raw.

The man below him moved out of his squat. He sat down on the floor with his knees up. One broad bare forearm lay over the point of his knee, and with the other hand he held the flashlight up, aimed at Oimu's face.

"We've got a kind of a split here," he said conversationally. "You know us ordinary people. We're not rich men."

"Please. Can I see Mr. Isobel? He's the night custodian—"

"Mr. Isobel is with us. Unofficially. Everyone is with us unofficially. Or they will be, as soon as they know the facts. We're not the governor's office."

One of the men standing near the door grunted. He was smoking a cigarette. Oimu watched it glow bright, then subside.

"We want to know where your wife is," said the standing man.

"I told you, I don't know."

"You didn't tell us anything," said the man on the floor. "Those people you told, they didn't really want to know. We really want to know."

"I don't understand."

Again he smelled the man's pungent breath. "They didn't

want to know. Because they don't want to do anything about it. They let Jonathan Goldstone die because they were afraid. Maybe they wanted him to die. Maybe they double-crossed him. Jonathan Goldstone and his family."

"I don't understand."

"Well, I'm not sure I feel like explaining. I'm not sure it's the time and place. I'll say this: The governor's office doesn't have much to do about this. The consul's office, the police. Sold us down the river, and they let him die."

"Tell us where your wife is," said the man near the door.

"I don't know. I'd tell you if I knew."

The man who was sitting down shook his head. Still holding the flashlight, he reached into the pocket of his shirt and brought out a loose stick of gum. He shelled it between the fingers of his right hand and put it in his mouth.

"We really want to know," he said. "We're not afraid of you. Five million, fifty. It doesn't matter. We can't allow you to murder our people. It's not going to happen."

He chewed gum for a few moments.

"But I didn't have anything to do with it," protested Dr. Oimu. "I was arrested before the first attack."

"But you fucking well know about it, don't you? How do you know about it?"

"They told me during my sessions. Please, my wife and I have separate ideas about these things. She's not answerable to me. I haven't seen her in a year. Nor do I approve of what she's done—I've never condoned violence. Naomi Gold-stone, I knew her. I—" He paused, then continued: "Who are you? I recognize your voice."

"That's because you know me. You know all of us. You met me many times, back when you were just another penis-licking Abo in a bad toupee."

"I don't recall. I—"

The man on the floor had laid the flashlight down. He had taken some black driving gloves from his pocket and was putting them on, smoothing each finger individually. Oimu listened to the slow champ of his gum.

"We really want to know," said the man by the door.

Oimu took several deep breaths, and then he opened his mouth to call out. Before he could do it, the man on the floor had risen up, had grabbed hold of his throat again in his right hand, forcing it closed. In his left hand he held the flashlight, and he brought it close now, shining it in Oimu's eyes, on his nose. Oimu felt the light pass over his face. It was like a finger on his face.

He closed his eyes. The man had grabbed him under his chin, and he could scarcely breathe. His mouth was open and he felt the flashlight slip inside of it. He felt the metal on his teeth.

"We built this country, and we're going to keep it," said the man. "Who's going to take it away? Cock-sucking mutants like you? No. We made you. Without us, you don't exist."

Oimu could scarcely breathe. He felt drowsy, weak. Yet how fine it would be, he thought, to tell the truth. Here at the end. Make them understand how small they are in the history of this place. If it takes a thousand years—they will go, we will stay.

Yet how can I say it? he thought, drowsy now, his brain starved. What human orator would I imitate? What human hero? Not genuine. How could they believe me if I spoke in English, or understand me if I didn't?

Yet it is terrible, to die like this.

"Dry . . . Water," he gasped, and instantly the flashlight was gone from his mouth, the pressure on his throat was less. "At Gundabook before. Now Drywater."

"Thank you," said the man. Then the grip on Oimu's throat tightened again, and he couldn't breathe or make a sound.

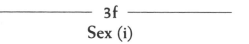

3f
Sex (i)

Drywater was the name of the demon ruin. In his stone chamber there, Simon woke up.

Katharine's face was next to him. She was not asleep. He could feel her breath upon his face.

He turned toward her. They lay knotted in blankets, her face inches from his own. One of her eyes was in darkness, hidden by the shadow of her nose as she lay on her side. But the other stared at him unblinking, a golden-orange ball, subtly strange, shining in the lamplight.

As usual, he had woken up with an erection. It was mostly urine, yet even so he was aware of it because she was so close. Her hand was very close to him, he knew.

She cleared her throat. "Tell me," she said. "Have you slept with many women?"

She spoke with no trace of shyness or hesitation. It was as if all that had been sweated out of her; he could feel that the blankets around her were damp with sweat.

"That day at Goldstone Lodge," she said. "Did you sleep with Natasha Goldstone?"

His tongue felt frozen in his mouth. He couldn't speak. An image of Natasha came into his mind, lying with a sheet wrapped around her. He had looked back as they pulled him to the door, his ears ringing as Harriet Oimu raised her gun again.

He licked his lips with his dry tongue. Nearby was a ceramic cup of water. He punctured the sphere of warmth that lay around them to reach for it. And then he stopped with his fingers just inside the rim, because when he moved he felt her. He felt her hand against the front of his pants.

He felt her fingers through the fabric. They searched for him and closed around him the best they could, gently, firmly. He was conscious of the fullness of his bladder, conscious also of the smell of their bodies, though he had lain in it all night.

"Katharine," he said, letting go of the cup. She had moved closer to him, so that when he brought his hand down again he touched her, touched her on the cheek. She turned her face into his hand, and he touched her almost accidentally upon her silicone-stung lips.

And he could feel himself shrinking underneath her fingers, losing his erection in the crude transition between fantasy and fact. He stared down at her face, suddenly conscious in his body of a knowledge that had been only cerebral to that point—something he had read about in books before he came here. These people were a one-sexed species. Katharine, when she was born, had had a penis similar to his.

He tried to pull away, to shift away a little bit, but she held him fast. "Katharine," he said. Then he lay still. His feelings at that moment seemed chaotic and undifferentiated, a cloud lit with sudden flashes. He sank down through it into a more familiar landscape of other people's expectations; he lay back and allowed her to fumble with his zipper, to pull it down, to reach inside.

"Katharine," he said. She had turned her face away into the blankets so as not to look at him. But he could see her throat and neck stretched tight, and he could see the old cuts on her skin, and he wondered where they had opened her to take out her organs of regeneration: was it there, that long old line above her clavicle? Where had they opened her to rebuild her throat, rebuild the hinges of her jaw?

Her hand pushed through his fly and spread open the front of his underwear. Then she was touching him, her fingers soft on his soft skin. She touched him carefully, like a doctor. She rolled each testicle between her fingers and her thumb. She combed her nails through his pubic hair. And then he felt her other hand undoing his belt, unbuttoning him further.

"Katharine, stop," he said.

Still she had not made a sound. She lay with her face pressed into the blankets. Almost it was as if her hands were not a part of her, were moving independent of her will. And perhaps, thought Simon, in some sense they were. When they were first captured, she had talked to him for hours about the convent school where she had spent her childhood, about the bell-ringing and the choir, about the stone chapel with the altars to the Virgin and to Saint Teresa of Avila and to Joan of Arc.

Her hands were gentle and so tentative. The feeling brought him a pleasure different from excitement; he lay back and let her do what she needed, because less than anything did he want to embarrass her, humiliate her. Only he lifted up his hips so that she could pull his pants down over his thighs. She pulled his underwear down too.

Still she would not look at him. But in time she rearranged the blankets, and then he felt her moving down his body, moving her head down toward where her hands had been. In time he felt her breath upon him and in time her tongue—it did not feel sexual so much as intimate. He felt as if she were washing him with little careful probings of her tongue, as if she were an animal, a cat. His skin cooled as the moisture dried—it made him feel clean. He bent down over her and put his fingers in her hair.

For a single moment she took him completely into her small mouth, bathing him with her saliva. Then she pulled back and tried to pull away, to turn her head. But he slid his hand under her cheek. Her whole cheek was wet under her eye, and he realized she was crying. Suddenly small movements of hers—small intakes of breath that he had assumed or hoped to be connected to some kind of passion—he now realized they were part of something else. Something more alien, perhaps. Or no. Something that filled him with remorse—Natasha had cried, too. Again he saw a vision of Natasha Goldstone tied in her white sheet. The woman at the doorway with the gun in her hand.

"Katharine," he said. "Please," but then he stopped, partly because he had no clear thoughts in his mind, and partly because her face slid through his hands now and turned up toward him, and all impulse to say something was amputated by the grief and anger in her eyes.

Amputated also by the sudden darkness; she rolled away from him to blow out the lamp. Then she got up. He felt her hovering somewhere in the darkness, but he couldn't see. He lay back, suddenly cold, listening to her ragged breathing as he pulled his pants up and tucked himself in. All the warmth from the blankets seemed to have fled away, and they were stiff and damp as he sat up and wrapped them around his body.

He couldn't see her except once, when she crossed in front of the barred window. But he could hear her in the darkness. He imagined her standing with her cheek against the wall, in tears. Her tear ducts were implants, he knew, and part of him wanted to be close to her, to see if he could tell the difference. He imagined her face contorted in a mask of hatred, and part of him wanted to reach out and light the lamp again, to see that mask. Instead, shivering slightly, he sat and looked out the window. He let his eyes spread open to the darkness. The glass in the window was frosted and opaque. Yet through a hole in it he could see a few bright stars.

Suddenly he felt tired. This was not a rare thing for him. Often he was overpowered by other people's emotions. Fear also made him sleepy. He was afraid; she lurked outside the circle of his sight, transformed by darkness into something monstrous. He sank back down into the cold blankets.

"We're in a difficult situation," he said.

So far, as if by agreement, neither of them had mentioned what was happening to them. Neither of them had offered any thought about the future, about the hidden past. It was as if this dark cell, ruptured only by occasional meals and trips to the latrine, existed independent of the world. The pressure of the world had given it a dark integrity. Had given them a closeness that was artificial, false—he saw that now. Perhaps it was because the integrity was broken now that he felt free to speak; perhaps also because he regretted the loss of it he felt compelled to mention the pressure outside, as if he could bring the effects of it back.

Perhaps also he couldn't think of anything else to say. And yet the silence was unbearable. "Listen, what are we going to do?"

He couldn't tell where she was now. She was close to him, gone in the darkness, breathing, crying, angry, sad, disappointed—no, he could not guess. "Listen," he said. "They are holding us for hostage. But the government won't do anything.

"They would have tried already," he continued after a cold pause. "They won't help us, and they won't buy us back. We're on our own. You understand that."

These words, so painful, made him tired. Each one liberated new words, new thoughts. "They're afraid of an uprising," he said. "If they come down on it. The NLC—so far it's localized in one small group. They are afraid that it will spread."

He could hear her breathing, raggedy and soft. "The consul set me up," he said.

Beside the cup of water lay the crumpled envelope. Even in the dark Simon knew exactly where it was. "He gave me a letter for Jonathan Goldstone and I forgot about it. I actually forgot. I found it in my pocket when you were asleep. It was one line. Anonymous. It said there would be an attack on Goldstone Lodge. It gave the time."

He could hear her breathing. "I thought about this when you were asleep," he said. "That's why Clare refused to go—he wanted some type of incident. He didn't want to use the police to track down the NLC. He wanted to keep it unofficial so that people wouldn't blame the government for the violence. Perhaps he thought they would exterminate each other, the Brotherhood and the NLC. Perhaps he thought he could kill two birds with one stone, and at the very least there would be a diplomatic incident if I was involved. So he could complain to New Manchester, perhaps. Or perhaps farther in. God knows, perhaps to London, though by the time they got the message . . ."

It was preposterous. He lay down on his back and put his hands behind his head. Nevertheless, just that word *London* gave him something. Not a memory, but just a feeling. An open, empty feeling. He looked out through the broken window at the sky.

"If I had given him the letter," he said, "perhaps this never would have happened."

He lay back. In time he saw an alteration in the darkness through the window. After a moment he could tell someone was coming, could see the flicker of a flashlight as someone crossed between the buildings. Then there was a noise at the door, a rattling of the lock and chain. The door groaned open and someone stepped inside.

"Quickly," someone said. "Let's go."

The light illuminated Katharine by the wall and then flicked back to him. "Get up."

He pulled on his shoes. It was cold, and he lifted up one of the blankets and wrapped it around his shoulders. Without looking he could hear Katharine in the corner, hear the sound of her breath. Moments before she had seemed strange to him, yet now he felt something in him reaching out. Especially in this situation where any news was likely to be bad, any change for the worse. He turned a little toward her and was gratified to see her come to him, come across the floor and stand beside him, her eyes wide, her teeth chattering. "Oh," she whispered, and then a few more words. Simon thought for a moment she was praying and perhaps she was, but then she stopped and looked at him. "Oh, Mr. Mayaram," she said, "I'm so scared," and then she smiled. He bent down again to pick up another blanket, and then together they rolled it around her body; it was stiff from cold, uncooperative. Then she took his hand and squeezed it, because they both knew something was different now, something had happened. Three times every twenty-four hours someone had come to feed them or take them out to the latrine, and even without clocks they had managed to establish a schedule. This was different.

The man at the door flicked his light impatiently around the room. "Come quick," he said, and he was making an effort to sound threatening. He was not someone they recognized.

They stumbled forward, their legs awkward from disuse,

their hands clasped. How strange it is, thought Simon, because he felt absurdly comforted by that small pressure. And because all other thoughts were full of anxiousness, he tried to think about that. Sex means something, he thought. No matter what it is, it always means something.

They had not been tied up or handcuffed since they had come over the rim; there was no place to go. But the man showed them his gun in the light. He was dressed in an orange down jacket. Someone else waited outside, in the alleyway that divided their stone jail cell from a larger ruin. A walkway of uneven stones, greasy with ice and frozen mud, led around the corner of the wall.

Hand in hand, they moved along it. There was a young woman in a baseball cap. "Adele?" said Katharine. "Adele Borgo?" But the woman turned away, her lips pursed, her face set. Other lights appeared up ahead; around the corner, the way led uphill. A long, low building sat at the top of a short rise. Light burned in a row of windows.

This was the command center of the National Liberation Coalition. Its flag, an upraised fist upon a green background, hung limply from a pole outside. The sky was purple up ahead, as they looked back toward the rim, the terminator.

And as they came up the walk, Simon could feel his heart rising in spite of his fears. The building was made of whitewashed bricks, a comforting combination that set it apart from the cold ruins of the demon city. It was a house built for human beings and perhaps by them as well; he didn't know the history. But the wooden door opened on hinges and the heat leaped out to greet him—so cold he had been for so long.

He could hear the thump of a gas generator. An electric bulb hung by the door. Inside, electric bulbs festooned the walls, their loose cords stapled to the plaster. A gas compres-

sor roared at each end of the hall, and the air included a petroleum stench that mixed queasily with another smell.
There were fifteen or twenty Aboriginals in the narrow room.

Some were standing, some were sitting on the floor.
Some held automatic weapons. Harriet Oimu stood in an
empty place. A man and woman sat cross-legged behind her.

Oimu was a woman in what human beings would have
called late–middle age. Her face was a product of less skilled
and less expensive surgeons than Katharine's—they had
modeled her on an amalgam of American film stars out of a
book. But the texture of her face had hardened and stiffened
over the years, and her features had realigned themselves in
subtle ways. Her left eye was higher than her right. She had
a bulge of silicone under one ear.

Her face was distorted also by a look of terrible sadness,
terrible malice, which confirmed some of Simon's fears. As
they were escorted down through the middle of the hall, he
tried to hold Katharine closer, to give her comfort and then
take some also. But she pulled away from him. She was making a noise deep in her throat that he couldn't analyze; she
pulled away from him and clasped her arm through one of
the guard's. She was hurrying forward as best she could. People were standing around, and soon there were several between him and her. She was hurrying down toward where
Mrs. Oimu stood talking to someone, her eyes scanning the
room. When Katharine came close she turned to face her,
and Simon could see she held an extension cord wrapped
around her fist.

At first he wasn't near enough to hear what Katharine
said above the noise of the compressors and the hum of
other voices. An Aboriginal wearing a fleece-lined vest had
his hand around Simon's bicep. He thrust him forward and
someone in front of them moved away. Now he could see

Katharine better. He felt it was urgent to be close to her. He was finding it hard to tolerate a dozen aliens together, was feeling a liquid rush of panic in his guts, was feeling in a new way what it meant to die so far from home. He stepped forward behind Katharine, hoping to stand close to her through whatever happened. So her hand almost touched him when she reached back to point at him, and he heard her distinctly when she said, "Don't leave me alone with him. Please."

To say *please*, he thought, was not in her character. It was a sign of her distress. "I need my medication," she said. "Don't you understand me?"

Mrs. Oimu took a step backward. The noise of conversation slackened, and Simon could feel a sudden admixture of interest, of concentration. All of these were transformed Aboriginals. All of them took various prescriptions. Inside all of them, Simon supposed, was a dark fascination that must also contain some pity.

"Please," said Katharine, and she reached out her hands.

Pity, he supposed, but it was hard to tell. There was no movement on Mrs. Oimu's face. "What do you want?"

"My pills. Please—I'm losing hold. You must have taken my pills from Goldstone."

Mrs. Oimu shrugged. "There was no time," she said. Then she turned away as if to talk to someone else, but Simon could sense a falseness there. Her eyes were still on Katharine, and in fact why had she brought them there, if not to make some revelation that concerned them? That took Simon back to their predicament—it was ridiculous how hard it was to concentrate. Hard to focus. Was he really more concerned about Katharine than about himself? More concerned that she might hurt him or reject him publicly or insist that he be locked up separate from her, than he was about his life?

"Besides," said Mrs. Oimu, "I can lend you some."

This was a joke. Aboriginals had sunk into comas, or died, or suffered permanent damage from such mistakes. Katharine made a little groaning sound, and Simon caught some echo of sympathy among the people standing near. Perhaps Mrs. Oimu caught it too. She turned around in disgust. "Medication, yes." she said. "I'll tell you—yes. Barivase, Mellarin, Activol"—here she gave the names of a few of the base compounds—"what would we talk about if we couldn't talk about them? But don't you understand?" Here she raised her voice so that she was speaking to the entire room— "These drugs are the work of the invader. They are the mark of slavery. But when the invaders are forced home, then they will be discontinued. They will be thrown into the sea."

"You don't know what you're saying," whispered Katharine.

Simon thought he could detect some flicker of uneasiness in the faces around him. One man looked down and moved his feet. Mrs. Oimu changed the subject. Her fist wrapped in the extension cord came up. She brushed back a strand of her black hair. "Anyway, it's not the point. To be frank, it doesn't matter one way or another. But it's ironic in the case of such a pretty young collaborationist. Has he been bothering you?"

She smiled. She unwound six inches of the cord and let the plug dangle. "Anyway," she said, "it doesn't matter. The fact is, I don't know what to do with you. My husband died in Shreveport yesterday morning, shot in an escape attempt."

She turned to Simon. "You," she said. "We've heard nothing from your people."

He said, "You've got to keep us, though. You can't suppose they don't know where you are."

This plea for mercy was complex because it involved a threat: only by keeping them alive to bargain with could the NLC avoid being hunted down and crushed. Simon had his appeal prepared. At scattered moments in the dark cell he had worked on it. Now was the time. But as he started to speak, he found that he no longer had Mrs. Oimu's attention. There was a disturbance by the door.

The ambient conversation had increased in volume, and many faces had now turned away from him. Some of the Aboriginals had gotten to their feet. Mrs. Oimu walked a couple of steps back toward the door, the extension cord restless in her hand.

He found himself near Katharine again. But she didn't look at him. She was staring back toward the doorway, and her expression now transformed to one of such abrupt horror that he also turned. For the first time, he saw the demon.

Of course he had seen the photographs from Goldstone Lodge and Gundabook, but he had not quite believed that they were real. Part of him had hoped, and now the hope came true. Despite all other troubles, this moment brought part of him back a long way, back to when he had been a hoping child, to when he had first seen the corpse of the Celestial Man stuffed in the British Museum. He had pressed his face against the glass. Now, looking back over the heads of the Aboriginals, he felt again the mix of nausea and fascination that had possessed him in the Hall of New World Cultures when he was eleven years old. And something different: a thrill of terror when he saw the creature move. It had ducked its head to come in through the door, and now it straightened up.

When Simon had first decided to leave London, his most potent hope was to find contact with these creatures—one of three sentient races in the entire universe, and the only one more powerful than human beings. When he left, they had been plentiful here. When he arrived they were all gone. This one was perhaps the last.

It stood almost eight feet high. It was very thin. Its back was bowed, its chest sunken. It was dressed in rags, and through them Simon could see its mottled skin, stretched over fragile bones. Its hard, thin hide, which could keep it warm to absurd temperatures as long as it kept moving. Its pulse fluttering among the cords of its neck. The demon's head was down, but then it pulled up suddenly. Its eyes blinked in the light—its big sunken eyes, its long snout.

The shape of its skull was evident under its white skin, pulled thin and tight over its high cranium, its bulging braincase. Knotted ridges lined its forehead and its cheeks. It had no chin, just a few thick rolls of flesh hiding the hole through which it took in its soft meals.

"Homo in Coelis," he murmured, suddenly elated. "The adversary," early colonists had called them, but Simon didn't feel it. He felt a small ache of fellowship, born of self-pity.

Beside him, Katharine put her hands over her ears.

The Aboriginals cleared away from it and pushed themselves back against the walls. Soon Simon could see its complete figure: its short body; its gigantic legs, muscular and long, which could carry it a mile in two minutes. Its ankles chained together. Its three-toed feet. Its long arms and hands. Its hands were raised. Simon knew some of this language, but he didn't know this word, and he didn't know the phrase that the demon was repeating over and over, molding it and shaping it between his fingers.

The demon had a halter buckled round its breast and shoulders. A chain hung down its back, and it was locked to the wrist of a man, a human being. He came forward now, leading the demon down the middle of the hall toward where Mrs. Oimu stood. The Aboriginals moved away, and all around him Simon could hear their outraged voices muttering and crying, muttering and crying.

Submissive, the demon bowed its head. It pushed its face into its shoulder. But its hands were talking always, making the same signs over and over, sculpting the air with motions so eloquent and precise that Simon, ignorant of the words, nevertheless received from them a jolt of meaning. Such heartbreak and such pain. Underneath, a layer of brooding anger.

"What the hell is this?" asked Harriet Oimu, and the curse seemed to emphasize a squeaky note of panic in her voice. "Martin, what do you think you're doing?" The plug hung down between her fingers, and Simon could see it trembling.

"He wanted to be heard," said the man. He was wearing denim jeans and a blue shirt, and he had a small cross pinned against his collar. His forehead and the top of his head were bald. What was left of his black hair was curly, wiry, pulled back in a short ponytail. His cheeks were full of pimples and his skin was pasty white, the product, perhaps, of too long in the fringes.

"God damn it all. God damn it—get him out of here. This is important."

"Yes, he knows. He saw the motorbike come in."

Simon was looking at the demon's hands. The motions had changed somewhat, had taken on a new embellishment.

"He has a right to know," said the man. "His sister's dying and for a week you've told him when the doctor comes he'll save her. But the wound's gone septic and he knows it. Please, Harriet, he's tried to help you out. Don't treat him like an animal."

"Tell him my husband's dead," said Mrs. Oimu. "He's dead and that's the end of it."

It was clear to Simon that the demon understood these words. He saw the meaning, then the implication, pass over its emaciated features. Its sharp face, so reminiscent of vicious and extinct terrestial creatures, perhaps a point midway between a vulture, a python, and a wolf. And yet in spite of that, or else perhaps because of it, more true, more natural, easier to read than Mrs. Oimu's half-human mask.

Simon became aware of Katharine close by him, and he turned. She must have come to him. He had not moved. But he didn't know whether it was out of a conscious wish. In fact she seemed oblivious to where she was. Her breath came hard. She sucked it in through her clenched teeth. It bubbled on her lips. Her eyes were rolled back in her head. A small humming came from her, and it seemed to emanate not through her mouth but from her flesh. It seemed to wrap her in a skin of sound.

He went to her—just a few steps. He reached out his hand. She shied away from him, then stumbled. He took her arm to keep her from falling, and then held on. She allowed him, and none of the other Aboriginals moved to stop him. Perhaps she had lost consciousness. It was hard to tell. He put his face into her hair and took some comfort from it. Took some comfort as he let her sag down to the floor, because he was afraid of Mrs. Oimu, and afraid of what she was going to do. The plug moved in her hand.

The man named Martin had said something, but he had missed it. The demon was agitated now. It wagged its head from side to side, and its hands moved faster, faster. "He's outlived his usefulness, I'll tell you that," said Mrs. Oimu.

She looked around the room. And perhaps she was concerned to see her followers so cowed, so panicked as they pressed away against the walls. Perhaps she wanted to comfort them or to assert her strength or to express her hate, her misery. The plug was dangling eight inches from her fist; now she stepped forward and she struck the unresisting demon across the face with it, once, twice, three times.

IV

⊠

---------------- 4a ----------------
Styreme and Clare

He was killed during an escape attempt," said John Clare.
"Excessive force was used, and I regret it. An autopsy was
performed, and now we are able to release the body for
burial. I sent for you to give you all the news we had, and to
ask for the names and addresses of anyone who might be interested in taking charge of his remains."

Junius Styreme shrugged his shoulders, a painful, slow,
exaggerated gesture. "Mrs. Oimu is hiding," he said.

He sat on the edge of a stool in the consul's study, his
cane between his knees. John Clare paced the floor. "Yes, of
course. But since news of his death was leaked to the press,
there have been disturbances, as you know. Yesterday three
policemen were injured in the native lines in Shreveport. In
addition, I just got off the telephone with Robert Garner, the
commissioner of the Ludlow district in the fringes. He has
requested military support."

Styreme blinked. Watching him closely, the consul interpreted this as a small expression of alarm. When the old man opened his eyes again, they seemed wider under his bifocals, more prominent than before.

He could not sit in the big chairs. The secretary had brought him a stool and he perched primly on it, dressed in an impeccable suit, his hands clasped on the head of his cane. His cappuccino, his croissant, stood untouched on the table beside him.

John Clare, in contrast, had ordered a big breakfast. Until the week before he had taken nothing but black coffee in the morning. But he had developed a new custom since the attack on Goldstone Lodge, one he hoped might overpower his others, might leave him less nervous and more effective. Since the news of the Oimu's death he had been eating steadily, and it had helped him sleep the night before. But this morning food nauseated him.

He sat down behind his desk and pushed his egg sandwich to one side. He had slept in his clothes. His tie was creased, his shirt was smudged. Pungent smells came from his body. Watching Styreme closely, he thought he could detect from time to time a small flare to the old man's nostrils.

"I thought you could help us," said John Clare. "Mrs. Oimu represents the violent arm of the NLC, and it is she who is responsible for these murders and for your daughter's disappearance. We know they stayed in Gundabook after the attack there, and used that as a staging area for Goldstone Lodge. Now they're gone."

He hesitated for a moment, then continued. "For all we know, her husband had no contact with her either. Certainly he had made an effort to isolate her politically, even from prison. He was more moderate, and he had kept his ties open to the business community. He was a friend of yours."

"I knew him."

The consul knew that Styreme had had tear ducts implanted, and part of him was waiting with a sad fascination to see if they were functional. He said, "We have prepared a list of his associates, and the governor has asked me to show it to you, to see if you can add anything to it. He thought you might be able to give us some more information, and perhaps if you knew anything about the disturbances last night . . ."

Styreme looked up, and with part of his mind Clare was gratified to see some moisture in each eye. "If I knew," the old man said, "why not think that I would tell you?"

There was a pause. Tears trembled underneath Styreme's spectacles. Because of the brittleness, the frailness of his bones, he had none of the easy motions of human beings. He did not raise his hand to brush the tears away.

"Tell you, tell me," he said. "I got a demand for ransom every day. One hundred thousand dollars—it is nothing. I would pay, except for you. This morning there's no letter.

"They said free Dr. Oimu," he went on. "Now Oimu is dead. What will they do?"

The consul cleared his throat. The stench from his egg sandwich seemed suddenly oppressive. He leaned back in his chair and raised his hand, an inexpert gesture of compassion. But the old man's tears were disappearing as fast as they had come. He sat staring at the pattern of the carpet.

"Believe me, I'm so sorry," said John Clare. "Simon Mayaram was like a son to me. Don't think we would have abandoned them. I can tell you our plan was to let Oimu go, and see if he would lead us to his wife. Now, of course . . ."

Overwhelmed suddenly by embarrassment, Clare let his voice subside. He was watching Styreme, and he saw the change as the old man started to turn inward. It was as if he were retreating to someplace inside himself, far from the surface of his skin. Already frail, already delicate, he seemed to diminish before the consul's eyes until he perched as dry and stiff as a spent pupa.

4b
Consequences

Drywater lay nineteen miles inside the rim. It was surrounded by a circle of low hills. Nothing had ever grown here. This was the unimproved surface of the world, and it was made of shattered disks of silicate and porous crusts of rock. The road wound in along the riverbed. To the pickup trucks and 4×4s coming from Ludlow Grange, the landscape seemed eerie, menacing. The beams of their headlights snagged on tall, brittle, mushroom-shaped excrescences of tufa from the ancient mere, and slid over hills of greasy pellets—the slippery shitstone that had so confused the first pioneers. Black in the darkness, in the light these hills achieved a mixture of queasy colors, reds and browns and yellows.

The first jeep pulled over at the top of the rise, next to the stone pillar. A man got out with a shotgun in his hand. He stood for several minutes watching his breath, looking over the lights of Drywater down below at the end of the straight slope, the scattered outstructures, the gleaming hall.

4c
Sex (ii)

At the bottom of the road, in a square stone chamber, Katharine Styreme and Simon Mayaram lay together in a nest of blankets. "Fuck me," she murmured. But her mind was else-where.

Her body was alive to minuscule sensations. But her mind was elsewhere. She was listening to music in the walls and in the air around her, the first few bars of an imaginary sonata, a sonata for four hands that was part Bartók and part Liszt, and you could never hear more than half of it at one time, and it was describing the staircase that would take her down.

Strange how her music had deserted her. Always before, it had given her comfort. Never had she been without it in the hard times of her life. But in that prison, lying in the cold, she had often tried to go through well-loved pieces in her mind. In the black, empty hours, she had tried to recapture potent and familiar melodies, and she had failed. Maybe it was as they said. Maybe music was a human concept after all, and she was leaving it behind. Leaving it behind her at the top of the stair.

The stair was ornate, gothic, narrow, wooden, of a type that she had seen in postcards of medieval churches. And maybe at the top lay the world as it truly was, and objects were solid and unsubtle and dead in their hearts, and the light of God played on their surfaces. Where human beings had souls and everything else was dead, inert. Where there were no angels and no devils, and objects at rest remained at rest. Where causes were clear and the sun shone, and another stair led upward, she was sure. But now she stood trembling on the first steps down, and maybe she had already reached the turning, the landing from which she could peer over into the dark. The music crashed around her, wild and restrained, pompous and spare, and she stepped down with it, feeling the texture of each step on her bare foot, feeling with infinite clarity also the touch of Simon's hands upon her stomach and her breasts. She was lying on her back among the blankets, and her hands and his had pulled away her clothes, her hands and his were touching her.

The stair was not a long one. At each step the temperature rose and dropped, so that when she stood at the bottom and allowed her eyes to get used to that new shadow, she felt both hot and cold. It was as if a capacity for mixing extremes into a single tolerable sensation was now lost to her, and might be lost forever. Ahead, the way seemed bright and dark.

And perhaps that's what hell was—the infinite ability to separate things out, so that nothing was muted by its opposite. Standing in that gray landscape at the bottom of the stair, feeling the ebb and flow of sensations in her body, she remembered a sermon of Saint Robert Bellarmine. Some words she had underlined at school: how mental suffering divided naturally into four kinds—that of imagination, of memory, of intelligence, of will. How fearful she was! How keen her remembrance, how bitter her regret, how desperate her loathing and self-loathing. Yet because there is a devil of compulsion in every living thing, she felt herself eager to go forward; she let go of the carved newel post and stumbled forward, feeling with utter clarity the shattered volcanic rock covered with rime.

Around her banged that old piano. She felt Simon's face upon her lips, and she opened her mouth to him and put her tongue into his mouth.

His hands were covered with his spit and they slid over her breasts, freeing tiny smells. "How can we describe the stenches of Hell?" asked Robert Bellarmine. She stood on the shattered rock with the mist curling around her, and in front of her two shadows were receding. One was her father, limping over the uncertain ground, leaning on his cane, peering around him through his huge bifocals. The other, larger and more ominous, was the figure of the demon, its eloquent hands gesturing her forward, pulling her forward as if by threads hooked to her body. "Mother of God," she prayed. And all the time she was conscious of Simon's weight on her, and she pushed her fingers down between his buttocks and licked the inside of his mouth and licked his chin, his shoulder, and his armpit.

———— 4d ————

Demons (iv)

It had been hard to leave her alone, even for an hour. Now it was hard to come back. Hard to enter in again to that sad storm. Cheeks freshly wounded, he lay down beside her.

He was sweating, even though the chamber was cold and dark. The heater's filament was just a yellow spiral. He had his back to it; now he pulled away part of her shirt so that he could touch her, so that he could feel her fire. He felt it inside his skin, and it was heating up his inside spaces, and it burned there like a yellow flame.

For days it had been sinking down, cooling as her body dried and stiffened from the outside in. Now she was stiff to his touch. But the fire still guttered in her heart of hearts, and as he held her close he felt it grow and change color and rise up through a spectrum of intensity. She felt him now. She knew that he was there. The connection, broken when he went away to fight for her with Harriet Oimu, was patched together now. He had felt that he must do something, that he couldn't just lie there waiting for her death. But since he had accomplished nothing but to feel once more his absolute humiliation and to hear once more that she must die, now he regretted every second spent away from her. Especially since, now he was touching her, every moment seemed a country, seemed an infinite landscape of shared recollection, of time and space, each one with its own lost past, its own lost future. It was how he knew at first that she had changed, that she had softened, and her will had softened. Because now their memory seemed to coincide, as if for the first and last time in her life she was letting him take the lead now, letting him control her, and she was hoping to find in that control some final comfort.

They lay together on the stone bed. Together now, hands clasped with him in front, he led her away through their lives together, choosing always the easiest path. He led her through their earliest childhood when their father was alive and they were living in the cave kept warm by the hot rocks and the hot pool. And Father would catch beetles for them in the trap and mash them to a paste. There were others of their kind then still alive in the black hills of the rim, and all around from far away you could feel them in your mind and feel their love and their anxiety. They were the little children, he and she, treasured hopes, and they felt it every minute, every hour; it was the starshine of their childhood in the dark.

Now he knew she was weakening because she lagged behind him. But instead of making it easier, instead of holding up, out of a kind of desperation he pulled her forward, trying to show her more and more—remember this and this and this—until she stumbled and broke free.

She had fallen by the path. He knelt over her and put his hand on her wrist. At first there was nothing inside her that he could feel, but only emptiness and darkness. Then something started to grow, a fire, an energy that jolted out of her and sent him sprawling backward among the rocks, where he

crouched and watched her. And even though he knew what
he was witnessing, and even though a part of him was sunk
down in despair, still another part was rising with her, happy
at this last explosion of life. The fire rose up around her,
burning on her skin, chaotic, red, and blue, and he could see
strange shadows and strange shapes in it as it grew hotter
and hotter and took on a false desperate strength. He could
see her kneeling curled up by the path, a black shape; he
could see the curve of her back, could see her hands above
her head. They were gesturing and making words that
seemed to blow away in gusts of flame, and he couldn't make
them out until he heard them roaring in his head and in his
heart: I AM I AM I AM I AM.

The fire burned away the rocks and the path, and burned
away everything except what was. And he was lying with her
on the stone bed, his naked skin against her skin, and he
could feel her skin burning him, her heat rising up around
him. He could feel her spirit rise up, filling the cold room,
filling him also with a storm of light and heat. He pulled his
hands back to hide his eyes. All around him colors were pulsing and breaking, primary colors with no piece in them of
red or yellow or blue, no piece in them of any tone that humans understood. They were colors which bring sound to
the silent, music to the deaf, food to the hungry, love to the
unloved. They moved in him and spoke to him and whispered his name and called his name with an increasing urgency. In his mind he cried out I AM HERE, but it was lost in
the storm that battered around him, that crushed him and
hurt his eyes until it finally broke, wavered, fled, and disappeared forever, and he was left in the dark room, in the dark
cold room, utterly alone next to his sister's empty body, and
he was lying in the dark.

Then, finally and irretrievably alone, he called out to her

once more, one time, with all his strength. Martin Cohen, waiting in the storage antechamber, heard nothing but his snuffling breath. Simon, half a mile away, curled up in his cell under the blankets, heard nothing. Near him and underneath him Katharine lay asleep, naked in the litter of her clothes.

She lay on her stomach. Her body, golden in the lantern light, seemed impossibly beautiful to him. He bent down to kiss her shoulder, still awed by the frenzy in which she had given herself to him. Awed by his acceptance of it. It is fear, he thought. We are forced together by our fear.

He moved his fingers over the side of her breast, down her rib cage and over her back, her buttocks. He scratched with his thumbnail the dried crust of his semen, spattered in the groove of her back. He touched her shoulder. He felt the urge to possess her again. Her body radiated heat. He brought his face down toward her. He couldn't smell her anymore. Instead he watched the breath push through her lips, which were flattened and distended against the blanket on the floor.

He bent down to kiss her cheek. But now she was awake, suddenly awake, painfully awake. Her eyes started open and she pulled away from him and clasped her hands around her head. And for an instant he was hurt to see what he interpreted as another spasm of ambivalence. Then he saw she was in pain, truly in pain; she turned over and her back arched off the floor. And she was clasping her hands over her ears and crying out.

The Brotherhood of Man

The man stood at the top of the rise, looking down over the demon ruins with a shotgun in his hand. He had left the engine of his truck running, the door open. He was drinking whiskey from a glass bottle. When it was done, he threw it against the rock post of the old demon gate. It stuck there without falling.

Other men stood around him, smoking cigarettes, chewing gum, drinking without talking.

Reverend Cohen Shows Compassion

Martin Cohen waited in the storage antechamber, wrapped in a blanket. He sat on the window seat among the cases of dried food, rubbing his mouth. It was a habit he had. He squeezed his lower lip between his fingers.

There was a doubt in him, or rather a conviction, that seemed in the lantern-lit darkness to be a permanent part of him, the permanent foundation of everything he'd done. The grit in him had formed the pearl, such as it was.

Once in school, his mind confessor had shown him how to pray without stopping, how to keep a prayer rotating forever through his hippocampus. It was a discipline invented by the Reverend Geoffrey Kiyungu-Christ, seventh primary avatar of Jesus Christ, not long before his murder in Addis Ababa. It was a mental trick, not difficult. But Martin Cohen, who had won prizes for scholarship, had never learned it. That slow wheel never revolved for him. It was another force that made him move and twitch, that had pushed him out into a world of service. The Peace Corps, the Missionary Corps; once he had been in charge of a community health program near Deseret. There had been an outbreak of tuberculosis among the Aboriginals, who were allergic to streptomycin and several other antibiotics. He had been lecturing to a room full of people, and as he spoke he became conscious of a slow interior chant behind his temples where the prayer was supposed to be. He stopped talking, as if for emphasis, but really to give himself a chance to hear the words: "Please, Jesus," which was good as far as it went. But then: "Let them all die, please, Jesus." He had finished his lecture in a loud and panicked voice.

He moved his fingers over his brow, rubbing at the wrinkled grooves between his eyes as if to smooth them away. He pushed his fingers back along his bald forehead. What had led him to this? he thought. Was it that prayer? There was a lantern on the window seat. It cast a circular light. What animal stirred outside of it? What moved? There was something; he was waiting, and in time the door opened and an Aboriginal came in, holding a pistol in its awkward hand.

It stepped into the circle: a woman wearing a down vest, a red plaid shirt. Her hair was long and straight and parted in the middle. Her face was quite beautifully done, quite expressive, which was the test. Emotions came to its false surface; she was afraid.

She stood in the light, and the light shined off her spectacles. "Is he asleep?"

Martin Cohen shook his head. She expected him to say something. He was looking at her, suddenly sensitive, he thought, to everything around him. The chill in the air. The coldness of the stone seat through the blanket. Time moved slowly, and he used it by trying to read the flicker of emotion in her face. She had not wanted this work. She did not believe in it. She did not think it necessary. And she was terrified.

"The revolution didn't come," he said.

Her brows came together and her left hand made a small gesture.

Harriet Oimu had told them that a single spark would set the world on fire. The people would rise up. But they hadn't. There had been an incident in Shreveport, but that was all. He had heard about it on the radio.

So what was left? To push on forward into the cold dark along the demon road? And perhaps the first step on that road was the murder of a helpless creature.

"Give me the keys," she said.

He produced them from his pocket, then shrugged, then rose to his feet. He paused. "I'll go and say good-bye," he said, letting his voice break.

Again she made a gesture with her hand. He was looking at her face, watching apprehension mingle with relief. He turned away and fitted the key into the padlock.

He pushed the door open and slipped through it and then pushed it closed again. Inside the little cell he stood with his back against the door, breathing the cold stench of death.

The demon had stretched his sister out on the stone slab. He had stripped her naked and stretched out her limbs. She lay on her back, her hands crossed on her breast, as perfect as a plaster model. The lines on her stomach and her thighs had faded to yellow. The pellet marks had puckered open as her skin had dried.

The room was cold and quiet. The demon had turned the heater off; he sat in a corner of the floor, huddled in blankets. Light came from a candle on the slab. There was no draft, and the flame stayed bright and tall.

Martin Cohen heard the clanking of a chain. The demon had altered his position, had thrown back a corner of a blanket to show his hands, and the chain around his ankle scraped the floor.

Without speaking, almost without thinking, Cohen stepped across the room and squatted down. He had another key in his hand now, a smaller one, and without saying anything he fumbled under the blanket. The demon stretched his leg out, and Cohen unlocked the shackle and pulled the chain free.

The demon made a gesture with his forefinger.

"I know, I know," muttered Martin Cohen. "I've got some cream." The skin under the chain was raw and worn away.

The demon shook his head.

"It will take the pain away," said Cohen, moving his hands. "I've got some in my bag.

"It's all right, you know," he said. "I spoke to Mrs. Oimu and she . . ."

The demon blinked his pale eyes once. His livid arm, evil, thin, and supple as a snake, slid out through the blankets and his hand grabbed hold of Cohen's wrist. It was a motion that made talking difficult, yet it was full of another kind of hard communication; he made no effort to pull away. He squatted there breathless, feeling as if cold fingers had slid their way inside of him somehow and closed upon his liver or his lung.

It was a communication that was almost sexual, at least for him, a hard sexuality that seemed to come out of his inmost fears about himself, his inmost guiltiness. Ah, he thought, take me, but then the pressure was gone and Cohen opened his eyes again.

The hands moved in close to his face, and perhaps it was a trick of the light, but it seemed as if everything else in the room had disappeared, and he was staring at those hands, following the smallest movements of those hands. Needing to understand, as if in those perfect gestures all meaning was condensed—"You don't know anything," the fingers said, flashing before his eyes, echoing his guilty thoughts.

"You don't know anything," they said. "You don't know, know, know, know, know. She is gone, gone, gone, gone, gone, gone, gone. You're here with your crippled hands. Never talk again. You are a creature from the blind race which never understands. Blind men with pictures in their minds, and we are hindered by our sight. We are weak from truth. We cannot resist. But you are caught on surfaces, upon the skin of time. You can't see reasons, the dark reasons, the light reasons, the soft reasons, the hard reasons, the ugly reasons, the sweet reasons, the slow reasons, and the fast."

Tell me, thought Martin Cohen.

"I can't tell you. Your eyes can't open far enough to take it in. What do you know about death? What you do know about the life in front of us? What do you know about the life behind?"

Nothing.

"Nothing, no." The hands were silent, frozen in that last configuration, repeating it over and over.

Martin Cohen turned his face away and closed his eyes. And in the sudden darkness new thoughts appeared to him: This creature never talked like this before. The dead one had not talked like this. Maybe these words, he thought, had come out of himself, part of his doubt and the hope that lived in it like an unborn child. He was not gifted in this language, where every tiny millimeter of every finger's movement made a distinction too fine for human brains. Perhaps these words had come out of his ignorance, had come out of his guilt, had come out of the intensity with which he had tried to understand the last conversation, perhaps, ever attempted in this language. No, thought Martin Cohen, he had been stupid, slow. He had formed words out of what he needed to hear, and at that moment his need for understanding seemed as urgent as a shout, a loud shot, but far away.

And in fact there was a noise inside of him, inside the quiet of his mind. There was a voice. "Let them all die," it said. Or perhaps it was something else half heard, heard at a distance, and some filter in him turned it into that.

He opened his eyes. There were no choices in these matters. "I have a cream for your ankles," he signaled hesitantly, but the demon had turned away, had sunk his bulging head into his blankets.

He reached out to touch the demon's knee, then hesitated, then stood up.

4g
Katharine (iv)

She had heard a cry out of the pit in front of her. The creature in the pit had shouted out a name, and though it was far away its voice had been intolerably clear, intolerably precise, had entered into her and pushed away all other thoughts. For a moment as she stumbled on the rocks that were both hot and cold, she saw in front of her an image of her own face as if painted on a billboard, or on canvas, or on plaster. It was pitiless, enormous. And she saw her own small spirit pushed out of that painted mouth into the world: a naked wormlike woman who clutched and struggled on enormous yellow lips and fought against the breath that was forcing her out.

"Fuck me again," she said. She was lying on her stomach on the floor. The man lay above her, and she could feel his hand stroking her wet back, and she could feel his penis against her; now he shifted his weight on top of her, and one of his big arms was tight around her neck. She couldn't see his face.

His weight settled on her back, pushing her into the floor. She opened her mouth and felt the breath rush out of her. It made a mist in front of her that writhed and curled into the darkness, glittering with crystals, and she imagined herself climbing down out of her own comfortable mouth into that mist.

In front of her somewhere was the pit. She smelled the sulfur. Huge figures loomed around her in the shadows and she recognized them. She had seen them in picture books and on prayer cards which her father had given her. She had prayed to them at school. Then they had been smaller, had been possible to reach, possible to talk to. But now they were huge, of a scale with her abandoned and inert body on the stones behind her. They bent over her abandoned body; they were wreathed in mist and so large that she could only see small parts of them. Yet she recognized them: Catherine, inscrutable, her wheel burning in her hand. Lawrence with his grill. Roch, covered in tumors. Thomas More. Hildegard of Bingen, who had tasted Jesus' foreskin in a dream. Saint Joan of Arc in polished armor with her long two-handed sword.

There was Saint Teresa of Avila, and Saint John of the Cross: old friends who had helped her with her studies and guarded her bed at night. She had consulted them often, had dinned their ears with moral problems, and they had never failed her. When she was humiliated or hurt, they had taken her pain into themselves, into their own racked, tortured, mortified bodies. But now they seemed disorganized and helpless. They blundered through the mist, commanding each other in uncertain voices that rushed around her like weather.

"Help me," she prayed.

They were enormous. She lay on the rocks, naked and exposed. She pushed her face into the rocks, hurting her lips on the rocks. But then she felt a shape gathering above her, and she felt a hand grasp hold of her hair and pull her head up by her hair. It was Teresa of Avila, and her hand was rough and strong, and her voice was harsh like wind, and she said, "This is not the place for comfort anymore. This is the path that we all walked alone. It led us through countries of temptation and sorrow, and it led underneath the devil's legs, and it led us to our deaths."

Then she was gone. The wind was still, and her fingers were like tendrils of mist, and the mist receded, and Katharine lifted her head up, and she could see more clearly now. First the stair that led you down into the darkness. At the bottom you moved forward over the stones that were both hot and cold. And then you heard the demon's voice that came out of the pit, and it entered your body and expelled you, naked, small. Then you continued onward through the forest of the saints, and the pit was out in front of you somewhere across the diamond sands, across the black glass, across the ice pack, and you would find it if you looked for it or not.

The man stirred above her and she could feel his strong arms, his strong hands and fingers. She was lying on her stomach and he was running his fingers down the cleft of her behind. His face was on the back of her shoulder, and she raised her head, and turned and felt his ear. She kissed him, and with her mouth close to his mouth she told him what she wanted.

"Wait a little," he said.

"I can't wait."

She could feel his cock against her leg and it was soft. At other times during the past day this had been a signal, and she had responded to it by moving her mouth down his body and taking him into her mouth and peeling back his foreskin. She had entered into a tiny little penis-sucking world, a world too small to admit any other phenomenon, a world at whose threshold she had to leave all ideas, hallucinations—all desires, even. It was restful in that little world.

There was a difference now. He didn't budge, didn't allow her access when she moved her hand. He lay with part of his weight on top of her, his arm clasped around her neck.

"Let's rest. Let's be together."

Together, she thought, and in the ghost world where she stumbled on the greasy rocks, she saw herself look upward to the sky, as if afraid that the word *together*, long and flat, heavy and meaningless, might fall out of the dark sky and crush her suddenly. What did he mean? Together? Where was he in that landscape?

There he was. A black dog standing on the rocks in front of her. A black Labrador with maybe some mastiff in it, big and dangerous, with brutal, stupid eyes. All black, black in every part, except the red tip of its penis as it shifted its leg.

This animal, this brute incapable of reason or compassion, this creature had raped her when she was most exposed. Again and again. How was it possible? What had brought her to this place? She had been playing the piano with her father.

She had an impulse to cry but could not. But a sound came out of her, garbled and harsh, an animal sound, and for that reason he responded to it. He spoke her name. "Oh, Katharine. Kathy, what's wrong?" and she squirmed under him. In the ghost country she squirmed on the rocks as these words fell on her out of the sky and the dog growled.

There was a knock on the door and a click as the lock unsnapped. The weight was gone from her back and she raised herself up onto her elbows. She started to laugh to see the man fumble with his clothes, pull his pants up over his dark hairy legs. He threw the blanket over her and then stood up; she turned onto her side. The door was open and another man was there, a human being carrying a lantern and a bag. It was the dissenter, the Kiyungu priest. She had seen him lead the devil by a leash. She turned her face into the blanket.

In the ghost world, another dog came slipping down the stones, tentative and slow, a white dog with a touch of orange mange, its tail between its legs, its lips pulled back, its fur high on its neck.

"Thank God it's not too late." In the ghost world, this reference to God had a curious effect, and she examined it with part of her mind while she watched the dogs trying to face each other down. Light splashed from the clouds, and it splashed onto the rocks and for a moment made the rocks glow before it seeped away. Ignoring it, the black dog stood stiff-legged, its heavy head extended, while the white one slunk around it in a circle. And she noticed that both their cocks were uncovered, and both of the long red tips had slid out of their sheaths.

"What do you want?"

"To help you. I can help you but you have to get ready. I'll come back—there's not much time."

"What do you want?"

She heard him pulling on his shirt, the click of his fingernails against the buttons. She heard him shudder as his sweat dried in the cold. The other one was breathing hard, and the lantern in his hand made a small clanking sound.

"You've got to leave. We all have to. I'll come back in ten minutes with some more food and supplies."

"Who are you?"

"I'm a man. My name is Martin Cohen. Trust me because I'm not with these people now. I never was. Not out of choice. I'm a priest."

"But I saw you."

"Yes, I know. I'll explain later but there's no time now. It doesn't matter—let me give you what I have. You've got to leave this place. We'll hide in the hills and back to Shreveport. I'll show you the way; I'm going too."

The black dog stood up straight. Its claws scraped the rocks. The white dog slunk down on its haunches about ten feet away, its tail between its legs. They were in the forest of saints, a misty place of broken trees and humid rotten smells. A path led back the way she'd come, straight and clear through the trees, and a line of glistening water marked it. There was a ditch beside the path, which continued also around the bottom of the pile of stones where she now stood, watching the dogs, uncertain of the road forward, whether to go, whether to stay.

"This all started almost as a joke. Harriet's crazy joke. But they're not playing anymore—they took me prisoner. Theodore Oimu is dead and there's been no word, not from her father, not from anybody. They were hoping for a strike at least, but nobody's heard anything about that. So now they want to cut their losses and move forward—you know what that means."

The black dog made no motion.

"Don't trust me. It doesn't matter. No, but take the clothes. Take the food and go because you've nothing to lose and not much choice. If you don't, they'll kill you."

A Murder

After Martin Cohen left, the demon sat rubbing his ankle. Earless, he did not understand that the door of his cell had been left unlocked. But with other senses he was aware of a gathering menace, aware of someone standing on the other side of the door.

It was an Aboriginal, and it was blocked to him, closed to him by its medication. He felt it as an empty shadow, a dark outline. No warmth nor light nor meaning radiated from it. The drug formed a black shell which kept all that inside.

Aboriginals were different from human beings. They were blocked, but you could feel them, feel their presence. Human beings, it was as if they didn't exist. Outside the range of sight they almost disappeared. So cold they were, so dark in their hearts, that it was as if they existed only as objects, like stones or trees. And when you sensed their movement, it was like feeling the wind in the twigs of a dead tree. Even animals, even insects had more life, had more color in them and around them as they moved.

This was an Aboriginal, a slave. It stood outside the door, waiting. Then it moved. Its hand was on the latch.

The demon watched the door open toward him. He raised his head off his knees. It was a woman. It was what they called "a woman", because of its long hair.

She was carrying a gun, a pistol with a long mechanism on its snout to deaden the shock. She held it down, pointed at the floor. She stood in the doorway.

She was closed to him. He sat watching her, opening and shutting his eyes, not blinking but rather breathing, summoning his forces, tightening his mind. It was a kind of breathing. He felt no fear. He had nothing to lose. His sister lay dead forever, gone away, apart.

In no hurry, the Aboriginal stepped inside. She moved away from him sideways along the wall until she was as far from him as she could manage in the little room.

She was shut to him. She stood with her back against the wall. Her left hand, up by her chest, opened and closed. Her face showed nothing, no color, and there was nothing in the air around her.

He closed his eyes. In the ghost world, he sat among the dark rocks. He sat on a concave bed of sand and stones, and he could feel the looming presences of the formations, and when he opened his eyes he saw that there were fool's diamonds and sharp pieces of basalt in the sand. He sat between two boulders, and there was ice on them.

The woman was there too. She stood at the bottom of a small embankment. Ice was there, a sheet of black ice, and she stood on it. She was difficult to see, almost invisible. And silent. And still. In this world he was the master. She stood frozen and invulnerable, unable to move, unable to change, trapped by her defenses.

Tentatively, slowly, he got to his feet. He dusted off his hands. He climbed down the embankment and came out over the ice.

The ice was the drug. It was Mellarin AZ, with some complex modifications; his sister had shown him the differences. His mother had shown him. It had a smooth black sheen, almost like graphite, and small particles gleamed in it.

He tested it underfoot. It was brittle, thick. He walked out over it toward the frozen statue, almost invisible against the black sky. Small shards of pyrite gleamed like stars.

The ice was thick on her. He walked around her in a circle and then came close. He could see her human outline, silhouetted against the lighter rocks—her long hair, her chin, her nose. Her neck, her big shoulders, and the bones of her face. But when he was close to her he could see it was a shape formed out of ice. Underneath, frozen inside, stood the Aboriginal, the little slave. Unmodified, with her soft face. The drug lay thick on her like a black armor, protecting her, giving her form. Yet it kept her from moving, from living, from the world.

He put his hand out to touch her breast, and then he moved his hand over the cold grainy surface. He bent down to peer inside. There she was. Her eyes were open, panicked, quiet.

He moved his hand over the surface of her breast, looking for flaws, crevices, joints, lines of a lighter color. He scratched his nail over her heart and felt something. An imperfection. He closed his eyes.

And when he opened them, he had moved a level deeper. This was the world of symbols. It was not dark here. The sky had one color only. The horizon was straight. There was ice here, too, though it was not as cold. It was more like glass.

There was no statue here. But still he stood on a surface of ice. It was perfectly round. He squatted down and put his hand on it. Inches below, he could see water.

The ice was smooth, but here too there was a tiny imperfection. What was it? A reaction. A rebellion. A side effect. He ran his thumb along it. He scraped it with his nail. He scratched a circle in the ice.

Then as hard as he could, he punched down with the side of his fist and then jumped back. The ice shattered along the line, leaving a small hole.

He waited a few moments. Then he stretched himself out along the ice and pulled himself out toward the hole.

He moved with slow care. The hole in the ice was six inches in diameter, lined with angry edges, sharp as glass. Already as he watched, small crystals were forming on the surface of the water. But still he waited, watching, waited. He pulled his woolen sleeve up to his shoulder.

He thrust his thin arm down into the water and then pulled it out. He had a fish grasped in his hand, a big mechanical carp with plastic scales and steel fins and a big mouth that yawned open to reveal its metal ribs, its clockwork guts. It flopped in his hand. He opened his eyes, closed them, moving quickly through the worlds until he felt the metal turn to meat under his fingers, and the fish was gasping, helpless in his hands.

The Aboriginal moved. Sensing danger, she raised her gun.

He sat with his head on his knees. Sensing danger, she raised her gun, took aim. But in another world he had the fish in his hand, and he was squeezing it, and it was gasping and dying in the alien air.

She slid to the floor. She gasped for breath, and her eyes were open wide. She sat with her legs stretched out, and she held the gun in front of her. Its long silencer thrust toward him.

In the cold cell he sat without moving. But elsewhere he squatted by some rocks, and he held up the fish with both hands and squeezed it behind its gills. Its stupid eyes bulged out at him, and he held it up and stared into its stupid eyes.

Slowly, deliberately, the Aboriginal turned the gun around. She held the tip of it toward her and prodded with it at her own lips, forcing the cold metal against her lips. He squeezed a little harder and her mouth popped open and she slid the gun inside. She slid it past her teeth, over her tongue, to the back of her throat, and her throat closed around it.

The demon held the fish up, and he was staring into its stupid eyes. DO IT DO IT, he said, perfectly silent, perfectly quiet, perfectly still.

4i

Spike Laudenberg

They had left their trucks at the top of the hill and then walked down. At first they had been careful; four scouts had gone on ahead. They moved down the ditch beside the road and then sent a message back while the others waited in the cold.

Wasted precautions, wasted time: The Abos set no guard.

It had made him angry. It made him angry as he stood in front of the roofless building and watched the flames gutter down.

It had made them all angry. They had felt like fools. They had squatted down among the rocks around the building and then set it on fire. They had shot ignition bombs through the window, and when the doors opened and the Abos came out, they killed them. They slaughtered them like animals. If only one had resisted, if one had braved the smoke and stayed back, if one had shot his gun or done something beside run like a rabbit or stand up straight with the flashlight in his eyes, then they might have shown some mercy, something.

And no doubt a couple had escaped, or run off from the outbuildings. There were eleven bodies when they counted them.

Now Spike Laudenberg stood in the darkness watching the flames settle down. The roof had fallen in.

Others in the Brotherhood seemed to enjoy the killing,

but it had disgusted him. When he was a child his grandfather told him how they used to hunt the raw Abos for sport, with bows and arrows up on the Wind Plateau. When he got senile, he told the story every day. The expression in his voice changed over time as age bleached out the boasting and added details until finally he just told it as if he didn't understand the words.

It had to mean something. Laudenberg had shot only one, but he knew which it was. He moved over to the front step. Beside it a girl lay on her back, dressed in a denim jacket. No wound was visible. She lay with her mouth open and her face was . . . what could you say? Convincing?

He had told them to gather the bodies into a pit behind the rocks, and they were dousing them with gasoline and setting them on fire. Two men in wool pants and red-checked shirts took the woman by the arms and dragged her away; her head lolled down. Laudenberg was drunk.

They had left a man up the hill with the cars. Now he drove bumping down the road. Laudenberg broke open his shotgun and turned out the shells. He did not reload. When the 4×4 pulled up, he walked over to it as if making a decision. As if he were the leader of this band of murderers. He opened the passenger door and got inside. "Take me back," he said.

The driver, a potbellied little man, wore a mask over his eyes. Like all of them, he wore his little armband and his little strip of linen knotted round his head. It seemed stupid all of a sudden; he knew the man's name and he felt like saying his name, felt like using any sentence that contained both the man's name and a curse.

They made a three-point turn. The car bumped over ridges of stiff mud. The driver flicked the high beams on, then off. Mist drifted over the road.

"How did it go?"

He shrugged. He was too drunk to talk. He put his fore-head against the cold side window and looked out into the dark.

The car drifted to a stop. The driver flicked the high beams on. Laudenberg sat back and tried to see. Two figures rose up out of the mist in front of them.

The driver leaned forward to rub some condensation off the windscreen. His hand made a noise against the glass. Then he sat peeking through the smear, his forearms on the wheel.

"What's this?" he said.

They sat for about a minute, looking. There was nothing mysterious about it. Laudenberg had searched for the hos-tages at Drywater. He had found what he guessed was their cell, but it was empty.

Now they stood in the dirt road. The headlights bleached their skin. They were dressed for the cold, in sweaters and long pants, and the man carried a small knap-sack. He made a gesture with his hand.

"What do we do?"

"We pick them up."

As soon as he spoke these words, Laudenberg decided that they wouldn't. They would leave them in the dark. A small nausea in his stomach, and there were reasons. He couldn't tolerate an Aboriginal just then, not alive. Not in the car with him. He had spent all his life with them. Now he had reached his own dividing line.

"Styreme will pay us," said the driver apologetically.

"No."

Just to look at her disgusted him. She stood staring into the headlights, a glassy, dazed expression on her face. Her mouth was open, her lips pulled back. Her white dentures—

yes. He knew all about her. His brother Davey had been at St. Kitts, near where she had gone to school. He said she had taken two football players into the trees behind the gym.

Inhuman. Aboriginal. She stood looking into the lights, her hair knotted and golden-red. Then she turned half away into the man's arm, and she rubbed her face against the man's arm. He held his palm flat out.

Laudenberg opened the door and let the cold air in. He took the unloaded shotgun from the seat and then climbed down, his head reeling. "Get away," he said.

"Thank God you've come," answered the man. Mayaram.

"Get away." Spike Laudenberg moved out into the light, held up his gun. "Get out of here."

She had her lips against his sleeve. She was rubbing her mouth into the man's sleeve. Her human mouth. "Get out of here," he said. He gestured with the gun, and with his other hand he touched his mask, grateful for it.

V

5a
Simon (i)

The priest went away and left the door unlocked. He told them to wait. Simon got dressed and then he helped Katharine with her clothes.

She struggled with her socks, and then her mouth opened and she was yawning. Her eyes closed and opened. He felt tired, too.

It was odd because time was crucial here. They were in danger; he knew it and the Kiyungu priest had told him. Cohen had left them coats and sweaters, had left the door unlocked. Time was critical. But Simon sat down again on the blankets to watch Katharine yawn. He thought: Strength is easy when you are the victim. When you could endure and that was all. But they had choices to make.

He lay down on his back and put his hands behind his head. Then suddenly he was asleep, a tiny piece of sleep. It consisted of a single image, and there was not much to distinguish it from memory, except for its clarity. The absence of emotional context: Once when he was in school they had taken a bus trip to the north. Years before his birth the city planners of Birmingham had decided on a military option; on Mirpaz Day they'd gone up to look, twenty busloads of children. The landscape was barren, lunar, deserted. Some ruined houses still stood—a county park. They got out at the site of an old power plant. He had stood with his gloves on the barbed wire, and then when nobody was looking he had climbed up over it and walked forward among mounds of red earth. He stripped away his helmet—unwise at the best of times because of atmosphere depletions in that area. His favorite teacher, twenty-four years old, died of leukemia that year. Many of his classmates had cataracts. But now he stood bareheaded, looking up at the bright sky.

That was the image: a little boy with his mouth open staring upward. When he awoke (and he awoke almost immediately, startled by the sound of a car door), he kept that image of himself as if in front of his eyes. A single frame as if from an old film, and he knew as he lay there that he could unroll it further, that he could run it backward, forward, backward, and it would bring with it a sense of loss. Yet why? What was to regret? What was to regret in that picture of that little boy?

He lay there in the dark with Katharine beside him. She was sitting with her eyes open.

He listened to the chunk of the car door.

He felt so tired. But there were other noises, yells. He turned to look at Katharine. She sat with her hair unbrushed, her auburn hair, her skin red in the lantern light, and there was something in her face. Left to himself, perhaps he would have lain there without moving, curled around that image of himself. He would have lain there till whatever happened happened. But just her face and her wild helplessness—he sat up to look at her. His hands were trembling. He felt light-headed, felt something rush up out of his guts, an urge to cherish that came up out of his dream, out of the place where he kept the picture of the boy, the little boy who stripped his hat off and looked up at the ruined sky of that world, that tiny distant planet where there were no mothers and no fathers anymore.

She was sitting with her legs straight out. She looked as if she were listening to something. She had the relaxation in her body that comes from listening. But she didn't seem to be concerned with the new sounds, the banging and the shouts. Now Simon felt them as if on his skin, and each one made him flinch, and there was a ticking in his body as he waited for the first gunshot. He was moving now. He was stuffing the blankets into the bag that the Kiyungu priest had brought. He was squatting in front of her, helping her with her shoes, and she looked up at him with a bleared expression that contained a smile. Or not. Or maybe just a little piece of recognition, of acknowledgment—that was enough, and he was standing up and helping her up, too. He pulled the sweater over her head and brushed the hair out of her eyes. It was full of static.

He took her by the hand and pulled her to the door, and she came with him, unresisting. Their prison was a square stone building with that single room intact; he led her out of it and down into the cold. Carrying their bag, he led her down some rough steps into a kind of corridor between two ruined walls.

They walked on wooden planks that had been laid down over the mud. They made a clomping noise. But speed was more important than silence; there was gunfire now close by.

Simon hurried forward along the corridor between the walls, and then they came out in an open space a hundred yards or so from the big hall where they had seen the demon.

The dry hills rose around them, sandy and dark. The sky was murky toward the east, a violet haze over the terminator, and a few bright stars shone through.

In the other direction, a hundred yards away, light spilled out of the hall through windows and the open door. A whitewashed building at the top of a gentle rise; Simon turned away from it and pulled Katharine downhill into the shelter of a dry creek bed. He pulled her down behind some boulders and then turned back to look.

Men had gathered at the hall where the road turned around. A white van was parked there and a man crouched behind it with a gun in his hand, a projectile weapon of some sort. Simon could tell he was a man. There was something in his stocky build, his posture that could not be duplicated. A brainless competence that hung around him and could not be duplicated, a brainless menace that seemed to cleave the air in front of him. He was pointing his gun at the door. A bright flame leapt out of it and disappeared.

Closer by, there was a screaming among the rocks. Simon squatted down. He put his hand on Katharine's shoulder. Too stunned to react, to turn away, they watched an Aboriginal come running toward them down the hill. He was wearing a baseball cap. His unzipped parka flapped behind him. It was Frank. His shirt was white. And as Simon watched, something exploded out of it, something red the size of a football.

There was a man standing in the rockfall twenty yards behind him, and he was holding in his hands a cylinder made of plastic. It was a more modern weapon, though still it had been banned in the area around London for a hundred years.

It cooked people from the inside, blew them apart and never made a sound. Instead, Simon listened to Frank's bubbling scream. He went down, his arms spread out.

Simon turned toward Katharine to cover her eyes, cover her ears, to make sure that she was hidden. As he did so, he had a picture in his mind of the way that she would look, cringing, terrified. So even in the midst of his concern for her, for them, he was startled to see her wide-eyed stare, the set of her mouth. She looked—what was it?—satisfied, somehow. But also as if she wasn't paying attention, was focused on something subtly else, was finding some subtle new significance in the harsh stark bloody fact—the kid was down right there. Blown apart. His chest turned inside out.

A quarter of a second, yet it was enough. She smiled and he couldn't bear it. He put his fingers to her lip to smooth the curve of it away, and then he touched her eyes to close them. He spread his hand over her face and brought her down behind the rock until it was all out of sight, the dead body and the man, and the man had gone back, and everything was quiet near them, and they sat in the cold air watching their breath. She had his fourth finger between her teeth, and he felt the steady sharpness of her teeth until he took his hand away. They were listening to the gunshots, and they were watching the flicker of firelight reflected on the pale surface of a rock above their heads. The white house was on fire. Its roof was on fire. He heard the snap and crash, the shouts.

"Meat," said Katharine, and for an instant he smelled it. Caught on a tremor of air, the cooked heart, the cooked lungs of the Aboriginal, and it was gone.

"Listen," she said, and he was listening, and his pulse was beating, and he couldn't hear anything except her strange hoarse voice, and she was humming something softly.

He turned to look at her, and she was smiling with her eyes closed. He let out his breath. He was frightened now. Frightened for two reasons. He reached out to hug her close. He put his face next to her face until he lost in her skin and hair the smell of the cooked meat.

The draw led down away from them toward the road. It was only a few feet deep, yet it gave some shelter. All light in the valley now came bursting from the roof of the white hall. Sheets of flame, currents of sparks flew up from it. All eyes, all words, all sound, and all attention, Simon thought, had to be gathered that way, and so he took Katharine by the hand and led her down into the draw. She came unresisting. Their shoes made a crunching noise in the dry sand.

The road came down out of the eastern hills. It ran over the draw, over an empty culvert half a mile away.

A car came bumping down the road. It crossed the culvert and pulled up in front of the white house.

"We have to get you back," said Simon. "We have to get you home."

From where he and Katharine stood, they were a day's walk from the terminator. And then what? There was a town called Ludlow, a hundred and fifty miles from anywhere. They had no money. They had clothes, and food in the rucksack enough for two days.

But the men had come by car.

"What do you think?" he said. He turned to face her and he took her by both hands, even though every instinct told him that they had to get away now quickly, because the gunfire had stopped. Her opinion didn't mean anything now, and yet he asked. He turned to face her, and again he was alarmed to find her smiling at him. A hundred yards away an altered Aboriginal lay dead, and she was smiling at him as if she trusted him. It was a dazed, starry expression, and her eyes were opened wide, and she came close and he could smell her breath, her hair, until he turned away. "We have to get you home," he said, only to himself now, because he knew that her physical closeness here was the reverse of intimacy, was the mark of how far away she was.

He turned and led her by the hand. They crunched down through the draw, through the sand, and there was silicate frost on it. A crust that gave way at every step. The boulders rose around them, but still they could see the burning house. The glow from it threw weak stripes through the rocks. Katharine came unresisting, and she was looking all around herself with a dazed smile, her eyes wide open, her face open, as if no sensation were lost on her, as if no idea could ever catch hold. Was that the secret of her mind? he asked himself as he trudged along. Was that, was that, was that the clue? "Was that the clue?" he asked himself, making a little song out of the words, repeating them over and over, feeling his lips move silently around them, feeling his fingers stir in his gloves as if he were typing them upon a keyboard, not paying attention to much of anything around him until he climbed up past the culvert and stood on the mud road out of breath with Katharine behind him.

A car came toward them from the fire, from the bottom of the hill. Its headlights pitched into the drainage ruts across the road, and he could hear the labor of the engine. It was a red 4×4. Mist drifted across the road, and the car came to a stop a few yards away.

Two men sat in the front seat. The glass of the windscreen was fogged up, and the driver leaned forward and rubbed it with his sleeve. When it was clear, Simon caught a glimpse of his own unshaven chin, superimposed above the driver's face.

He could see that they were talking to each other but he

couldn't hear what they said. He put his hand out like a policeman, more for Katharine's sake than theirs; she was looking out past the car into the darkness beyond the road, where a rubble of mud sloped down out of sight.

The passenger door opened and a man stepped out. He was dressed in boots and blue jeans, a black shirt and a leather vest, and the top part of his face was hidden by a strip of cloth. He came forward into the headlights, and he was holding a shotgun pointed at the sky. Through the holes of his mask Simon could see his eyes. They were so blue that they seemed blue even in that light; the holes were messy, big, and through them Simon could see the small skin puckered in the corners of his eyelids. His eyes seemed so expressive, and they contrasted so strangely with the blankness of the mask; Simon knew him, and as soon as he opened his mouth, Simon recognized his voice, although he couldn't place it or give the man a name. It was just that he had heard that voice before and seen those eyes, and during the conversation that followed there was always part of Simon's mind that was worrying this problem, as if he could have seized some advantage or avoided some pitfall just by knowing who the man was, by naming him, by giving him a context.

"Thank you for stopping," he said.

The man had a gun and he was drunk. Acrid smells came from his body, sharpened by the cold, and with part of his vision Simon watched Katharine turn her head, watched her nostrils widen, watched her throat knot for an instant. Simon himself felt magically alert, magically sensitive, as if everything around him contained information he could analyze, and it could help him. He felt the focus of his concentration resting on the tip of the drunk man's gun, trembling and moving with it in a complex weaving pattern, and then moving out from there and touching everything. He saw the burning house half a mile away at the bottom of the road. He heard a dozen distinct noises from down there. He saw the driver of the car scratch his face through the dark windscreen. They must have parked the cars at the top of the hill, he thought. They must have parked there and walked down.

"Can you give us a ride?" he said.

The gun tip pitched and weaved and made a little circle in the air. The blue eyes blinked. "This wasn't for you," answered the man. "You two."

"Can you take us back?"

The drunk man moved his lips, forming what looked like words, although no words came out. And then: "Why? Just so you can see how screwed up things can get? There've been riots every night in Shreveport since Theodore Oimu died."

The gun tip made a circle in the air. The man had more to say. "Why? Just to show you. You and that faggot Clare. You and your Abo friends. It wasn't for you." The gun tip made a circle. "You could have died. Who cares?"

"I understand."

"Shut up. You're not even from here. Are you fucking her?"

"No."

"Yes," said Katharine. It was the first time she had spoken in an hour.

The blue eyes closed, then opened. "Please," said Simon. "She wasn't part of this. She needs her medication. There'll be money, too."

"Go fuck yourselves," said the man. "You think that's what it's all about? We're not savages. We're not like you. It's the principle—you had your chance. If you had done something about it, we wouldn't have to . . ." He gestured back behind him with his shotgun.

The words came out of him. "You want an incident?

You've got it. You want something to complain about? And as for you," he said to Katharine. "I wouldn't cross the street to save your fucking life. This fight is coming and it's got to come. Just remember when you look into the mirror. Just remember whose side you're on. You've got a liar's heart, every one of you. Inhuman. Oimu told us to come here. He told us where to find you."

"I understand," said Mayaram. "We won't say a word."

"You bet you won't. Fuck you—say what you want. You think I'm ashamed?" The gun tip wove a crazy pattern in the air. "No. This was for Jonathan. Jonathan and his family. You think their lives meant nothing? And what I want to know is," he said, turning toward Katharine again, "how did they know? Didn't you tell them? Didn't you give us away? You and your father? Someone turned off the electricity. We had one change of shift at Goldstone Lodge, and that's when they hit us."

Laudenberg, thought Simon, and all at once he remembered everything. He remembered Natasha Goldstone with her white shirt unbuttoned. He remembered her standing at the window, turning toward him, the breeze pulling at her shirttails. He remembered the man in the doorway, the woman behind him with the gun in her hand, and the image pressed together with another image—the boy in the baseball cap, his coat flapping behind him, his heart exploding from his chest. He looked at Katharine and she was staring at him with an intensity so sharp it hurt. "Please," he said. "We won't say a word about this. Just take us back. She needs her medication. She needs a doctor, and you can't just leave us here."

Then there was silence, because of course he could. As if to emphasize that possibility, the driver of the red car turned the engine off. He left the lights. He opened his door and got out, and stood with his hands in his pockets next to the front wheel.

Human chaos, thought Simon, staring at Katharine, at her orange eyes.

5b
Katharine (v)

Once at Ursuline in her senior year, she had been in a play, and she had played Medea, and she had stood alone on stage with the red dye on her hands, and the lights had been all around her, shining on her, shining in her eyes. In that crowded auditorium, the lights made her alone. Here on the cold road with the headlights in her eyes, she threw her head back in a gesture from the play. She was alone in the past, and alone in the ghost world, and alone in the real world where the men stood around her, frozen by their wants. On the road, with the light in her face, she stood as if on the apex of the earth, and the earth curved away from her on every side, and as if from an enormous height she could see the road and the cars parked on the pass and the line that divided dark from light. She could see the fire and the burning house. Down below her she could smell the sulfur swamps, the source of misery and life, the devil's pit, and beyond the swamp she could feel the devil waiting. He was waiting in the diamond sands, and in the real world and the ghost world and the dead world too, that colorless place where the dead crowded around her. Down the road, toward the burning house, she could see them mustering around the white van, and she could see their white faces, and even at that distance she could hear their voices as they talked, a hum of amiable conversation. The men had dragged their bodies to a gasoline-soaked ditch, but in the dead world they stood and talked: Adele Borgo and the rest, and Mormon Thomas, and Frank Blair, who had been to prep school with her cousin.

Closer to hand stood Mr. Goldstone and Mrs. Goldstone and Natasha Goldstone, and because they were human beings their spirits had no physical reality, but could only gibber from the throats of the men who stood around her in the real world, in the car's headlights. But she knew them, and Mr. Goldstone was the man with the gun who had used his name, and Mrs. Goldstone was the other man who got out of the car—he had her movement in his hand, the way he put his hand up to his neck. And Simon Mayaram was Natasha, and she was living inside Simon Mayaram as a reproach to him, a punishment to both of them because he had slept with her that day while Katharine was playing the piano. Now she was speaking with his voice. "We won't say a word about all this," she said. "Just take us back. She needs her medication. She needs a doctor, and you can't just leave us."

The dead world had no color in it, and the air was thick and full of a speckled mist. She felt she was safe in it; possessed by the dead, the men couldn't move, and so for a while she listened to the Goldstones as they talked—there was tension, as always, and Natasha wanted something that her parents couldn't give her, and they couldn't understand what she was saying. She wanted things, she wanted things for Katharine and herself, and her parents couldn't understand her. "Just forget it," Natasha would have said. "Walk away, just walk away from them, because let's face it they're incorrigible," and it was like that time when Natasha had wanted the keys to the car so they could go someplace— "She needs her medication; she needs a doctor": What a crazy excuse, when all they needed was to have some fun.

She needed to go forward, not back. And in the dead world
the dead called to her through the grainy mist, and "It's all
right," they said, and nothing lasts forever. These soulless
creatures, these men who live in one world only, how can
they touch you with their guns, their hate? "Look at us," they
said, and "We are free." So she turned away from the spotlight, slowly, histrionically presenting her unprotected back,
and she walked down the mud slope.

She walked down the mud slope. With every step downward, it was as if the air got warmer and it was as if she were
sinking through layers of gradually increasing warmth. In
the dead world she could feel the clear gradations on her
skin, and it was as if the world there existed as a series of
continuums between harsh opposites, but just a few—there
was dark and light and heat and cold, and there was hunger
and a kind of glutted bloat, and there was fear and the reas-
surance that comes from tiny options, from clarity, from sim-
plicity, and there were human beings and the amiable dead.
Away from the road they existed not even as separate spirits
anymore, but as a roaring in her ears, a warming pressure on
her skin: more and heavier and hotter as she walked down
north and east toward the dividing line.

As she descended, she became aware of new sensations,
and sounds in her ears that were not the voices of the dead.
But they were more distinct and sharper, and her sneakers
made squelching sounds in the rough mud, and clots of mud
and gravel slid away from her down the slope. She could
hear the slamming of the car doors above her and she started
to move faster, unsure now that the spotlight was no longer
on her, now that it no longer protected her and made her
separate, now that the worlds came together and above her
there were men with guns, and below her there were dangers
too. She raised her face, and the mists of the dead world

parted above her and showed her the sky, and showed her the vault of heaven hung with stars, each one aching, holy, and inviolate. She looked toward one, the rat's red eye in a constellation called the Ratcatcher, and at that moment she smelled something that seemed also to come from limitlessly far away, and it was distinct from all other smells, just a ghost of something on the freshening wind, a sharpness which was gone, and she turned away from the rat's eye and turned down the slope, and walked down the slope toward that hinted smell of sulfur.

This place, this strip of land inside the terminator which the sun sucked and pulled at like the sea gnawing a beach, it was the source of the world's life. These sulfur pools which dotted the dividing line, from their hot dark bitter water life had come, born out of the mud, feeding the carnivorous earth. At one time these hills were full of life, rare now in the real world. But in the ghost world Katharine turned down the slope. The forest of the saints was far behind her, and all that comfort from her human life was past. In front of her, small vicious beasts lurked in the rocks, and she could feel their tiny sensibilities. Oh, God, she thought: words now empty of significance in this dark, crowded landscape, and she knew it. Creatures scurried in the rocks, and there were big ones too, vague presences. And one creature above all, so quick, so strong, so purposeful, so close—"Are you there?" she called out, and she raised her head up toward the rat's red eye again.

"I'm here."

It was Simon. Disappointed and relieved, she waited for him. He came down stiff-legged, frightened by the slope. He whimpered, his tail low and his slick black fur splashed with mud. An odor came from him, a sharp smell of fear, yet even so she found herself reassured by his bulk, touched by his loyalty; low to the ground, he made a circle round her feet and lifted his muzzle up to touch her hands.

The car started above them, and then it drove away.

"Look, we have to stay close to the road. Where are you going?" And he kept on like that for a little while until she reached down and seized him by the muzzle, and held his mouth closed. Vanquished, desperate to please, he sank down into the mud, he turned over onto his side and lifted up his forepaw and his back leg too, and she could see the red tip of his cock slide out. She squeezed the front of his head, and she left him with new thoughts when she let go, and he was happy just to be with her. Happy to do what he could.

Yes, and she took comfort. It felt good to let her body move. Good, and yet it hurt. Those days in the frozen dark she had been bent and closed, and now she was opening up. Her jaw hurt, her face hurt from smiling, and her limbs were weak and awkward. Her sneakers, clogged with mud, were big and heavy, and she stomped down to the level ground and the dog followed her, and then he took the lead. Yes, that was right. There were creatures in the rocks, subtle and cerebral, and they shied away from his dumb physicality.

He took off north and east and she followed him. The land opened in front of her and he moved into it. Twenty yards ahead, he turned back to look at her. He stood frozen and expectant, then he went on. She followed, watching his footprints lose their clarity as the damp clay turned coarse and dry. The horizon glowed in that perpetual twilight, and they were heading toward it, and the land dried out. The road ran behind them down toward the burnt house, and the dead were there. It ran down an artificial causeway of banked mud; they had crossed the road by the big culvert and now they left it, and they turned away east. They crossed the dry channel and climbed up through the collapsing sand, and the valley closed up tight. And then later it opened up around them, a barren desert landscape studded with rocks and mud formations which in the sunshine might reveal dramatic colors—gaudy reds and oranges and browns—and which even in the murky half-light seemed to hold pregnant or imprisoned inside of them a kind of rich warmth. The sun had not touched them in years. Yet when they wandered through a ring of polished boulders, the dog still twenty yards in front, Katharine seemed to feel a secret warmth seep out of them and gather on their surfaces, and whether it was just because they kept some memory of light locked in their rocky hearts, or whether she was sensing the subtle outcome of some geothermal disturbance, or whether there was some radioactive principle she could now perceive with her new eyes, they seemed almost to glow. She clambered over a lip of basalt and along a basalt shelf; it seemed coarse under her fingers, scoured by the wind, warmed, perhaps, by the wind's friction, by the grinding of the sand. Breezes came out of nowhere and subsided, dry air with grit in it which chafed her skin.

They were moving uphill now. The dead house was lost behind them. Fierce stars burned through the horizon veil. Behind her in the purer dark of the west sky, constellations roiled and battled above the distant ice pack, and she turned often to look back at them when she stopped to rest, or to preserve the twenty yards' distance between her and the black dog. They uncoiled in her memory, a girdle of fighting beasts, named by human beings and revealed to her first in the planetarium at Ursuline, where she had memorized them and memorized the crude dramatic outlines which the stars themselves could only hint at. Now she seemed to see them like a row of cartoons in the sky: the ratcatcher, the archer, and the crab, and the lines seemed to glow above her as she turned back to look. Now also she was aware that this was night, that this was really night, and she was looking at it and seeing it almost for the first time. The night wind on her face, drying her face, drying her breath. Before, near the dead house where they had been locked up, she had not thought about it, and she had concentrated on the other things. They had been locked up as if inside a closet or a cellar, and she had seen that kind of dark before. But now the door was open to the night outside. Now it was night, and even though for the moment they were headed back into the day, still she turned often and watched the beasts fighting in the sky. She felt sensitized by darkness, as if in order to collect the small warmth, the intermittent photons, her eyes, her mind, her body had to open up, to dilate, to unsheathe, to swell.

They climbed uphill, and there was sweat on her face and the wind dried it. They climbed for many hours, and she did not get tired. The sky lightened in front of them, and a slender yellow line formed on the horizon, a single line which drew the bulges of the hills.

The stars were dimmer here. They walked along a path, a gray line through the middle of a gray valley. Swells of dry mud, dry ash surrounded them. To their right, seven basalt spires stood in an artificial row, placed there by some demon hand. And while lower down it had seemed that there was some warmth, some tiny radiation that was seeping from the stone, now the effect was stronger. Katharine could hear a noise, a small hum at the lowest frequency her new ears could perceive. It shocked her; she stood still to listen, and as she did so the whole landscape began to change, to come to life. Light gleamed on the gray hills. Water flowed far underground. The rocks themselves seemed halted in the midst of movement. The ground seemed insecure under her feet.

She looked along the line of the path. The ground had

split there; a seam had opened up in front of her, and the path ran along one edge. She skirted it carefully. She peered over the lip and then stepped back. The mud shelved underneath her out of sight—not a long way in the half darkness. Looking ahead, she could see how parts of the path had collapsed down, leaving an irregular, scalloped edge. In one such place she could see six feet or so of newly broken mud where the overhang had slipped down, perhaps when the dog had passed. It oozed a liquid which was not water, which gleamed as if it were itself a source of light, which dripped from a sharp nipple of embedded rock with a peculiar greasiness, forming a viscous string.

Katharine walked forward to this place and squatted down. Flowing over the fresh break, the liquid liberated a bitter smell. Here where the overhang had already subsided, she felt safe to squat down by the edge, safe to look down. She could not see far. Yet it was as if at the limit of her sight another sense took over, something which was not as dependent as sight upon external circumstance, and it carried her down deeper, combining with sound and smell and memory to form a new amalgam of perception. This new sense still revealed itself in visual images, which seemed at times flatter and flimsier than normal sight, at times heavier and more solid. Projection and anticipation gave form to these images, while memory gave them mass, and sometimes she relied on one more than the other, the future more than the past; she squatted down and watched a wet green bug clamber out of sight, and then she followed it down inch by inch over the sculpted granular surfaces and down and down, and down there a cleft opened up, and it was small but very deep, and the bug waded down over a delicate slope of sand and ash, starting minute landslides as it stumbled down. At the bottom of the slope it shook its feet free, and stood unsteadily next to the lip as if unsure whether to proceed down farther into that narrow, knife-edged hole, and there was a wet sound down there, a tiny acrid smell.

She could hear the dog barking up ahead.

She squatted back on her heels and closed her eyes. During the past few hours, whenever she had blinked she had been conscious of a flash of dull red light. Now with her eyes closed she looked around herself at a red landscape. Its contours were the same, or at least the differences were subtle and elusive: a new sharpness perhaps, an absence of detail, an impression of two dimensions only. But the main difference was not in form but in color; it was a landscape composed of aftcrimages, and they were formed of riotous and unnatural shades of pink, purple, green, orange, red. There was a shudder in the air, also, a far thunder, as if a jet were breaking the sound barrier high above.

She reached her hand out in front of her and spread her fingers—strangely flat, a livid green. And qualities of light were now reversed: East toward the horizon, toward the dividing line, the sky was an undifferentiated purple. Overhead, it lightened in perceptible bands, an enormous spectrum. Back behind them, back toward the ice and endless snow, back along hills the sun had not touched for a hundred years, there was a soft white line. Beneath her feet the ground was a dark sienna, except for the chasm where the bug had gone. Something burned down there.

Simon stood above her, holding a water bottle. "I've found someplace to rest for a few hours. Have something to eat—you must be famished." She smiled up at him with her eyes closed, and watched that one word *famished* come alive and stand its ground, while the rest skittered away. Simon's flesh seeped from him until his hips were too thin to hold his pants and they fell down, revealing pale thighbones. Yes, she thought, and opened her eyes, and smiled up at Simon. Such a handsome man, she thought. His dark eyes and dark cheeks. His chin covered with coarse hair.

He bent down to touch her head, to bring his face down near her head. "I love you," he said, and she closed her eyes. Yes, there he was again with his famished bones. She brushed her cheek against the porous surface of his hip. He was standing near the hole, and as she watched, the words he had spoken took on the shape, again, of insects, and they climbed painstakingly over his ribs and down the empty pel-vis where his sex had been, and clambered down his shins and down over his shoes and over the red break in the clay and down the strange and radiant hole. He moved his fam-ished hands over her hair.

Later she walked in front of him with her eyes closed, following his double line of footprints.

Later she found the place where he had left the pack, "out of the wind," he said. But the wind sucked at her no mat-ter where she was, sucked at her without touching her, for her hair and clothes were still. There was a roaring in her ears, and it was not less when she sat down on the sand in a place enclosed by basalt boulders. Exhausted, she leaned back against the rock.

He forced her to drink, forced her to eat. She wasn't hun-gry. He gave her a wet bologna sandwich. She held a piece of it in her mouth, her teeth clenched around it, and she thought perhaps the acid in her mouth, the acid wafting from her stomach when she breathed, might dissolve it down to nothing, and she could spit it out. With her eyes closed, she pictured the long ringed column of her esopha-gus and there was nothing in it, and it was blessed, empty, sacrosanct.

She spat the food out and lay back with her eyes closed.

She felt an enormous relief to find herself surrounded suddenly by darkness, by images of her own making, and it was
as if darkness had filled up the red landscape and come
around her like a fog. Perhaps it was sleep, and sleep was
coming; she gave herself to it, and soon she was asleep. But it
was as if there were no change in her consciousness, no relaxation of the frayed stretched fabric of her thoughts, but
just a new kind of pattern, a new imagery—a dream of the
real world, the small, unopened world when she had been a
child, and she had lived with her father in Shreveport in the
sun.

Not, in fact, so long ago. Her dream was of Goldstone
two summers before, where she and Natasha had spent part
of their vacation. She dreamt that she was sitting with the
family in the breakfast room and that Natasha had given her
something to wear, a summer dress that was too short, that
left her naked from the waist down. She squirmed her naked
behind against the wicker seat. Mr. Goldstone was leaning
toward her across the table, and he told her that her father
was expected any moment, that he was at that moment on
his way, and Katharine was filled with terror because she
knew that she would have to jump up to greet him when he
arrived, would have to run across the floor to him and help
him. It was a tiny dream, almost reassuring in its small anxieties, and she welcomed it almost gratefully, for she had had
it before. She welcomed it, she grasped at it as if it were a
thread, as if it were Theseus's thread when he was in the lab-
yrinth and the Minotaur was close. One end of it was
wrapped around her hand. It was so thin, so frail when it
stretched tight, and it stretched back through the rocks and
up the strange slopes and through the forest of the saints and
up into the light, and it led her back to memories that were
far from pleasant, yet she needed them. Now she was no lon-

ger asleep; she lay back, inert, and the images of her dreams faded imperceptibly into memory—just a subtle fading of the colors. There she stood. There she stood at Goldstone Lodge, and she had come in from the swimming pool. Natasha and she had spent the day there reading magazines and putting sunscreen on each other. Natasha was wearing a black bikini; she had a demure one-piece which her father had picked out, and she had gone back to the house to get some Cokes. Mr. Goldstone was there, and he was standing in the kitchen in some kind of uniform, some kind of khaki camouflage, and he had a khaki hat on his bald head. He took it off. He was an enormous, terrifying man, and he had a diamond earring in his left ear, and she stared at it as he came close. He was asking her some questions, but she knew; it was no surprise when he put his hands on her. She stared at his diamond earring as he touched her. He took the top of her bathing suit down and felt her breasts, palpated them as if for cancerous lumps. He kissed her neck, and his breath had a sweet antiseptic smell, and he was saying, "You are something else. You're a hot one, aren't you? You're a wildcat"—whatever that was. His equipment belt had dug into her ribs.

She opened her eyes. She was leaning back against a slope of sand, and someone had covered her with a wool blanket. Boulders loomed above her. She had lain down out of the wind in a small dell of sand, and there was no noise anywhere, and everything was still.

The black dog was curled up near her. He lay in a hollow in the sand. He was asleep. He was dreaming, and his feet made tiny kicking motions. His eyes were open, his pupils jiggled rapidly. She stripped off the blanket and knelt down close to him. His breath was unsteady. It smelled dirty from the sandwich he had eaten. His teeth were covered with a film. His breath was heavy, and at the back of it she could hear words, strange words. "Do not forget that you are mine, my property, my tool, and I claim you. Separate, we are helpless nothing."

5c
Demons (v): A Voice in the Dream

YOU ARE MY THING MY NOTHING THING AND THE THREAD TIES US. WITHOUT ME YOU ARE GONE ALONE BACK WHERE THEY HURT. HELPLESS. I AM HELPLESS. YOU STARVE. I AM STARVING.

5d
Simon (ii)

When Simon woke up she was gone. Asleep, she had been shivering, but now the blanket he had put on her was thrown aside.

He looked for her for hours, coming back again and again to the small shelter in the rocks which he had found for them. He used the flashlight from the knapsack, but the sand and clay had not taken her footprints. He could not follow her; other people had come this way, and the traces were unclear.

He had no sense of which direction she might have chosen. For the past day her thoughts had been disordered, and he had led her as a mother leads a disordered child. Perhaps she had gone out to urinate and then got lost, or gone a little way into the rocks and then got lost. "Katharine," he shouted. It was easy to imagine her helpless and in danger; as time went on, his worry and his self-recrimination took the place of thought, and he moved out from their resting place in widening circles, returning often to see if she'd come back. His worry and his guilt combined together in his chest, and made a pressure that affected him and brought him close to tears. He mouthed strings of silent words.

He climbed up toward the east, where it was getting lighter. The horizon was approaching, and the golden line over the hills was thickening.

"Please, God," he said, "if I find her, I will not let her go. I will not fail her."

He was standing at the top of a rock wall, shining his flashlight around him in a circle. He thought, If I could build a fire, then she would see it and come back. She'd see it from far away.

But in this world where all life came out of darkness, there was nothing to burn. Oil and gas sometimes leaked to the surface, but not here, not in this place, and he was standing in a wasteland so barren that there was nothing even at home to compare with it—he had seen pictures of the Spanish desert, but even there things grew. There were remnants of houses. People lived there. And if there was no future, then at least there was a past.

He sat down on the sandy clay and looked toward the horizon line, where the golden outline of the hills bled upward into darkness. He sucked in the cold dry sour air, and he felt as if it were starving him, starving his human brain, making him vulnerable to false fears and hallucinations. He rubbed his eyes with his fists and imagined himself climbing up onto some rock ridge to build a fire. He imagined himself finding something there, something to burn. He imagined finding the body of an enormous insect covered in the sand, a creature perhaps twenty feet long, and so old and fragile that its shape could only be guessed at. Tubes of chitin lay about like bones, and they were so dry and abraded that he thought, Yes, I can put a fire to them, and they would burn, and the fire would be visible from miles away. Yes, he thought, and in his half-dreaming state he felt the relief that comes from action, because he was already lighting a fire in his mind. The flames were leaping up.

Yes, he thought, and he said it too. But because he was half asleep, the word didn't come out of his mouth fully formed. It was just a noise he made, and then he was awake and standing up. He was peering down below him through the rocks. He had heard some answering noise down there, and it was not part of the dream.

"Katharine," he said. He waited. And then he heard the noise again, a human voice.

He scrambled down off the rock wall. Below him there was a channel in the sand, and it led down sharply and then evened out. He could hear the voice talking to him, and in his mind he made it into Katharine's voice, so that even before he reached the source of it, his mind had already raced ahead in time. He had already comforted and consoled her, already chided her not harshly but firmly, and explained to her how important it was for them to stay together. He had even spoken to her a little bit about their plans, about what they would do next, about how they were going on toward Ludlow and then home. How they would find Dr. Klemper at the Shreveport clinic, and she would regulate Katharine's medicine and bring her back. He found himself mumbling as he clambered over hillocks of rough sand, searching for her voice. He found himself rehearsing and rejecting certain phrases.

It was not her. It was the priest. It was the Kiyungu priest, and he was in a bad way. Simon shined the light into his face. He was huddled between two car-sized rocks. His black sweater was torn, his face was bruised, and there was blood in his hair. A beaded cut ran across his scalp. His eyes were closed. He shied away from the light and put his hand up. And he was talking constantly; his voice had led Simon to him over a litter of sharp stones.

"Don't," he said, "just leave me. Just no more. Just don't touch, my God," and then he lapsed into one of the native fringe dialects, speaking rapidly and indistinctly through his battered lips. Simon could make out the odd word.

He was a small, pale man. His hair was pulled back in a rubber band. His complexion was jagged, rough and bruised, and pitted with small holes and sores; his beard was growing out in patches. The flashlight threw the imperfections of his face into relief until Simon turned it away and turned it off. The sky was light enough to see without it.

"It's Simon Mayaram," he said.

That shut the man up. He sat huddled with his arms around his chest, nodding his head and taking short, snuffling breaths.

"Are you hurt?"

Silence.

Simon knelt down by him. "Can you walk?"

"Yes of course I can," said Martin Cohen. "How do you think I got here? I walked all the way from Jim's Gut. Almost to Ludlow. But you can't get through and now I'm walking back."

Jim's Gut was a town in the fringes, the site of a copper mine. "That's where we were heading," admitted Simon.

"Well you can't. They're on strike. The Abos killed Bob Garner and they're going out into the farms. I heard it on the radio. People are gathering at the Boy Scout camp at Ernestine and Ludlow Grange. There's the militia there."

"We've got to reach them."

"Well you can't. You mean Katharine Styreme? They'd kill her and they'd kill you too. I know what I'm talking about."

"We have to go. She needs her medicine."

"I bet she does." He opened his mouth wide and picked something out of it and flicked it away. "They must have closed the road. Here." He took a pack of cigarettes out of the front pocket of his pants, and then a small box in a leather case. It was a shortwave radio. He lit a cigarette and fiddled with the radio, searching for a band.

"Here," he said, moving back and forth between two identically worded announcements: exhortations to remain calm, to progress with a minimum of baggage to certain landing fields.

The staggered voices and the static in between made an eerie effect. The same words over and over. After a moment Cohen spun the dial, looking for something else, and then he turned the radio off.

Simon stood up. "You must be pleased." He was thinking about Katharine.

Martin Cohen blew a stream of smoke. He studied the lit end of his cigarette. "No. Oh no. It didn't have to be like that." And then he shrugged, not dismissively, but as if he were trying to say something. He started to talk again after a pause, to explain himself perhaps, but that small gap was enough to shake Simon's attention. He was worried, and anxious to get moving. He didn't listen. He stood rubbing his hands together until the cigarette was done and Cohen got to his feet.

They went back to the place where Simon had left the rucksack. Katharine wasn't there.

"I came back along the trail," said Martin Cohen. "I

would have seen her. As soon as the sun comes up, then you can see for miles. There's only one way to go and I'd have seen her."

"If you were looking for her."

"I was. I was hoping you would come this way. I was trying to head you off."

Simon stood holding the small bag of food. He called out her name a couple of times, and then he opened it. "I'm afraid she's lost. She needs her medication—she's a bit disoriented right now."

They started eating the sandwiches in the bag. They ate them all, and Simon wrapped the blanket up, and then they drank the water. After that, there was nothing left to do. Simon shined the flashlight in the air. Suddenly he was impatient to get going, though he didn't know where.

"She must be out of earshot," said Martin Cohen. "She probably went back."

Why probably? thought Simon. What's "probably" for her? He felt close to tears. It was very sudden, like sudden nausea.

"Well I'm going back. We can't stay here. There are more supplies at Drywater and I know where they are."

He started walking, and Simon followed him. More than anything he didn't want to be alone.

Cohen knew the way. They started walking down the valley. Cohen limped and talked, and often they stopped to rest. Simon felt an urge to follow him, believe him, do what he said. Cohen knew this country, and he had seen nothing as he came across the line. Unless he lied, oh God; all the way down Simon gnawed at his misgivings and kept the flashlight burning, and shouted Katharine's name when they stopped to rest, and listened with half his mind to Martin Cohen as he talked. It was enough. Later he would remember things, days later when he was crawling out over the ice toward Shackleton Station, and he was so exhausted that his eyes were playing tricks on him, and the face of the moon seemed to vibrate, and huge sheets and swirls of purple and orange spread out from it, and the ice glowed red and took shapes that were not real. There where the rent in the ionosphere was almost visible, and the wrecked stars glowed beyond it, and the radiation seemed to glitter on his skin. Then he would remember parts of Cohen's monologue. After cold and exhaustion and despair and the wild wind had taken away the possibility of speech, then he ate his memory like food. And Cohen's words didn't stay with him because they were important or wise or even true, but perhaps because when he first heard them they seemed the only part of his environment with any reality at all. The journey back to Drywater took an intolerable time, and even after he thought he had discovered one of Katharine's footprints headed in the same direction, still his worrying and wondering seemed to blot out his perception of the landscape. He moved through the half-lit clay hills as if through an empty room or across an empty stage.

"It didn't have to be like this," said Martin Cohen. "No, if men weren't men. If we didn't touch it with our poison—no, I was in Jim's Gut today. The Abos smashed me up but they'd have killed me if they had been men. You're not from here. Do you think I should be sorry? You of all people? You should know it more than anyone—you come from the place they destroyed. We destroyed it and I've seen the pictures. I've read about it. Forests. Oceans. I saw a movie about Borneo, and they were in this forest and the trees were fifty feet around. There were huge red monkeys in the trees. Small ones—they ran through the branches. There were pigs and snakes. So many things were growing that the people got diseases. They were carrying packages full of some equipment and then they came out into a small village with carved wooden houses and the children ran to meet them. There was water everywhere—it was on their skin. It puddled on the ground. Everything was covered with flowers—I saw it. Don't tell me it's still like that."

"Not much," admitted Simon.

"Yes I know. We wrecked it, didn't we? We used it up. They made plastic bags and diapers out of the oil and then buried them. They cut down all the forests. The air is gone, the sky's gone, and there's nothing in the ground and nothing in the sea. It's just dead water rising, and nothing lives and nothing grows. People's skin just burns. Yes and they're dying. I saw the movie about eye cancer. It was a hospital, very clean with all the air filters. Outside it's a garbage dump with people fighting in the garbage."

"That's not true," said Simon.

"They found six worlds in the universe over a distance of a thousand years, and they wrecked them all. Sure. Don't tell me about it. Don't tell me because I know. I know it because here it's just the same no matter how you try. Here it's like the house of Circe in the myth, human beings into animals, and you don't even have to be an evil person for it to change you. There were two races here. Two ancient, subtle races millions of years old, and we've massacred one into extinction and drugged and enslaved the other. Two cultures destroyed utterly, maybe the only two outside our own that ever existed. Two cultures linked in a way we never even bothered to understand—it took us a hundred and fifty years, that's all. The break in the atmosphere over the ice field, the fact is that's already from industrial pollution. Even insects, foreign species outnumber native ones by ten to one now. We're killing this place. Do you know why?"

They walked in silence for a while. He said, "Because we hate it."

He said: "Do you smell that smell?" Simon didn't; he was thinking about other things, and soon the priest went on: "That's the sulfur. It's here in the fringes on the dark side of the line. A hundred years ago it's where they lived and it's where their food chain starts here in the mud. Did you know that? It's not like us. It's a different kind of thing and we will never understand."

"It's not so different," said Simon.

"No. I bet I know: You're thinking about that girl. You're thinking about her and wondering where she is, and you're thinking she's not so different. Maybe a little strange now, maybe a little confused. Maybe she's had some strange hallucinations but if you can just get her home and shoot her full of drugs well then she'll be all right. She'll be fine. I saw her—no. She's a different kind of organism. It's only the way she looks that makes you feel the way you do."

There was silence for a long time as they trudged through the dark clay. And then Cohen started up again, as if his words had been building a new pressure. As if they soothed his battered lips: "I know you know it. But does it mean enough to you? What does it mean? They live forever, almost. They don't eat. They don't sleep or else they're sleeping all the time. They're one-sexed. They see in the dark. They never get cold."

"Be quiet," interrupted Simon. And then: "I know you're right. But then you're wrong as well. I still feel it. All the rest, it's like a trick. Her mind is playing tricks. It's not her real self. If it was, why would she be afraid? Why would she need me?"

They trudged in silence for a few minutes. "I once saw a movie about brain activity," said Martin Cohen.

He had a water bottle. From time to time they'd stop, and he would bathe the bruises on his face. He would touch them gently with his fingertips. Once he drank and spit the water out. He cleared his throat. "It was about us," he said.

And then a little later: "Human beings are like gods. That was the core of Geoffrey Kiyungu's message and it's true. We give and we take away. We create and we destroy. Whatever we touch we transform. Irrevocable. We're unique that way."

They climbed up a slope of coarse white clay. Martin Cohen put his hand out and they stopped. He stood silent for a while, then lit a cigarette, and the words came quicker. "I saw it in the movie. The electromagnetic impulses of the brain. They had an outline of a human brain and lights played over it to show normal activity. Waking, sleeping— little lights flashed on and off and streams of lights made up connections, red and blue. People say we never use more than ten percent of our brains, and I saw why. The lights were just in a few areas. Whole sections of the brain stayed dark. But then they showed an Aboriginal—unaltered. Raw. The whole surface of its brain was lit up all the time; it was like lightning playing over it. The point was to show how those medications were first developed, to block out that activity, to close it down. To make it dark except in a few areas and we succeeded. Of course we did; we can do anything. We're like gods, but the actions of gods are always limited. Limited and predictable—a tiny range and in that range we demonstrate our strength. It's like the one muscle in a crocodile's jaw. Implacable." He blew out a stream of smoke.

"We've blotted out nine-tenths of our experience," he said. "And then we force the world into the tiny space that remains, and everything outside that space we claim it doesn't exist. We claim that that's what's real, that space where we have power. But it's a lie. The world—God, don't you know how big it is?" They stood on top of the white hill, and he gestured toward the darkness all around.

"In dreams you see it sometimes," he continued. "In madness—crazy people sometimes see it. Drugs and drinking sometimes. When you starve yourself or if you can't sleep. Everything that makes you weak and everything you do to relax that muscle, and you can see glimpses of it. Geoffrey Kiyungu in his prison cell. They starved and tortured him and then they killed him, but he caught a glimpse of it. The world opened up a little bit and he saw part of it. Like the Bhagavad Gita, where Arjuna first sees Lord Vishnu and he fills up the whole world. Kiyungu said we were all Christ, that Christ was born in us again and again through lifetime after lifetime until we figured it out, until we carried our own cross to Calvary. Until we no longer worshiped him or anything outside ourselves, and understood that heaven and hell, that the spheres of the universe were part of us not just in metaphor but in medical fact, part of us, part of our brains. Oh God is that so difficult? Every man and woman has moments when they know and the world seems as if it just might split apart and show them something new.

"Hallucinations," he said, "you think she's having hallucinations? I saw an unaltered Abu once, and he was holding something in his hands I couldn't see. But it was real. Scientists go crazy trying to explain why there is so much oxygen in the atmosphere here, why there's so much oil and even coal. They say that the world has changed, that the 19,000-year rotation is new, that it killed off life that was once plentiful; they're wrong. The fact is that the world is full of life outside of our small blinkered range, that doesn't show up on our instruments. We're the one whose eyes are closed. It's as if we closed our own eyes and the images we see in the darkness on the inside of our lids, we make them real. Through an effort of will. We make our own consensus and we make it real and we force the world to live in it. We force the world into a space that's bounded by our tiny minds. And it gives us power because it allows us to talk, to think, to communicate in concepts that are as artificial and self-referential as mathematics. It gives us a frame of reference that is false and we live in it like gods because we made it. It's like building a house where the electricity works and there's food in the refrigerator, and everything outside is the wild forest of Borneo. The wild forest. Of course she's frightened. Frightened and weak. Crazy people, addicts, saints—their worlds are separating out."

"How do you mean?"

"I saw her. Katharine Styreme—I saw her eyes. And I've seen it before. They're raw Abos in the fringes and you see them sometimes. They can't do anything. The fact is they can barely function. They are so alone. Hell, they lived like animals before we came. They didn't even have fire or spoken language. All that came later; in forty years they were building houses even in places that the pioneers had never gone. So quick. That's when the demons first appeared. That's why they needed them, or they used to. To make maps. To pull out what they wanted and to make it real."

"What do you mean?"

"You called them demons but they were gods. They're gone now."

Later, on the ice, Simon would wonder what this meant. What maps? They all needed maps. At times the landscape on the ice seemed more mental than physical after the eye lost any sense of progress or distance, lost the horizon line, lost the difference between forward and backward, and the ice was like a black ceramic underneath his boots, and the light from the drain made a blizzard all around him, roared in his head. Then he would stagger on a few steps, and it was as if the world around him was transformed into a moral allegory, and he was struggling through the mists of ignorance while pride rang in his ears. And he was taking steps that left no imprint on the hard plateau of despair. Cohen was swallowed up. He had slid into the pit, and his voice was still forever. Katharine was a deadweight in his arms. And the walls of the world rushed toward him until they lay on his own skin and covered him.

In this country around Drywater, also, there was nothing much to see. It took hours, but finally they saw a single light, and they stood on a hill overlooking the road.

"I stole a car," said Martin Cohen. "After I left you I couldn't come back. The men were coming down then. I saw another man and I knew it was the Brotherhood. I listened on the radio. They were burning out the native lines in Shreveport. People were burning native businesses. I knew they'd kill me. That's why I didn't come back for you. I just went straight out and hid. What happened?"

"What do you think?"

Martin Cohen touched the bruises on his face. "I went up the road. I thought I was lucky. They had parked their cars over there at the top of the hill, and I found one with the keys in it. I didn't know. I didn't stop till they stopped me, and even then I thought I could explain. At Jim's Gut. They didn't care."

"Who?"

"The Abos, man, the goddamned Abos. They had put a ditch across the road. It was just stupidity that made them let me go."

Martin Cohen talked all the time. This is one of the signs of emotional bankruptcy, thought Simon later, after the man was dead. Now Simon was grateful for the noise.

VI

⊠

6a
Katharine (vi)

She left the black dog curled up on the sand. She went to see the sunrise.

She followed the trail. It continued on toward a low place in the hills, and she left it and climbed up onto a shoulder on the right. It was high enough so that at the top the sun came up, bisected by the hills in front of her; she stared at the immense golden hemicircle of the sun until it started to appear dark to her, a hole of darkness from which, nevertheless, a sense of joy and warmth and life continued to flow. It seemed to her at that moment the source of all the darkness behind her, and it was as if a warming stream of darkness flowed over her, pushing her hair back, roaring and whispering in the caverns of her nose and ears. She sat down cross-legged on the hard, thin crust of sand; it turned to powder under her. She closed her eyes, watching the afterimage of the sun fade from her retinas.

She was in the land of voices now. Everything around her had a voice. In some voices sound predominated over meaning, and in some the reverse; the sun was like a puckered red mouth on the horizon, and its lips opened and pulled back and disappeared, and the darkness in its throat expanded, and its voice flowed in a pulsing wave. It whispered in her ears, tingled on her skin, and blew her sweat away.

She turned her head and combed her hair back from her ear. She allowed the wind to enter in. It carried meaning in it like dust, like the grit that blew into her nose, and grain by grain she felt it find its way inside, and push its way down the soft corridors.

She could hear the voices of the rocks around her. They were slow, harsh mournful voices, and every syllable took generations to express, and it was only by slowing down her breath and stopping her heart and letting her blood drip like honey through her veins that she could even hear them. They were elemental voices; they rose out of the ground, and she knew what they were saying, or she thought she knew. She heard the noise and it was enough. She heard the noise and the tone and the intent, and she supplied the words. You will die, she told herself. You will starve and die. You will burn in the hot sun. The black dog will fuck you again and again and again.

In that slow world, living creatures were as insubstantial as ghosts. One came from nearby, along the path that led into the sun. He was invisible. The light bent around him and his voice was softer than a whisper. To perceive him was an act of faith. He came up the hill and stood in front of her, looking down at her. He spoke, and she couldn't hear him over the noise of the rocks. Her interest was slight. He spoke again and kept on speaking, and in time she allowed herself to rise up toward him, and she let her blood flow faster and it was as if she were rising underwater with the sounds of the water in her ears. It was as if she were looking up through the surface of a pool toward a man who was standing on its bank. As she came up closer she could see him better, and the roaring in her ears was less until she broke the surface. She broke the surface and could hear him too. He was the man that she had seen in Drywater with that creature on a leash. He had brought them sweaters.

He was holding a radio in his hands. The voice on it was covered in a web of static: a woman's voice. "Residents are advised to proceed toward the landing field at Ludlow Grange."

"I must have followed you up from the valley," said the man. "I guess we all had the same idea. But did you hear what's happening?"

He put his hand out as if to halt some kind of interruption. He moved the dial on the radio, and the woman's voice came clearer: "Luggage is limited to ten pounds per passenger. Please secure all property. We advise you to remain calm. We advise you to lock all doors when you leave. These are precautionary measures only, until those responsible have been apprehended. We repeat: Please remain calm."

"Where's the guy from the consulate?" asked the man.

He listened to the radio as it subsided into static. "Maybe it's not such a good idea," he said. "I don't know. Are you tired?"

"It was a climb," he said. "But your eyes get used to it."

"Where's Simon Mayaram?" he said.

"I followed you up," he said. "I figured we could go together but I'm glad I brought the radio; now I'm not sure. We ought to think about it before we just go up, even though it's tempting, sure. Listen: There have been raids on five farms around Ludlow and the mine is closed. The miners have

gone out and the report is that Robert Garner has been mur-
dered. I don't think it's safe, not for any of us."

After a while he turned the radio off. Katharine was glad,
because the sound of it and the sound of the man's voice had
been distressing her. It had been scratching at her nerves.
Maybe because he was right: She was very tired. Her skin
felt bloated, fat. She had fat fingers, and she slid the cuff of
her sweater back along her fat wrist.

"Don't blame me for what happened," he said. "It wasn't
my decision and I was a prisoner as much as you. They kept
me locked up. At Goldstone they had a gun on me all the
time and it was never my intention. I'm sorry about your
friends."

Her fat wrist, her powerful fat hand.

"I don't know why I'm wasting my time talking to you,"
he said. "I might have known. What did you do—run off?"

She opened her eyes. She looked up at him; he was an
ugly little man with pale skin and a bad complexion. A cross
was pinned to the breast of his coat.

The cross was in the center of his chest, and it divided
him into four parts. She got up off the sand. She stood up in
front of him, stretching her fat legs, shifting her fat feet, and
at that moment her fatness was a blessing to her, a source of
power and solidity and strength. A deep slow anger was
burning in her, a furnace stoked with animal fat. The fire
crackled and flared up unreliably, and it was fed by all the
drugs and chemicals in her polluted body, and all the man-
made plastics that the doctors had spliced into her, and all
the bone grafts and the leaking artificial viscera. The fire
sputtered, wet and toxic, and it was generating heat and
harsh synthetic colors and foul smells—strange farts and
burps. An expensive furnace that was burning garbage, and
maybe there was such a goal as purity if the heat rose high

enough, and maybe garbage was the only fuel there was and ever would be.

She could feel all that inside of her, and it hurt so much. It hurt her with an aching pain, and as she stood there in the sunrise she felt that pain travel backward through her life, and felt it travel forward also.

She stared at the little man in front of her. A human being. A man of God. The cross divided him into four parts. One part was his ugly body, and one part was his occluded soul. One part was his past, and one part was his future; she reached out toward him and then pulled her hand back.

She reached out again and touched him in the top right quadrant. It was his future, and he stood before her. He was wearing a strange plastic suit, padded, with a visor. The cross gleamed on his breast. The suit was colored green, and the part that closed over his face and over his head was bright orange. It almost glowed. The faceplate was clear, and she could see his face. His cheeks also seemed to shine—perhaps the glass or the plastic was treated with something that magnified the light. She had heard of such a thing.

The man was tired, gaunt. His beard had sprouted over his black cheeks. A curl of black hair hung down over his eye.

Beneath his feet, behind him, a dark plain stretched away as flat as the surface of a pond. There was white powder in the air, and some of it was sticking to the man's suit. A clump of it stuck to the grid over his mouth where his breath came out; it made a cloud.

Katharine felt the pressure of her anger rise. Her guts ached. She reached her hand out. "Don't touch me. What?" said the man, his voice amplified and strange. She joined her hands together, and hit him on the plastic ridge of his survival suit near where his clavicle might be. Then with her hands together she hit him on the face, and her hands were as bloated and solid as a loin of pork, and she hit him many times.

He tried to defend himself; he dropped his radio and put his hands up. She hit him once more and knocked him down, and with her plastic fingernails she slit the skin on his bald scalp, and then she walked away. She walked away and then she started running, and at first she ran forward into the light and the rising sun. She climbed uphill, and the sun was enormous and pink and hot and radiant and bright—too bright. She had wanted to see it. She had climbed from Drywater to see it. Just to see it. Just to be sure. Just to feel it burn her eyes and crackle on her skin. Just to feel the sweet relief of turning away. She turned away, turned back, and hid from it beneath the shadow of the hills.

—————— 6b ——————
Sulfur Pits

The demon sat rubbing his ankles in the room where his sister lay. He kept the candles lit hour after hour. These were the only lights in Drywater now that everyone had gone. The men had gone, the cars had driven away. The slaves were dead. He had dragged the body of the dead slave into the anteroom. The wound from her mouth and from the back of her head had left a slick trail of grease when he pulled her out. It left pollution in the air and he lit candles. There was a store of them for some reason. There were cases of them in the anteroom, along with many other things.

He put nine candles on each windowsill. He put eleven candles at his sister's head, six at her feet. The wax made puddles on the table and the cold floor.

The demon sat cross-legged. His hands were restless. He was rubbing his feet and talking to himself. His hands made patterns, sometimes fast and frantic, sometimes slow. And he would get up to light new candles and to touch his sister's face.

He had put out the candles when the men had come. Blind, they had not seen him in the dark. They had not come this far. Now they were all gone, and everyone was gone.

The light attracted men but repulsed other beasts. Now that the men were gone, he had covered the floor with candles. Men were not the only creatures in the world. Not yet. Now the light would keep the animals away. Now he felt them sometimes outside the window. They had come for the dead slaves. The men had taken the bodies to a hole and doused them with gasoline, lit them on fire, but now the fire was out. Gasoline still lingered—you could see droplets of it in the air. It could sting your eyes. But the fire was gone, the men were gone, and now the animals had come out of the rocks.

The animals didn't like men. It was not fear. They had no reason to be afraid. They lived outside the range. They were too light, too quick, too sly, or else too coarse and base ever to be caught in the net of human senses—a small net easily avoided, but tight once it caught hold. He remembered living in the cave with Reverend Martin, and he watched an animal come into the light. Unwary for some reason, brain-damaged, maybe, or too young to understand. He didn't know the real name of it, nor did his sister; no one had taught them. But they had made up names. This one was Snout. It had no eyes. It had a long, pointed, hairless snout, and a squat body close to the ground. Squat, powerful legs—it was as long as his arm. It came lumbering into the light, sensitive to it, he thought, because it paused at the edge of the circle of the fire. They were burning chips of oilstone which gave off a red light, and the beast paused where the shadows moved across a gap in the rocks. It stuck its snout into the air, turning it this way and that. Its snout was thin and naked at the end, like a finger.

Reverend Martin was talking with his clumsy hands, his agile lips. Maybe he could hear it, and maybe he could smell it too—the demon was not a judge of such things. But he was watching carefully, and though the priest didn't stop talking, his hands slowed a little bit, and he showed a tiny uncertainty there, and also in the movement of a frown across his forehead.

Snout stumbled forward into the light. It disturbed some pebbles on the edge of a crust of mud and they rolled down. The priest could see that. He looked over that way. His frown deepened but he didn't stop talking; Snout stood quiet for a few moments, reassessing, but it wasn't afraid. It stumbled forward next to the priest's outstretched leg. It touched his leg with the end of its nose, and the man hesitated, and then kept talking. But with one hand only; with the other he reached down to scratch his leg. He made a sudden movement, and his hand came in contact with the beast's flank. His fingers seemed to touch it, yet not touch it. The beast's flesh eluded him. It receded from him as the beast recoiled, as it turned and lumbered away into the darkness, disturbing the stones, the sand. Reverend Martin stopped talking, one hand lifted up.

Reverend Martin had a theory. He said there was no food chain in the world, no chain of evolution. He said there was a gap. He wondered whether the masters and the slaves had come from someplace else, some other world. But the snout had been under his hand. He could perceive the crude forms of life—small insects, beetles, and the one-celled creatures of the sulfur holes. And he could perceive the most complex. Everything else did not exist for him, and in his arrogant sad human way he made a science, a theory to explain his own deficiencies. He had explanations for the entire universe.

Now the animals had come to Drywater, and they were nosing around the dead slaves in the pit. One had slipped up to the door. He could feel it on the steps outside. He could feel the heat from its body, feel its small movements, the small vibrations of its brain.

—————— 6c ——————
Talk

I've worked for every cause there is," said Martin Cohen as they stumped down the road. "The fact is I'm the patron saint of lost causes—I've been a volunteer ever since I was a kid. I was in the Peace Corps; I was a teacher for the Ludlow Mission School. I ran the program for alcohol abuse. I helped organize the clinic there—all volunteer. I was always a pacifist, and I still am. I don't believe in violence. But problems are so deep. I've worked all my life for some kind of communication, some kind of cooperation and I know more about this than any man alive or any woman. I know all the languages. And the Coelians, I know all about that too. By God, I lived with them. I'm the only human being who can make that claim."

"Tell me about that," prompted Simon. He thought: If he weren't so boring, he'd be interesting.

"Yes I will. I was working at the mission with Mrs. Oimu—that's how I met her. I was organizing a community outreach program—what we call CIE. Communication, information, and education: it was a vaccination program, but we did other things all through the fringes. They caught diseases from us and we cured them. Harriet said that there were communities on the other side of the line: I don't mind working by myself and so I went. I had a six-month grant. I set up twenty miles south of here and waited for them to come to me. Abos can be curious. I was busy with some language research and I was studying for my spiritual exams—what we call 'interface.'

"I met a man named Paul Smyth. He was a hunter. He worked on a ranch outside of Ludlow but he would spend weekends west of the line. He was interested in archeology; there are a lot of demon ruins around here from the time of the first pioneers. There've always been rumors, but he swore there was a demon family still alive in back of Rodman's Gorge. He'd been poking around there for months. Then after a few days he'd come back to my place just to pass the time.

"One day he came back with this big greasy bag and I thought he was drunk already. He played a game with me: 'What's in the bag?' He wasn't going to show me. But he fell asleep in about an hour and I dragged it out. It was a demon's head, just fresh, decapitated at the neck. I set it up on the table of my little cabin and I stared at it. That long high skull. It was a magical moment I can tell you, with Paul snoring on the cot. And the wind. And the dark. It was a female, I could tell.

"So then he woke up and he was angry. But he was drunk you know, and so I forced him to tell me where it was, where he had found it. He said he was going back to get some money, his vacation time was up. The fact is I don't think he remembered he told me—I packed a bag and went up as soon as he left. I scoured that whole area until I found the body. And then I found them: two adolescents living in a cave. A long cave with a tiny mouth—I almost missed it. But it went back and back. Huge shadows in the light. And there they were."

They were coming down toward Drywater now, along the road.

"I took them to a safer place. They were hungry. I hid them in a ruin near my cabin. I could talk to them. I'd read that book of Reverend McElroy's—I'm fluent."

He made a few gestures with his hands. Simon recognized "Hello."

"It was sad," said Martin Cohen. "If I had had more time—there was so much I didn't understand. They were just beginning to show me about the world, about how they see the world. I was writing it all down. And I could understand them, that was the amazing thing. Not like the Abos, where every word is false. No—it would have been a great work. It would have made me famous. It was incredibly important."

"What happened to it?" asked Simon.

"It was my thesis for the Kiyungu-Christ exams," said Martin Cohen, rubbing his battered nose. He sniffled, rubbed his eyes. "You know it's not like the fucking Abos. They look so terrifying, but I could understand them. I thought there must be some kind of connection. They're not from here, I know it. They're like us only better. More developed. Open. They don't kill what they touch."

"They kept slaves," said Simon.

"So do we. Besides, it wasn't like that. Do you really think the Abos needed coercion to make them hate us and attack us? No—it was more mutual. Symbiotic. You have to understand. The Abos—this was my thesis, really. Kiyungu says we must worship the Christ inside of us. Atman, you know: that's what the demons are. The world is so confusing, and we have our way of dealing with it which is to block it out. Block out nine-tenths of it. But the Abos don't do that; they're like sponges that soak up everything. Too much, in fact; too much to understand. But the demons could make sense out of it. They could make patterns; they were like gods, really; you could think of them like that."

"I see."

"No you don't. Slaves and masters, it's the same thing. In a sense the Abos created them, like we created our gods. And it worked; you read McElroy. The Abos lived like animals until the demons raised them up. They were living in caves and eating beetles from the sulfur water. But the demons made a pattern for them and showed them how to think. The real world and the false."

"They were slaves," said Simon.

"You don't understand. Sure, we read all about it in school, the chapel of bones, the labor farms, the terrible way the demons used to treat them and control their minds; but you know that was just since the conquest. The fact is there were never very many of them. Human beings were here for forty years before they even were aware demons existed. All that building, that came later. Maybe their culture changed when humans came. Their kings, their council, their palaces at Drywater—all that they copied straight from us. There were never very many of them, and we hunted them so mercilessly that we forced them to become creatures like ourselves. Coercive."

They were coming into Drywater now. The white van was still parked outside the hall. One of the brick walls had fallen down, and inside there were scattered beams and glowing cinders.

A Sequence of Dreams

Katharine had come back a quicker way. While they were fussing in the hills, while they were waiting for her, while they were resting, while in places they mistook the trail, she had come back straight. She had thought to lose them after she had hit the Kiyungu priest across the face and knocked him down. She assumed that they were going on toward what was right for them, that they had found the trail and gone on, up into the sunlight. Across the dividing line. Up into the human world. Up to the landing site, and up to Shreveport in a plane.

She had doubled back to lose them, to avoid them. She had kept to the bottom of the washes, and she had moved without stopping until she saw the candlelight at Drywater. She was burning the resources of her body, burning the fat, burning the chemicals away. It was a painful fire. But still it pleased her to exhaust herself, to render herself down.

She came into Drywater along the bottom of the wash. Up behind the smoldering hall, among the rocks, there was a pit with seven bodies in it. But she crossed the road and crossed the turnaround with the white van in it. She had to elbow her way through dead people, and they were standing around the doorway of the hall. Mrs. Oimu was there, and she wasn't so frightening as she had been. Her features were softer, and the rage that had been her animating principle had seeped away. Or she had vomited it up. Katharine remembered seeing in the library at Ursuline a reproduction of a medieval manuscript, and it showed a naked man in bed. At the moment of his death, a winged creature was crawling from his mouth, was expelled into the air.

Those seven dead people had been bloated with rage, fat with bitterness and hate. It had formed them, formed the contours of their faces. Now they were vomiting it up. They were vomiting it all up, and with it came all the inert synthetic gels out of the ruptured sacs, and all the dissolving plastic joints and tubes. Their faces were collapsing and their bodies were shrinking. Katharine moved through them. They were reaching out to her. Their fingers slid along her arms. But their voices were foreign, and they were talking in the language of the dead. And they were happy; she knew they were happy, but it was happiness she couldn't share. It was a reproach to her.

The light was burning up ahead, up a sandy slope behind the hall. A window in the darkness: It was the window of a square stone cottage with a corrugated iron roof. Nearby an older wall, decorated with a carved frieze, stretched away— too dark to see where.

Long stone steps led down from the door, which hung ajar. It also was a sheet of metal, suspended crookedly from hinges made of chain. A length of chain hung loose from a hook in the door frame; a padlock lay open on the top step. Candlelight flickered through a long triangular gap inside the frame, and flickered also through the window. It cast a yellow glow.

Exhausted, Katharine sat down on the bottom step. She concentrated on the light flowing out over the uneven stones. In a little while the memory of the dead was less clear to her.

She sat with her neck bent, staring down at the rocks between her sneakers. In time she brushed her hair out of her face and gathered it in her left hand, and held it at the nape of her neck. In time a shudder wracked her body and opened her up. She bent down low between her knees. She opened her mouth wide. But nothing came out, or just some long strings of saliva.

How many times had she done this? The taste in her mouth was the same. She pictured herself in the pink-tiled bathroom of Au Gascogne, where her father had taken her once. She pictured herself on her knees in the upstairs bathroom of the Goldstones' house in town, the night of Natasha's graduation. To sit down in front of the toilet, she had had to slide her dress up almost to her waist. It was her backless yellow dress. She'd been afraid she'd be discovered.

Spasms shook her. But then she quieted down. She slumped back against the steps. Exhausted, she let herself slip down into a waking doze. And primed by memory, unimpeded by her slackened will, a new flow of images came out of her. They were more toxic than the bathroom ones, which had at least some element of pride in them, some element of control.

She was fifteen. She was standing in front of the mirror of her bedroom in Shreveport, after her shower. She was brushing her hair. It was longer then. She was wearing a bathrobe. Her clothes, which she had selected with anxious care, lay on the bed—blue jeans and a white angora sweater. She was already wearing her cowboy boots, trying to break them in. It made no sense, she now conceded as she sat helpless, watching herself from the steps.

Her father was behind her. She could see him in the mirror, standing in the doorway behind her, leaning on his cane. He was casually dressed, which meant he had no jacket on, no tie.

Peering through his glasses, he inched forward into the room. Did he know that she could see him? He was looking at her with a tentative, shy, rapt expression. He must have known it drove her crazy.

"Where are you going?" He knew. Or at least he knew

the first part of it, which was that she was going to be picked up in an hour by Andrea McClain, whose mother had lent her the convertible while she was out of town. And maybe he knew the rest, too. Maybe in some unconscious way he knew the whole thing, which was that they were going to buy cigarettes. Then Andrea was going to drop her off at her mother's apartment, where her cousin Tommy was staying during spring break. And Katharine would have sex with Tommy and maybe one of Tommy's college friends if anybody felt like it, and she would have to drink about a quarter of a glass of beer.

She shivered on the steps and put her arms around her breasts. In front of the mirror she ran her brush through her long hair and then laid it aside. "I told you," she said. "Andrea is coming by." Then she reached for her hair dryer and turned it on, partly to drown out the words of his response. But he came toward her over the floor, inch by inch, and he stood behind her, and he leaned his cane against the top of the desk.

"I like Andrea McClain," he said, and the hair dryer was not loud enough to cover his voice. He was standing behind her, and she was brushing her hair out and drying it strand by strand. "Here," he said. "Here," he said, "let me do it." He was looking over her shoulder, meeting her eyes in the mirror until she closed them. She turned off the hair dryer and lowered her face until she was staring down at the syringe cases on the tabletop.

"Here," he said. "Let me do it." He took the hair dryer out of her hand. He picked up the brush. He started brushing her hair out and drying it on low heat. He was so gentle, so frail, and so embarrassed. She also was dying of embarrassment, and she was anxious, too, as if something terrible might happen at any moment, something irrevocable.

There were other feelings too, muted by memory and

time, yet still strong, still poisonous. Guilt and tenderness and a desire to protect, though he had never protected her.

These feelings were chaotic in her, and subarticulate, and there was only one that rose out of the mass and formed into a thought and broke upon the surface of her mind. How does he know? I can't believe he knows how to do this. Because he was as gentle and thorough as any hairdresser. He must have watched me, she thought, conscious of another small pang of bitterness and guilt.

She sat on the steps at Drywater, hugging her chest. Even half asleep she could feel the soreness of her body. Often in her dreams, her emotions were as clear as primary colors. But at that moment, sitting in the cold starlight, her mind felt like a sewer, a cloaca, a drain.

Purge me with hyssop, she thought, and I shall be clean.

In her dream she heard a sound behind her. She didn't turn around. She didn't have to. She sat with her eyes closed and watched the light change. She was descending to a new level of sleep. She felt her fingers, which had been clamped around the muscles of her upper arms, loosen and let go. She slouched back against the steps, and the cold stone seemed to give a little bit, accommodate her shape. And in a little while her veins and entrails felt less constricted and less cramped. Blood carried oxygen to her cells. Waste moved through the passages reserved for it. She breathed, and her head lolled back.

She didn't have to turn around to see him standing behind her. He was just there, enormous, powerful, and the light flowed from his body. She didn't have to look.

He came down the steps behind her and moved past her and walked out across the sand. Light played on his high cranium. She didn't have to look to watch him go.

In time, with her new sleep, she seemed to achieve a new

kind of dreaming also. In her dream she opened her eyes. He was moving out of sight along the old wall, striding with his long, enormous legs over the sand and stones.

In her dream she found herself gathered to her feet, newly refreshed. She stood light-headed, out of balance on the bottom step, and then she turned around. The door was open now. She slipped through the gap and slipped inside.

She stood in a small chamber. Its walls were covered with shelves of canned food and other supplies. Coats and survival gear hung from a row of pegs. A case of wax candles had been opened, and most were gone.

Nearby, a woman lay face down on the floor, her jacket pulled over her head.

Across from her was a door to another, inner chamber. It was also made of metal. Yet it was more substantial than the outer door, more solid in its frame. It was pierced through with five small holes, and light bled from them.

This door also hung ajar. Light coated its edge. She pulled it open and light spilled from it, and she stood on the threshold of an inner room.

She was on the threshold of an inner chamber. Dozens of candles burned in it. They lined the windowsills. They stood in rows upon the floor, along the walls, and they left patterns of carbon dust on the bare stone. Some had guttered down to nothing. Some were freshly lit.

A stone table projected out from the opposite wall, and it was covered with candles. Long beards of wax hung down from it. The wax made a hot smell.

Among the candles on the table lay a naked corpse. Its long hands were folded on its breast. Its eyes were closed. The flesh on its head was sinking down, exposing the outline of its bones. A cage built to hold its thoughts, but they had squirmed away. Here is the body, she told herself, and she could feel her lips move. The spirit is gone. The soul is gone. But she didn't have the opportunity to say anything more; she moved into the room, and then Simon Mayaram was there.

He was behind her and she turned. Because dreams are disjointed he could supersede everything with his sudden presence. Everything around him disappeared or was subsumed in him: The wax smell seemed part of his smell. The light seemed to exist only to illuminate his living body, his lustrous dark skin. I am black but comely, she thought. Look not upon me, because I am black.

He put his arms around her and she put her face into his neck. Candlelight glistened on the dark skin under his ear, on his rich hair. She closed her eyes down to slits, breathing in his smell, and she felt the strength in his arms and the labor in his chest as his breath rasped out of him. It shook and trembled as he said her name. "Katharine," he said. "Katharine."

She closed her eyes completely, but only for a moment, only to reassure herself for a moment that there was another world too, and in that other world she could feel him coughing like a dog, growling like a motor. Then she opened her eyes again and she was staring at his miraculous curled ear. "Oh, I'm sorry," she murmured. "I'm so sorry."

"You've got to stay with me. You can't go running off like that. I was worried. I was afraid I'd never find you."

"I'm so sorry," she said, and she meant it. Because it was a dream, she could express herself perfectly.

"Just don't do that anymore. Please. We've got to stay together."

He kissed her lips for a moment, and she opened her mouth to him.

"I'm glad you came back here," he said. "That was the right thing to do."

But I was not afraid, she thought. In her dream she loosened his thick, heavy coat and ran her hands underneath it and across his belly, and down into his pants. She held him in her hands and made a sheath for him between her fingers, and he was penetrating her with his concern, fucking her with his concern, his need, thrusting into her again and again. "Stop it," he said. "What are you doing? Talk to me. I was so worried. We can't let ourselves get separated." But he was as hard as steel in her hands. "I love you," he said, words like that, and they leaked one by one out of the end of his cock and made a lubricant; she closed her eyes, and he was like a steel piston in her hands.

―――――――― 6e ――――――――
Candlelight

W e can't let ourselves get separated," he said. "You're all I've got. You understand that. I love you." She was tugging at his belt buckle. He pushed her hands away, enclosed them in his.

The demon lay on a slab, surrounded by candles. "What did you think you were doing here?" he asked. "Why did you come back here?"

"I don't know."

"I thought you got lost. Were you heading toward the road? Martin said he didn't see you when he came back from the line."

"He lied."

"I'm so relieved. Somehow I knew that you'd come back. That you'd know I'd come here to look."

"I thought you were going on," she said. "Ludlow Grange—that's what you said. I thought I lost you. It's what I wanted. That's why I came back."

"No. I'd never leave you. Trust me. Please have faith in that."

Her hands and cheeks were hot, feverish. She was looking at his face but not at him. He let go of her hands and brought his own hand up to move her chin, so that she could see him more clearly. But she closed her eyes.

"It's good you didn't go that way," he said. "I met Martin Cohen on the trail as he was coming back. There's an uprising in the fringes around Ludlow. We heard about it on the shortwave."

"Yes. He lied to you."

"What do you mean? He was there. They beat him with an axe handle. They barely let him go."

"I beat him."

She was delusional. Standing there holding her hand, touching her chin, looking at her closed eyes in that room full of guttering candles, Simon felt himself overtaken, overcome by tenderness. He put his fingers on her lips, and she opened her mouth.

"It's all right," he said. "It will be all right."

"He followed me. Up where the sun was rising. I hit him on the face because he lied. He was at Goldstone."

These were new symptoms. She spoke in a soupy monotone, as if she were describing a dream or a reality she knew was false. Her voice held no conviction, though her words were rational.

"You hit him?"

"He was following me. He never went up there."

Simon put his arms around her and hugged her for a minute without talking. He looked at the demon over her shoulder. It had lain there for days, perhaps. Its skin was drying out. Its long hands, crossed on its breast, were drying into claws.

"We owe him a great deal," he said. "Perhaps our lives. Harriet Oimu wanted to kill us."

She stood there, rocking slightly in his arms with her eyes closed, her head tilted up. "Is that what he told you?" she said.

"It's what I know."

He had only been away from her a few hours, yet he'd forgotten how distressing it was to see her like this. He would do anything, he thought, to bring her back.

He would do anything. He remembered the first days of their captivity, how she had fought so valiantly against these fantasies that now consumed her. She had lain with him in the dark, talking in her hoarse, queer voice—he would do anything to reinject that tone of hoarse intensity into her voice. It was the sound of her struggle, and this new soft voice was the sound of her surrender: "I thought you'd go with him up to Ludlow. You belong up there with him. In the sunlight. That's why I came back."

She was delusional. She needed him; she knew it. And he knew she cared for him. She could not say so, could not admit it. But he understood it in the way she always touched him, even when it was inappropriate and strange. It was the way the woman shut inside of her still signaled him, told him she was still there.

Yet it was distressing. He left her and walked over to the stone table. He held his hands over the dying candles; many had gone out. He held his hands over the strange corpse. Dully he examined it: mouthless, earless, chinless, and its eyes were closed. Homo Celestis. Its long face. The ridge of its cranium. Its bulging skull. Long neck, short abdomen, and big legs. Its three-toed feet. Celestial Man—yet this time he felt no excitement, no disgust, almost no interest, and it was as if these emotions were so fragile that they could not exist in the same small space with his distress, his disappointment, his anxiety. He stood looking at those shrunken cheeks, and the only thing he thought of was what Martin Cohen had said: how he had never felt a single failure of communication with this creature.

Behind him Katharine rocked and swayed a little bit, her perfect human face tilted toward the ceiling.

"He can help us," he said. "He knows this country. He's lived here."

"Help us?" she said in that little tone of voice. He turned.

"Yes. And we need help. Perhaps you don't quite trust him, because he was with the NLC. But it doesn't matter now. We need each other, and we don't have to like him to let him help us. The point is he has valuable expertise. He can give us choices. We were listening to the radio on the way back, and there are riots all through the fringes. So it seems that we can't go there now. So either we can wait here until things settle down, or else he knows some other places we can go to wait. He knows how to get to Shackleton Station, across the ice. It's an observatory two hundred miles west of here, and I know them. They were on the ship I came on. They'll have a helicopter there, and a full infirmary—the closest one. There'll be a doctor for you."

"I don't need a doctor."

"Yes, you do." He raised his voice. Now that he had found her, he was full of anger and impatience. Mixed with guilt: "How can I help you—how can I know what you're going through if you don't share it with me? If you don't talk about it? If you run away from me, and try to push me away? Don't be ashamed; there's nothing you can't tell me."

"I am not ashamed." Still in that small voice. He felt anger building up in him, and to find a way to let it come out he moved toward her again and put his arms around her from behind, and held her a little too tightly, too stiffly.

"Please don't turn me away," he said, and put his lips against her hair.

She laughed. It was a sound that was strange to him, that he'd not heard come out of her before. It was like a spasm of coughing in her restructured throat. "Turn you away? I can't get rid of you. You're like a dog. You're like a black dog. I go away; you follow me. I come back; you follow me."

He said: "They would have killed you up there. Reverend Cohen knows; they beat him. He said they beat him with an axe handle just because he was a man. What would they have done to you or me? He said they put a roadblock up at Jim's Gut. He said that they were pulling people from their cars and killing them."

"He lied to you," she said, rocking in his arms, talking in a dreamy singsong. "He was never there."

Martin Cohen was in the antechamber. Simon could hear him through the metal door. He was looking over the supplies there. Now he turned on his radio and spun it through the bands of static until he found a rock and roll station in Shreveport.

"Yeah," it said, "Johnny be good."

The sound started moving, coming closer. There was a knock on the door and Martin Cohen stood there, holding the radio.

6f

Dreams (cont.)

In the first place, he had no conception of her greasy, knotted guts. The steel and plastic that was tangled. The leaking seam. She listened to the radio. The man was there and she had hit him, and she had bruised his cheeks. In her dream,

Simon Mayaram let go of her. She moved away from him and crossed her hands over her stomach.

She turned her back to them. The demon lay on the stone table, and she was naked. She had been shot in the belly. Katharine could see that now. Black stripes in the yellow flesh, and they led away from holes that were empty and dry now, and their edges had pulled back.

The music on the radio stopped, then started again.

Simon Mayaram was angry. "Don't just come in here," he said. "You'll scare her. She's very sensitive right now."

"And you know best."

"At least I care about her." In her dream, Katharine could feel his anger. It was anger he had tried to give to her, but she had refused it. It was like a source of heat in that part of the room. She was looking at the candles as they burnt out one by one, and then she closed her eyes.

"You don't like me," said the man with bruised cheeks.

"For God's sake, what do you want? You're the reason we're even here. You and your friends. How we feel isn't the point. Just try to be honest with us, and we'll be honest back."

"Yes," said the ugly man with bruised cheeks.

Katharine was standing with her eyes closed and her hands on her stomach, moving to the music. "I don't claim to be a saint," he said. "But I didn't kill anyone. If it wasn't for me they would have done a lot more harm. I warned them, and even after that they would have shot them all at Goldstone if I hadn't stopped them. I was a prisoner as much as you."

"I don't believe you."

Katharine listened, moving to the music. It was a story about a man driving a train. He had just received his medication. And there was a lady in red—what did that mean? Was that the name of the train? Or was that her?

And you know it crossed my mind, she thought. In her dream she saw herself standing in the middle of the dark track, dressed in a red satin cloak, wearing red lipstick and red earrings and red high-heeled shoes. She stood unsteady and awkward on the cinder bed between the railroad ties, and from behind her she could hear the noise and feel the wind and see her long shadow thrown ahead of her into the darkness as the lights of Train No. 102 lumbered onto the wrong track and headed toward her, its engineer out of his mind from the cocaine, and he had two good eyes, and he still didn't see

"Stop that," said Simon, and the music stopped, subsided into static, and there was quiet in the long dark summer night. She stood with her eyes closed, listening to the static, the crickets, the cicadas next to the railroad track.

"The fact is it'll be all right," said Martin Cohen. "We have food here and the van. I found the keys in the pocket of her coat outside. But my Christ, where is he?"

"Who?"

"The other one. She was going to kill him. Harriet sent her to kill him. Where is he? The body should be here."

"Who?"

"The other demon—is he gone? Who lit those candles? Was it her?" asked Martin Cohen, meaning she, Katharine.

6g
She Wakes Up

There was part of the dream that she couldn't remember when she woke up and found herself on the steps. She sat on the steps and listened to men behind her, behind the metal door. She had promised something that she couldn't remember, an important promise and she couldn't remember. So that she woke up already with a sense of failure and foreboding, and she sat on the steps hugging her chest.

What was it? In the dream world she had promised something to Simon Mayaram. Almost she felt like asking him about it; he was behind her in the little room, counting out supplies. But there was something else that she had taken from the dream, an image of impending, violent catastrophe; as she sat on the steps her whole body ached, and she looked out into the dark dry hills, and down the rough slope and the trail that led west toward the black glass, the diamond sands. In front of her lay the ruins of the demon hall, which had been blown up by the pioneers when they had got this far. After Barivase was first invented, and they had poisoned the water supplies, and doped and poisoned all the fringe Aboriginals, and broken the link. Then their long war was over, and they had driven uncontested up the demon road, and she had learned about it at school, at Ursuline, and they had sung songs for Pioneer Day and learned the history. On August twelfth of the eighty-sixth year after landfall, the Rainbow Battalion had driven up that road and no one had stopped them. The link was broken, and the demons had fled away into the darkness, and the pioneers had blown it all up. They had blown up the aqueduct and blown up the theater and the dam and the gathering hall and the mausoleum and the Drywater bridge. The queen was sick with measles, and they had hunted her down.

Katharine sat on the steps of the stone cell, which was all that remained of the mausoleum. At Ursuline she had made a map, part of a sixth-grade project, and it showed the single intact building and part of the stone floor. The pioneers had not left one wall standing or one statue whole or one tomb unviolated. In her project she had included photographs from that time, showing the frescoes on the great lyceum wall, showing the tomb of Amat III. She had made a plaster reconstruction of the famous Crypt of Bones, whose walls were built out of the bones of slaves, the bones of twenty thousand of her people. In her class presentation she had quoted from the hymn of thanksgiving, which the first Aboriginal Council had offered to Governor Marr.

She listened to the sound of the two men moving in the cell behind her.

Perhaps there might have been a time, an opportunity. But those base drugs had proliferated even after the demons were all gone. There were always better ones, new ones which allowed more work and better organization. People took them voluntarily; that was always the excuse. It wasn't until thirty years later that people could afford a new kind which did more than offer them dull pleasures, dull passivity, which did more than combine potently with alcohol, which allowed them to begin to question the basis for these things. Not that she ever had. It was too frightening to give up what you were.

Too frightening, especially at the start. But she was in control now, and she felt in control. After all, it was not a foreign part of her that allowed her mind to move from one thing to another, to make chains of reasons. The conquerors had not given her a new mind. This had always been part of it, but there was more.

She was sitting on the steps and her guts ached. She had made a promise which she couldn't remember, and so she closed her eyes and let herself sink backward a little bit, back until she heard her own voice saying, "Yes, I'll stay right here."

With her eyes closed she felt again a sense of terrible foreboding, a presage of catastrophe. It was like vertigo. She opened her eyes, got to her feet, and watched the landscape change around her. She must have gotten up too fast. The blood drained from her head.

When her vision cleared, she was in the living forest. The peaked roof of the mausoleum rose through the trees. The sun lay low on the eastern horizon, and it pushed red shadows through the branches of the small, slow-moving, naked trees—their bark was like skin, and they slid along the rocks and left slippery trails. There was wind in the forest, wind among the trees, but it seemed to move slowly and to be made of something more solid than air. She felt it as a steady, invisible pressure. The trees also responded to it. Their bloated trunks seemed to swell to catch it, and they were all moving in the direction of the wind and sliding over the stones, an inch, perhaps, each minute. Small pieces of flesh seemed to fall from them sometimes, pieces which flopped onto the ground and lay still, and in some places they made piles.

Katharine closed her eyes and the trees were still there, bleached of color in that world, and in that world also she could hear their soft, bitter voices, and she could smell them too. It was a world of symbols, and the mausoleum was no longer there, but the trees moved over the perfectly round stones, and round drops of flesh fell down from their branches, and blood flowed from their bark, and in that black-and-white world the ground was littered with the souls of her slaughtered race, the souls of the twenty thousand from the crypt of bones, and the souls of all those who had died building the demon walls and towers, and the souls of all those who had been killed by men. The wind moved through the trees, and in the world of symbols it was music. Eddies, currents of notes moved through the trees, and when she strained her eyes, when she turned inward, she could see the wind break down into its tiny parts, its basic particles and they were notes, clusters of notes as small as molecules. She turned the focus on her eyes and they came larger; she could see the quavers and the semiquavers trembling on tiny wings. Streams of notes floated like bubbles, and she recognized many of them by sight: The piano part for Chopin's funeral dirge floated by, and it caught on a twig and hung there for a moment like a rag of gossamer.

She relaxed her eyes. The music disappeared, and she could feel the wind. And something else: There was danger here. Then she saw it: Birds were flying through the branches, black crows with greasy beaks, and they dove down to catch the falling drops of meat. They would light upon the branches and slice gobbets of meat from off the trees, and their beaks were sharp as scissors. They were the souls of dead men, dead human beings, and they were hunting Katharine through the trees. Six of them flew together and Katharine recognized them. They were the souls of the Brotherhood of Man, ravenous and starving because they had not been dead more than a single day. They were screaming with their open beaks, angry and passionate and full of hatred for her and for her kind. They had been ambushed on the demon road near Jim's Gut, and there had been a ditch across the road, and they had been surprised by people hiding in the ditch, and they had been beaten to death with axe handles; she knew it. It served them right, she thought, and her thought escaped out of her body and drifted up above her, noxious as a fart, and she could smell the cruelty in it.

The birds could smell it too. They veered and changed direction toward her, and they swooped toward her with their beaks stretched wide. She opened her eyes and stumbled forward with the wind at her back, allowing the wind to push her. But with her eyes open she couldn't see the birds, though she could still feel that they were there around her. The trees seemed stunted and smaller here, and she pushed through them with her arms held out, and they shifted away from her, and she ran through them over the uncertain ground, and the sky was full of thunder and lightning and roiling clouds. She closed her eyes. The birds rushed around her. They couldn't see her; they were blind, but they were following the smell of her thoughts, her evil thoughts, and her thoughts were leaking out of her as she ran down the slope. I'm so afraid, she thought, and a bird came squealing past her ear.

But then she smashed into something. A rock caught her on the shins and she tripped and fell and opened her eyes. She was in a rock landscape full of colors that had no name, that did not exist on any palette or spectrum that she knew. She felt danger all around her but she could not keep on running with her eyes closed; she got up and stumbled forward with her arms clasped around her head. She had ripped her pants, cut open her leg.

She climbed down into a gulley. She thought the rocks might offer some protection overhead. The sand was damp at the bottom; soon it was mud and she slogged through it, disturbing little animals that lived in it, that came up to the surface as she passed. Some were made of light, and they left trails of orange light as they escaped over the mud. Once she fell down and lay still for a moment, and watched them jump over her outstretched hand.

Even in the violent times, she thought, there can be single moments. She rested on her back, feeling the minute tickle of the light creatures as they jumped over her fingers; she looked up and almost saw her thought drift into the air. It hovered on the lip of the protruding rocks. Then it was gone and she climbed to her feet, encouraged, strong enough to find dry ground. She had lost one of her shoes; it didn't matter; she was encouraged; she could feel the life in her, and every part of her was alive. The sour smell of the mud was a living creature, and she almost saw it sliding and tumbling through the air, its ungainly, mottled body, its small wings. Little noises jumped around her and they scuttled down into the crevices, packing themselves into an undifferentiated mass.

The walls of the gulley sloped down. It led out into a broader wash next to the road. She followed it as it curved around, running her hands along rock surfaces that also seemed subtly alive, that seemed to cringe away from her by millimeters. Above her, the sky broadened, and she tried to still her thoughts, quiet her thoughts, throttle her thoughts and crush them down to nothing. Yet still they escaped, small and weak, and they left her and drifted up, food for the birds. The birds gathered around her, and sometimes she would close her eyes and see them—they were men, the souls of men, the brotherhood of men, and they sliced down out of the sky toward her, attracted by her rage, her fear. One wheeled close; she opened her eyes.

The sun lay on the horizon behind her. She opened her eyes and stood up straight and followed her long shadow down the draw and concentrated on the tiny things, the crust of silicate over the sand, the small release of pressure as she crunched through it. She was limping a little bit until she stripped off her other shoe. Then she felt better. She stilled her breath. She quieted her heart and stood up straight and let the tension leave her shoulders and her unprotected back, and she followed her shadow until the sun set and it disappeared.

When her shadow was gone, she followed a smell. It

came from somewhere in front of her, the smell of sulfur. She relaxed and let it fill her, and she moved toward it over a rubble of small stones. Then the smell was sharper; she stood on the lip of a hole that went down into the ground. Mud pulsed in it, and she could smell the hot mud, and she closed her eyes for a moment and watched the birds slide aimlessly overhead, their little minds focused on nothing at all.

She was standing in the sulfur pits. These small holes in front of her were vents from the main cavity, joined to it by subterranean passageways. Wisps of steam rose up through the basalt chutes, but the main fumarole was over to her left beyond a shoulder of white mud. She could hear water roaring over there. All around her the rocks were coated with a copper sheen. Grit fell out of the sky, and there were bugs in the air, too, tiny insects that landed on her skin and died. Down by the sulfur holes the rocks were full of them. Their packed bodies formed a crust over some of the small pools.

To her right the road led west over the diamond sands. The light was dormant now because the sun was down behind her and the moon had not yet risen up ahead, and the starlight was not strong enough to make the diamonds shine. She felt she was standing on the border of a new country that perhaps was not yet real, that perhaps was being formed just as she stood there, and everything was still implicit, unpolluted, a desert of potential. She walked downhill with her eyes open, hurting her bare feet and not caring. Hot stones fell down on her, and she walked through them feeling safe and secure and proud. Not everyone could have come this far and seen what she had seen. Not everyone could have borne this pain in her plastic guts. Not everyone could have endured this man-made cancer in the muscle of her heart. Not everyone was strong enough; she looked down at the border where the sand met the rocks and saw a footprint there, a line of three-toed high-arched footprints leading off into the sand. At the same time a desire rose out of her, and it mixed with her hope and her pride and her pain into a cloud of gas as toxic as any sulfur fume, and it rose into the air.

Then she was hit from behind, once, and then twice more. The birds came down. Katharine lifted up her arms to protect her head, her eyes. She stumbled over the sharp basalt and stumbled forward over the line onto the sand. She fell to her knees and bent down to the sand with her arms clasped over her head. She could feel blood seeping down her back under her sweatshirt. The birds had cut her, and she felt the blood drip down her ribs.

She couldn't look at them. But in her mind's eye she gave them cruel beaks and human faces, and she made their claws into outstretched human hands. Black skin covered their wings. They sliced the air around her head, and she stared down at the sand between her knees. The sand was black between her knees, and a carbon crystal lay on top of it. Even in that frightened moment she could not fail to see how beautiful it was, how precise, how sheer its sides. It seemed to hold inside itself a fragment of light, incipient, implied, part of the moonlight that was coming, yet not part of it, not yet. The walls of the crystal seemed inviolate. They could not be penetrated by anything but light. Looking down, helpless with the birds around her head, she saw as if for the first time the three spirits of matter, which came together and made up everything. One was the spirit of resistance, one was fire and force. And one—she lifted up her head and looked toward the horizon, toward where the moon trembled on the rim of the world, and it was rising, and silver light cascaded from it, and the sand around her burst into a diamond fire.

Openness was everything, she thought. She lifted up her

head. The birds were high shadows now, chasing each other, making patterns underneath the stars.

Near her a rivulet of water ran down out of the rocks to lose itself in the sand. She could hear it now. She could smell it. She sat back on her heels and then rolled over toward the water, where it had made a pool. Bugs lived on its hot surface.

She stripped off her clothes. She pulled off her sweatshirt and her pants and left them crumpled on the sand, and then she washed herself in the water. She rubbed the water into her skin and then lay out in the hot moonlight. She stretched out on her wounded back, exposing her man-made breasts, her man-made vagina to the sky.

And she must have been comfortable there. She must have fallen asleep, because she was in the dream world, and soon the white van came bumping down the road. It caught her in its headlights and turned onto the sand, then circled back toward her. The men were there, the creatures from her nightmares, the dog men, the black dog and the white dog. The van stopped and the side door slid open. Simon called out to her. He came toward her over the sand.

The headlights overpowered everything, and all the other lights. In the dream world everything was gray and drab and confusing and unreal, and most things had no meaning. Things happened for no reason, and you could not understand why they were happening. Or else you almost understood, and things seemed desperately important for a moment, before they disappeared without a trace. People talked in riddles.

Simon knelt down beside her and put his arms around her. "Oh, Kathy," he said, "what are you doing? You're all cut up—where are your shoes? What have you done to yourself? Can't I trust you even for a minute? You promised to stay put. Then I take my eye off you for thirty seconds, and you're gone."

She reached up to put her arms around his neck. "Don't do it again," he said. "Please, or just tell me. Tell me what you're feeling, what you need," he said, and kept on talking until she put her hand over his lips.

VII

⊠

―――――― 7a ――――――
Human Chaos

For the second time in two days, Junius Styreme and John Clare sat together in the consul's study. Clare raised his hand. "I wanted to give you the most recent information," he said. "Because I feel you have a right to know. To be honest, I want to beg you to help us. I don't know how to tell you this and perhaps I shouldn't, but perhaps you know it anyway. The disturbances around Ludlow are greater than we had anticipated. We've had to evacuate our people there. Robert Garner—that's the district commissioner—may have been killed."

The old Aboriginal bowed his head.

John Clare kept his hand up. He stared at the back of it. It looked very small, very white even to him. What did the gesture mean?

He had not slept the night before. The pain in his back

and shoulders had been so intense that he had been forced to take his medication hourly. He had exceeded the correct dosage, clearly; now one hand trembled on the top of his desk. The other, upraised, seemed unconnected from his body, seemed oddly far away.

"I'll tell you everything," he said. "Because you deserve to know."

He felt pity for the old man. Perhaps this gesture with his hand, that's what it meant. "The riots broke out at the copper mine," he said. "I can't think it's a coincidence that the NLC turned up in Drywater, on the other side of the line. It's not thirty miles away."

Or perhaps, thought Clare, the hand gesture was to ward off the small hope that now appeared in the old man's eyes. It was a tiny movement of his upper lid, but poignant, powerful, and grotesquely clear, as if magnified by the thick lenses.

"It was a massacre," said John Clare, chosing the word deliberately, as if to see its effect on the old man's eye. "The Brotherhood of Man attacked the place, utterly without authorization. Harriet Oimu was killed."

He stopped speaking and let a silence solidify between them, a transparent wall. "And Katharine?" the old man said finally, the words harsh, a whisper in his throat not forceful enough or powerful enough to scratch a hole in the wall.

"We had a report from the police station in Jim's Gut before it was overrun. They had been in unofficial communication with the Brotherhood after the attack. That was after Oimu's murder, but before the road was closed. They didn't find either hostage at the site, though they searched carefully."

Again the solid silence. The old man made some noises in his throat, but they meant nothing. John Clare raised his voice, lowered his hand. "We would have liked to question them. But they were ambushed, apparently. They were coming out of Drywater along the road. That part of the fringe is quite chaotic now, and no one knows where they are. They didn't get through, and they weren't with the evacuees. Perhaps the rioters are holding them."

"But," said Junius Styreme, perched on his stool, his hands clasped over the crook of his cane. The consul leaned forward to interrupt him.

"As I say, I want to beg you to help us. You have a great deal of influence in your community."

Styreme cleared his throat. "It is outside me," he said. "You have police, the soldiers. Have you not sent a message?"

The consul's hand was spread flat on the surface of his desk. He put pressure on it and stood up. "I will tell you," he said. "You deserve to know. It's more urgent than that, and no one has been honest here. The governor has told me— this is a secret, you understand. But I feel I will—some of our people were here yesterday, and I said that I'd received no word. I felt like telling them, but I did not. But perhaps I trust you more than I trust them. Men like that might take the law into their own hands. Whereas your interests are the same as ours. Believe me, I am sorry about your daughter. About Mayaram. More sorry than you could know."

A tiny expression of distress moved over the old man's face, distress tinged with something else. The consul felt that he could read it clearly, a mixture of irony, contempt, alarm. "We think your interests are the same as ours," he said again.

"I see."

"There is something about a terrible loss. With most people it is important to maintain that we can expect help from other sources."

As he spoke, the consul moved across the room. His hands and feet and body seemed to find no resistance in gravity. He slid through the air and had to apply an effort to stop when he reached the wall. With an adroit flick of his fingers he closed the window blinds. When the room was dark he turned and stood with his back to the wall. He dug out the remote control from the side pocket of his coat, and then the video screen came to life.

They watched the chip in silence. "Is that Earth?" asked Junius Styreme when it was done. The consul thought he could detect a shudder.

"It's a lake in Africa," he said. "Don't pay attention to that." He flicked the chip backward until the Nordsee official sat at his desk. "We've been abandoned," he continued. "You'll see—perhaps New Manchester itself."

The official on the tape opened his green mouth. "O.R.M.," he said. "No positive, 988 no change, John Clare. D.B. (#4) Short end cargo limit total. Pay schedule reflect, toto. Quick shit vite, no reason. Emergency is permanent, X.L.L. Hablamos Nyet. Fuck u (2) two. 20 hour here. No authority (101010xp6.). No request until this end, you no. Adio good-bye. Thirty seconds up."

John Clare froze the image, and the silence was filled with static from the screen.

"I do not understand," said Junius Styreme.

The consul shrugged. "This is actually an archaic example, meant for me to understand. It's English. They use it to express emotions rather than facts. Most of numbers are emotional states, emotional quotients; that's the important part. The grunts and clicks are punctuation marks or qualifiers. Mayaram explained it all to me. He said the anagrams and words are memorized. They print lists of discontinued meanings every day in samizdat."

Painfully and slowly, Styreme turned backward on his

stool, so that he could look at him. What was contained in his expression? The consul fiddled with the blind so that he could see.

"What is the other film?" asked the old man. "This I understand. The red birds. The flamingo."

"Yes, that's nothing," answered the consul, impatient. "It's a mistake. It was an error in transmission—no one talks like that. Not on New Manchester; certainly not on Earth."

"What do they talk on Earth?"

"They talk the other way. Or who knows? It's always changing. Life is changing there."

The old man stared at him. There was something in his face, something so mournful and so wounded that the consul closed his eyes and put his fist up to his mouth.

"Life is changing," hissed Junius Styreme. His voice was painful, dry, and harsh, as if expelled under pressure. "What am I? Then what is Katharine?"

"Dead," answered the consul, and he pressed his fist into his mouth so that the words had to squeeze out around it. "Dead. And Mayaram too. My friend Simon. I blame myself."

The old man stared at him. "Did you know of the attack on the Goldstone Lodge?" he asked.

"Abolutely not. Nothing concrete."

"I heard a rumor," said the old man. "But I went. I trusted you—why did you not tell me? Did you owe me anything at all?"

"I'm sorry."

"She was all I ever have," said the old man.

Shreveport

He had an appointment with his chemotherapist, but at the last minute he decided not to go. His chauffeur drove him past the hospital and then on toward home. "Please go by Magna Carta," said Styreme, and they turned onto a long commercial boulevard. A bomb had gone off in a theater halfway down the strip, and Junius Styreme turned stiffly in his seat to examine the burned-out marquee.

That was the extent of it. The rest of the human city was intact. Shoppers were out.

The civil militia had put up barricades at the end of the street. The car turned east through a neighborhood of warehouses and then stopped at the checkpoint. A chain-link fence stretched across the road, new since the day before. Armed policemen stood at the guardpost, but they waved Styreme through. He didn't have to show his pass.

He turned his whole body in his seat to look at the policemen. Then they were through, inside the native lines. They skirted the river for a few blocks. On the other side, across the bridge, the native shantytown had been leveled by bulldozers.

Then they were in among richer houses, though some of them were empty too. Fair Haven, especially, had a forlorn look. Styreme's human gardeners had not shown up for days. The lawn was drying out.

There had been some vandalism also, up and down the street. Styreme's neighbors had had a smoke bomb thrown through their window. The sidewalk outside of Fair Haven had been spray-painted with graffiti: GEEKS, LICK MY DICK, etc. The governor himself had promised Styreme protection, and there had been a militiaman outside the house on the first day of the disturbances. Now he was gone. Hateful and obscene messages covered the walk to the front steps. Someone had painted on the door itself. Someone had broken his bay window.

The chauffeur opened the car door for him and helped him to his feet. She helped him up the walk. "Are you all right, sir?" she asked. She was older than Katharine, he decided. A little overweight, he thought, but pretty just the same. He had not seen her before. The agency had sent her round.

"Are you sure you're all right?" she asked. He gave her his keys, and she opened the front door. She was pretty, he decided. She had freckles, short black hair. A big, solid body. She was not tall.

"What is your name?" he said. He stood on the front step, out of breath, leaning on his cane. He had his back to the open door, and he looked down the walk again, toward where the car was parked at the curb. He blinked and looked up at the sun.

"Cathy Thier," came the girl's voice.

"Katharine," he said, "is my daughter's name."

"I know. I'm sorry, sir."

"Don't be sorry." He smiled a little and turned toward her. "It suits you," he said.

Inside his chest, his heart labored to beat. "Will you like to come in?" he asked. "Is that against the rules?"

"No, sir. I'll get you settled, if I may." She made a gesture that might have alluded to the graffiti on the walk. "This is so terrible."

"It is not important." He took her arm and allowed her to help him over the threshold. He looked down at the point of his cane as he did so, and only once did he sneak a look at her face, to see if he could gauge her expression as she first entered the house. Human beings often had adverse reactions, he knew. But she gave no sign of anything, and perhaps that was a result of the air freshener his housekeeper used. Or perhaps she was keeping her face impassive out of politeness. She barely glanced around the atrium.

He smiled. "Is it the first time you are inside one of our homes?"

"No, sir." And she smiled, too. "Though I can't say this is typical."

"Let me demonstrate some things," he said, and took her through the living room. A baseball had come in through the bay window. She left him to pick up some of the glass.

"This is terrible," she said.

"It doesn't matter. Please don't concern. Let me show you my daughter's room."

They walked through the dining room toward the French doors, and then they stood and looked at the piano and into the spare bedroom. "She came out of my body," he said. "You understand it."

"Of course."

"Of course you do. You're slightly young for working, aren't you?" he said, embarrassed suddenly.

"It's a summer job."

"I see. That explains it."

He didn't know how to continue, and she seemed restless also. "You are kind to an old man," he said. "I want to offer you a recompensation." He fumbled in the pocket of his suit. "I bought a present for my daughter if she came back home. It's very good. It's platinum, you see. I keep it with me—do you have a father?"

He fumbled for the case, but he was prevented from drawing it out of his pocket by the expression on her face.

Not disgust, exactly. Yet he had felt compelled to offer her something. Compelled almost to expose himself, humiliate himself. "You see I keep it with me all the time," he said, watching her closely.

"I'd rather not. You save it for her."

After she had left, he made the slow journey down to the music room again. He had seen a letter on the piano bench a few minutes before, when he had stood with Cathy Thier at the French doors. Now he went back to pick it up. He had been waiting for it.

The word BETRAY was written in blue ink, in small letters, in the upper right-hand corner of the envelope. It was sealed, difficult to open, but he persevered. Inside, a lock of hair, just that. It was stiff and dark with some dried fluid.

His study lay on the other side of the dining room, in an addition that projected into the back garden. He limped across the long, empty floor and then sat down carefully at his desk. He put the envelope down on the blotter where he could see it. And for two hours he went over his tax statements, his computer files. He had retired from his businesses ten years before, when he had gotten sick. But this past week he had been working many hours a day. The money didn't matter. But there were still some things.

The tears ran down his face. The chair was too deep for him now. He had to rock forward to get out of it. Then he shuffled down toward the music room with the envelope in his hand. He didn't even glance at the piano as he went past it. He went into the spare bedroom and stood by Katharine's table while his body chugged and clamored from exertion. He put down the envelope, and he took the platinum necklace from his pocket and took it out from its case. It really was beautiful. It was set with emeralds. He laid it on the table and arranged it around the base of a small statue, a pot-metal crucifix from central Africa, distorted, crude, and ugly to his taste. But Katharine had loved it.

The clock in the dining room chimed two o'clock. Time for his medication. Past time, really, but it didn't matter. He took out his pillbox, but his hands were shaking and he dropped it. But Katharine had a big supply in her cooler on the table. He didn't exactly know what they were. But he took a dozen or so of the most brightly colored capsules, and chewed them together in his mouth until the sweet liquid came out.

─────── 7c ───────

A Pair of Pliers

She lay in the back of the white van, listening to them talking. She lay on a bed made of blankets, ropes, boots, clothes, cracker boxes, fuel canisters, packages of dried food, and equipment of all kinds.

The road ran smooth over the diamond sands, and they were driving fast. Her head was below the level of the rear windows, but still she could see a little filtered moonlight. It made a mist over her head. From time to time Martin Cohen played the radio, listening for news reports. From time to time also he smoked cigarettes, and the smoke drifted down behind him. They were in the front seats, but there was no partition. It had been removed. She lay listening to their voices, watching the backs of the red vinyl seats and the smoke drifting down.

Then she closed her eyes and concentrated on the smells. They lurked around her in the muted darkness, and when her eyes adjusted she could see them. They were like roaches and rodents, slugs and snails, hiding in the corners of the van. Little odors: turpentine and gasoline and oil and wax and cardboard and steel and rubber. The gasoline was like a snake moving in the spare tire pit. The cigarette smoke perched on the back of the red seat, a strange thing like a bat or a bird. It spread its wings.

From time to time Martin Cohen rolled his window down, and new smells came into the van when he did. The wind off the diamond sands was like a banner of soft cloth blowing in through the window. When he rolled the crank he cut it off, and a scrap of it blew back through the van and was lost. Other smells from the outside were painted on the banner: complicated and suggestive ideographs for *mud* and *water*.

"It's getting cold," said Martin Cohen.

They had been listening to the radio. "Well that's that," he said. "We might as well just go."

"No really." He continued: "We've got the car; we've got the supplies. We can make it. We could be in Shackleton by Sunday. It's not even two hundred miles. It won't even be that hard."

"I don't know."

"Shit, you heard what they said. It might be weeks till they get through. And when they do, you know what will happen. All those Abo rioters will come through here. They'll come back across the line."

"It's not that many."

"It's enough."

With her eyes closed, sounds were like smells to her. She listened to the two voices, and one was a damp, sooty smell, and one was hot and perfumed, as if it hid some other odor.

"What I don't understand is, why don't you have some kind of contact with them? You were on their side. Why are you afraid of them?"

"Shit," said Cohen, and she smelled it underneath the

perfume. "There wasn't any side. There's no organization there, no logic. It's just feeling coming out. They don't care about me: they'd kill me. Harriet Oimu and the others were the brains such as they were. They were the ones who knew me. Now they're dead."

Katharine put her hand over her nose.

"Leaving you in a difficult position, I suppose."

Cohen laughed, and the sound released a thin, acrid smell. "I sure am. That's why I've stuck to you. I figure if I get you out and Ms. Styreme, then you'll put in a word for me. You know I'm a man of peace. I never wanted any violence."

"I don't know if they'll believe that. Jonathan Goldstone is dead."

"They'll believe it if you tell them. I never was a part of that. I was a prisoner as much as you."

The silence filled up the whole car.

"Besides," Cohen continued, "I warned you. I sent a letter to your consulate and told them everything I knew about the attack. I gave them the time."

Solid silence. Then: "I don't know whether to believe you."

"Well of course not. How can you believe me? But let me tell you this—the fact is Jonathan Goldstone was a worthless bigot. A piece of shit. He was the founder of the Brotherhood of Man. He was the one who started all the killing."

"Hmmm," said Simon, and the sound was like a rush of car exhaust, poisonous in that small space. It overcame the smell of Jonathan Goldstone, the smell of his armpits and his crisp khaki uniform when he embraced her that time, and felt her breasts. Then it was overcome by another smell, a softer smell when he said, "And his family?"

Then there was another silence, which had an odor all its own.

"So I'm depending on you please. I can help you but I

need something in return—I can't just live out here forever. I'm no saint, I admit it. I'm not a Geoffrey Kiyungu or a Mahatma Gandhi. I'm even thinking there'll be a reward if I can get her back. You know, from her father."

Again he laughed, and the sound mixed with his cigarette smoke, which spread its wings on the top of his red seat. "Damn," he said, "I can't shut up. I'm just so nervous. You make me so nervous, and she does too. I mean we'll do our best for her, but don't you think . . . I mean even considering. She's dangerous too. And not just to herself. She hurt me that time."

Again a pause. Then: "What?"

"Oops."

Cohen must have opened the window, because many new sounds came into the van, and then they faded. The rush of the night. The clean air. They were like body smells, the exhalations of some human landscape where the dunes were made of shoulders and breasts and hips, and the sand was made of skin. Coarse black skin sprinkled with glitter. Natasha had worn glitter for a party once at Tom McClain's.

"What do you mean, she hurt you?"

"Man, I didn't think you would believe me. I saw her when I was coming back over the line. She went crazy. She attacked me. That was why I got so broken up before. Look what she did."

"But you told me it was—"

"Shit no. I never went there. I was too scared. I didn't have to go. I never stole a car. I heard it on the radio. They were killing human beings. I thought they'd kill me so I followed you."

Then he said, "I'm sorry, man." And he was. Katharine could smell it. She could smell his fear. It was in his sweat. She could smell his doubt and his self-loathing. It was in his blood. She could smell his sorrow, and it had two parts, and one was fragrant, and one stank. He was sorry he had been so stupid.

She had lain in a doze between dreaming and waking. Now she fell deeper into sleep, and the men's voices started to fade. Smells and sounds receded from her, and she lay on her side among the boxes and the bags, feeling the small jolts and shocks as the van slipped over the dirt road, over the sand.

Near her, inches from her eye, a hubcap lay propped up against a burlap bag.

The moon cast an even light. It slipped in through the rear windows of the van, and it fell on the chrome surface of the hubcap. Everything was still. The hubcap didn't jiggle as they flew over the sand, and in the middle of it was a circle as smooth as a mirror, and she lay looking at herself.

She looked at herself for a long time. There were no thoughts in her mind but only feelings. Vague urgings and impressions—she opened her mouth and examined her teeth.

And a little while after that, she sat up. She reached down behind her and pulled the toolbox out from behind one of the spare tires. She made no noise. She slipped the catches and pulled open the box.

In the bottom, among the screwdrivers and vise grips, lay a pair of pliers and a pair of shears.

7d

Simon (iii): He Fails to Communicate

He happened to look backward before she had done much damage. She had cut her hair short with the tin snips. Her scalp was bleeding where some of it had pulled out. He hit the brakes, stopped the van, and turned it off. He jumped into the back.

She had pulled out two of her molars and two of her fingernails. When he took the pliers from her hand he found them secreted in her palm: two disks of plastic polymer and two perfect plastic teeth. Sadder than that, though, was what she had done to her face. With a pair of shears she had made slits on each side of her nose next to her eyes, and she had dug out the excess moisture ducts. They were in her other hand. He pulled her fingers back and there they were, two exquisitely miniaturized valves, two tiny sacs made of synthetic tissue, still fat with unshed tears.

The incisions she had made were careful and precise, but the holes were deep. Blood dripped from them, less blood than he might have guessed.

"Oh dear," he whispered. Then almost for the first time since he had come into this world, almost since before that deathlike journey from his own place and his own time, he spoke some phrases in the disposable language of his childhood: "O.o. Daylook may daybright day 71 point o.o. 761 killum."

Then: "761 cu 762 cut 761 concha."

He mumbled these things under his breath. At the same time he was taking the sharp tools out of Katharine's hands, and he was rubbing her poor hands.

Martin Cohen was leaning over the back of the passenger's seat. "You see what I mean? She'll hurt herself and it's no joke. Maybe we should tie her up. Restrain her."

"F.f.foo fu fuk n2 (2)," said Simon. "You be quiet. Please." He yanked open the sliding door and let the van fill with the cold, clean air.

Katharine's breathing was steady, and she lay back

against the long seat of the sledge. Her eyes were yellow lines and she was sluggish, barely conscious.

He stepped out onto the road. The sand stretched away into the darkness around him, black sand full of iron and diamond crystal shining in the moonlight. The moon was almost full. He looked up at it, aware of its beauty almost for the first time. All he had seen since his arrival here had been its bleached carcass on the day side of the world. But now it rose above the road, huge and blue and silver, and all around him in the darkness the accumulations of crystal snatched at it and stole its light and gave it back in a myriad of tiny ways, shifting and unsteady as he moved his head.

"O.U. my Lune lute lutta metablack," he said softly, missing for the first time in remembered consciousness the small moon of his childhood, which perhaps was rising even at that moment over the empty ruins of North London.

The road ran straight in front of him without a bend. He could see it stretched out like a steel rule, gleaming in the moonlight. Crusts of ice had formed over its surface, and in some places the roadbed was slick and wet; it was not cold. Perhaps forty degrees, and the wind felt strangely warm. Bitter smells flowed with it out of the east, chemical and hard.

"U.#(2)," he said. "U.t. two point 2."

"It doesn't have to be tight," said Martin Cohen. "Just for her own good. Just with strips of cloth. There'll be a clinic at the station."

"Yes, I know." Simon squatted down and put his palm flat on the road for a moment. Then he stood up. "You sit in the back," he said. "You can go straight through. It's marked, isn't it? Even on the ice?"

"Oh, sure, of course. How do you think they got their equipment out there? They came right along this road."

"She'll ride in front where I can see her."

"Sure." Martin Cohen opened his door and got out, and together they helped Katharine into the front seat. She was docile, passive. She was breathing easily, and her eyes were almost closed.

But when Simon tried to open up her hands, she locked her fingers shut around the treasures in her palm. He tried to pry them open, but then stopped when he realized that he couldn't without hurting her. "What are you going to do?" he asked, not sure whether she could hear or understand him. He looked up at the moon for a moment. "What are you going to do, cut it all out? You'll have to pull your stomach out as well, and your intestines. Like one of your saints— there's not much you have a right to, once you start. There's not much that belongs to you."

The moonlight shone on her sweet skin. Her head lolled back. Perhaps it was just a trick of sympathy when she moved her head, but the cut on her nose opened again on the right side, and a drop of blood ran down from underneath the scab.

He stepped back and slammed the door. Then he walked around the front of the van to the driver's side, and climbed into the seat. Martin Cohen was making himself comfortable in the back. He had spread out a couple of blankets.

He was talking, but Simon didn't listen. He started up the van and drove on straight and fast. The road was dirt and cinder, and he listened to the rattle of the pebbles thrown up by the wheels, and he listened to the engine, and all the little creaks and whirs. They surrounded him in a cocoon of noises, and they overwhelmed Cohen's voice and the sound of Katharine's breath and the sound of her shifting in her seat. What was she thinking, what was she feeling now, right now, as she sat up and stared out the side window? What landscape did she see? My God, people were so lonely, and they never knew.

He drove on through the dark.

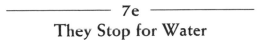

7e

They Stop for Water

Stop for water up ahead," said Martin Cohen. "It's an Aboriginal village in the hills there. It's okay."

After they had found the girl again, they had rested and slept at Drywater for a few hours. They had put together some supplies and listened to the radio. Now they were going to find water. Someone from the Brotherhood had dumped a corpse into the well at Drywater, and so they had to go and get some. They had gasoline and oil and tires, and once they filled up on water they would have everything, he hoped.

He had never been onto the ice. On the dark side of the world, you came out of these desert plains into the hills, and you climbed slowly up to altitudes of six or seven thousand feet. A hundred miles in, the ice began. It covered half the world and this was dangerous shit, he thought. There were breaks in the ice close to the edge of the shield. There were fluctuations in temperature, he'd heard, as winds from the melted deserts on the day side of the world were sucked down from the higher atmosphere.

Above the ice there was a rip in the ionosphere, and the radiation was intense there. Shackleton Station was on the edge of the plateau where the ice shield leveled off, perhaps a hundred and eighty miles from the van as it slid and hurtled down the road. Mayaram was driving fast, hunched over the wheel, chewing his lower lip. From time to time Cohen could see flashes of his teeth as he pulled his lips back in a nervous rictus, as he mumbled snatches of his incomprehensible slang. Cohen smiled as if in sympathy. Yet Mayaram was a stranger to him. Maybe when you came from a place where no one had anything, where no one lived long enough to grow old, where there were no fixed social boundaries, where all culture disappeared and people spoke a terrifying and obscene argot, maybe all those pressures did something to your mind, changed it in some way. Maybe it broke you apart into fragments of prejudice. Cohen had always hated the traditions, the intolerance of his own place, but at least they existed, something to rebel against, an edifice whose only function was to give you something to burn down. It had been a long time since he had wanted to go anywhere else.

He smiled again because it was all bullshit, what he had been thinking. The headlights pierced into the night. He lay against a coil of rope, listening to the chug of gasoline in one of the canisters, looking at the back of Mayaram's head as he stared through the windshield. What kind of a man was he to have come all this way? To come backward as if in time, to speak a dead language so well? A misfit. A reactionary. Surely he was as blinkered as anyone here. At Goldstone Lodge, in that upstairs room, he had been making love. Harriet Oimu killed the woman just while they were having sex. She shot Natasha Goldstone in the head, right before his eyes. Had he seen it? Not at all. Now he was in love with someone else.

"Maybe men are changing," said Martin Cohen. "Maybe the blinders are failing now—stripped away as it all falls apart. Maybe that's a kind of evolution."

How ominous and dark he was, how threatening and strong and persevering. His hairy hands gripped the steering wheel.

"Do you hear me?" said Martin Cohen. "Stop up here. There'll be water at this village."

Like it or not, they had something in common. Here they were, driving too fast toward Shackleton Station, which was full of men and women like Simon Mayaram. Certainly they had had a vision. Certainly they had come for something. Something had forced them out onto the ice, where they were drilling holes that went down three thousand feet into the shield. They were looking for neutrinos, and they dug them out a couple at a time. Or they had their radio telescope sheltered from the sun's noise, peering out into what? They were like Simon staring out through the glass into the darkness. From their vantage point outside the galaxy's plane they peered out at the black hole in the center of the Milky Way, and for half the local year they could see clearly, unimpeded, the destruction that surrounded it. And wasn't it sad, human and sad, that they had come all this way just to count the photons that escaped out of the galaxy's black core, out of an incomprehensible nothingness as big as Earth? He thought: It is our blindness that makes us move, that makes us hurt ourselves.

They had come twenty miles across the sand from Drywater, and the road turned among the first low hills. The van tunneled through the dark. Part of him felt like saying, Let's go back, let's take our chances. But it was a seductive power that had pushed them forward. Their own human love of darkness. Or else who knew? Maybe it would be easy. Men lived out there, after all. He had caught their station on the radio.

"Pull in here." The hills came down. The van had labored up a long, slow slope, but at the top there was a place to pull over. Mayaram turned into a level area as flat as a parking lot, and he slowed down to five miles an hour. He drove in an uncertain circle. "It's okay," said Martin Cohen. "I told you about this. They're raw here; they're raw but they're harmless. We'll just take what we want and then go."

The van slid on the rough cinders and then stopped. The moon was out of sight behind the hills. Mayaram sat with his hands gripping the steering wheel. "It's okay," said Martin Cohen. "I'll get it. You stay here."

He had a ten-gallon container in the back of the van, behind the electric sled. He struggled to pull it out, and then he slid open the side door. Mayaram was standing there, putting on his windbreaker. "You'll never be able to carry it," he said.

He got a flashlight out of the box. Cohen stepped out of the van and straightened up. "What about her?"

"She's asleep. She'll stay here for a minute."

"She might run."

"She might. I'm not her jailer. It's important that she feel trusted. And besides, I want to see."

He had put the sharpest tools in the pocket of his windbreaker, together with a small revolver that he had found at Drywater. "Sure," said Cohen. "It's quite a sight, but we'll just take the water. There's a spring in that nearest cave."

Mayaram shined the flashlight over where he was pointing. In fact these hills were riddled with caves. In fact there were Abos all around, though as usual they didn't show themselves. As usual they didn't seem to give much of a damn.

"They'll probably be doing their thing," he said. "Just be prepared, and don't think of it as sex because it's not. Or it is, but it isn't. It's more like eating or lactation. Nourishment— it's what they do."

"I've read about it."

"Sure," said Martin Cohen. "It's quite a sight. Sometimes I think that's why we started doping them at the beginning.

Not so we could fight the demons like we say. But a lot of those first pioneers were Mormons here, I mean in the fringes. Neo-Mormons or whatever. Barivase was invented by a Neo-Christian chemist, and I can imagine her figuring it out just to stop them from doing *that*."

The sulfur smell was overpowering here. Mayaram took the plastic water can. He walked over to the first hole in the rock, carrying his flashlight in his left hand. The light wasn't necessary outside, but Cohen followed it anyway. He had his own pocket flashlight, which he didn't turn on until they stood outside the hole in the red rock. They had to stoop to get inside.

It was what he remembered. A short tunnel led into a larger chamber, maybe ten feet square. A number of rock basins had been carved out of the opposite wall, and each contained a different kind of water. The springs themselves were farther in: The end of an old pipe, filched, maybe, from Drywater, stuck out of the wall. Near it loomed the black entrance to another tunnel.

He had been here several years before on one of his linguistic expeditions. It had not changed. Aboriginals still squatted among the stones. There were half a dozen of them in the rock chamber, naked, their skin bleached livid in the flashlight beams. It seemed as if you could only see parts of them at one time as the beam passed over their bodies: a back, a thigh. They turned their faces from the light. One stood erect. He (and Cohen persisted almost against his will in characterizing him with that meaningless human pronoun) was about five feet tall, and he stood under a natural spout in the rock where water seeped down. He had his hand on it, and the water seeped down over his face and chest.

He turned his face toward the flashlight beam, and it was blank, soft, naked, hairless, smooth, almost featureless. The sight never failed to shock Cohen and disgust him, again al-most against his will. Disgusting also was the second Aborig-inal, who knelt down in front of the first, nursing on his "penis," a bloated organ maybe nine inches long. It was stiff, engorged with blood, and certainly the motion, the method-ical sucking of the second Aboriginal, was evocative to human witnesses; Mayaram held his flashlight beam on the conjunction of that lipless hole, that fat red prick.

"They live on water," muttered Cohen, feeling that he must use up the silence, if only to explain what Mayaram already knew. "It's got those diatoms or whatever in it, al-though only about half of them ingest it directly. The others drink it after it has passed through their bodies—there's a gland that adds something to it apparently, enriches it."

His voice trailed away, but then he started again, uncom-fortable in the silence, made uncomfortable also by the mer-ciless way that Simon Mayaram had placed the light upon that toothless sucking mouth and kept it there, and moved it back and forth along the length of the animal's penis. "Like it's reverse entropy and it's sickening to see," he went on. "So let's just get the water because we should get back." The last time he had been here he had come alone, and it had not been nearly as embarrassing. There was something about watching it next to another man. He turned away and took a few steps toward the water basins. They smelled of sulfur, among other minerals.

But he had not reached them before he was interrupted by a new noise. He turned around and shined his flashlight, and there was Katharine with her eyes wide, her hands to her face. She was bleeding from the bridge of her nose and from her scalp, and her eyes were shining in the light. Cohen stepped backward, suddenly terrified, and Katharine was there.

He pulled the beam of the torch away from her and she

disappeared. He felt a movement near his face; he shied away. Then she was gone, and Mayaram's flashlight swiveled round and caught her back as she moved past them into the mouth of the far tunnel. She had shed her jacket. She was wearing a white T-shirt. It stuck to her. The damp air glistened on her arms.

7f
Demons (vi)

I AND I AM IN THIS PLACE. The demon stood up straight and flexed his arms. He was tired after his long run from the dead mausoleum and the crypt of bones. He had run over the hard sand, and with every step his chest had seemed to swell, his stride had lengthened, as if his muscles fed from being used, and the open spaces fed into his body after his long confinement. As if the pain of death and solitude had fed him, had liberated him, had made his legs strong so that he could run without stopping under the rising moon, and the crystal stones were glittering around him, and he was running through the black sand hills, and it was as if his arms and legs were growing as he moved, and all the powers of the world were growing, gathering strength.

He had come into the sulfur hills where the slaves lived. They were defenseless, and he could enter into their bodies and their hearts, and seize hold of their hearts. There was no ice here, no man-made ice, and when the moon rose over the hills he could still see traces of the world in its pristine beginning, when everything was right.

The slaves were defenseless, and they had opened themselves up to him, had welcomed him with love, and he had entered in and fed upon their thoughts.

A Reunion

She stepped into the mouth of the tunnel with her eyes wide
open, and even though the way divided and then divided
again, and even though it ran through chamber after chamber back into the heart of the hill, still she did not choose or
falter or hesitate. She was following a silver thread of light
that ran through the middle of the passage without touching
its sides, and it ran through the packed solid blackness without altering it, like a streak of something shining in a seam of
coal. But as she moved on, these threads of light began to
multiply and to combine into a cable that was drawing her
forward, and just the bulk and weight of it was filling the
passageway and showing its sides, and showing her the other
creatures that were moving through it toward the source and
anchor of that cable of light. They slid along the smooth red
walls, small, slow hairless beasts of many different species,
and some were tumbling over each other in their eagerness,
and some were blind, drawn forward by another phenomenon, a thread of sound that was combining like the light. Yet
it didn't seem to grow louder as she moved on toward its
source, but it acquired bulk in a different way: a voiceless
hum that seemed to occupy more and more space in her
mind even as it receded out of earshot, that expanded
through the corridors of her brain and pushed her little
thoughts aside, stampeded them and drew them forward,
and they were captive, blind.

She came around the corner and then there he was,
standing in the middle of an open chamber. He was enormous. A stone fire burned in a pit near the far wall, and the
smoke escaped through a fissure in the cavern roof that led

up to the sky. Part of the sky was visible, and the air was fresher, colder here. Water seeped down through the walls. The floor was crystal grit and coarse black sand; she noticed all these things because she was avoiding looking at his face, avoiding his fingers which seemed to gather up the strands of light between them, which seemed to gather up the strands of sound.

Others were there, many others. They squatted around him, or knelt or lay or stood, and he towered above all of them. His face seemed as big as the whole world, his lidless, burning eyes.

And she knew that she was present at a birth. One of her people knelt in front of him with a bulging chest and throat, and he had pried open its jaws, broken them, detached them at their hinge. He rubbed his hands together and the light flowed from them, and when he slipped his hands into its throat, Katharine could see them glow through the slack skin. The creature was frightened and in pain. Yet he calmed it, and sometimes he withdrew his hand to stroke its head and stroke the sweat away. Its hands were locked around his knees.

WATCH THIS; THIS IS FOR YOU, he said, his silent voice exploding in her mind. She looked at him and looked at his enormous head and his unblinking eyes, which seemed to stare directly at her, directly into the open and defenseless face of every creature there around him. And she imagined that his mind was big enough to spread his thoughts to each of them, to offer each of them a different word or phrase, to convince each one of them that he was there for them, only for them, only for their needs and no one else's. WATCH THIS NOW, he told her, and she watched. She watched his hands sink down the creature's throat, down into its chest. She watched his hands light up the inside of its distended chest, and seize hold of the fetus there and drag it out, and pull it out through that long broken throat, until the creature's bloody mouth formed an impossible exclamation, and its crushed voice box managed to cry out, to utter the small infant in its caul.

He pulled out the unformed, glowing package, and he bent down and bit the cord off with his tiny invisible sharp mouth. He held up the infant on his right hand, and with the fingers of his left hand he ripped into the leathery caul and ripped it open. The emptied parent, meanwhile, had sunk down between his feet, and it was being cared for by others, perhaps under his direction; they spoke soft words of encouragement. But he ripped back the leather caul to expose the infant's face, and it was blank, unformed until he put his hand on it, and pinched some features onto its blank skin. WATCH THIS, he said, and she saw a face appear under his hand that she almost recognized; it was her father's face. Just for a moment before he smoothed it away, but in that moment she was sure of two enormous things, and the first was that her father was dead in Shreveport, and the second was that his soul was in the demon's hands.

Yet with another part of her mind she was wondering whether every person in that red rock chamber had the same idea, whether every one of them had almost recognized the face of the new child, whether every one of them had found themselves at that moment almost convinced of the truth: that the soul lives on forever. And as if to emphasize that she was not yet and maybe never would be free of the human part of her—the part of her mind that was like a manacle of interlocking doubts, a chain that dragged behind her—those two human dogs slunk after her, as if she had dragged them after her into the chamber. The black dog and the white dog, and one was black and fierce, the other wretched and complaining.

The demon stood and stripped away the leather caul. He stroked the limbs of the newborn until it made a snuffling noise. Then he gave it into the care of another creature, a blank faceless creature who wrapped it in a piece of paisley shawl. YOU STAY WITH ME, said the demon, but his silent voice was less insistent now. He was staring at the dog men, and under his metamorphosing gaze they started to conflate, to become one dog only. It was a dangerous and dirty animal, poised on the verge of fleeing and attacking. Its head sank low, the fur rose along its back, and it was snarling and whining, treacherous and loyal, and it would kill you and then die for you.

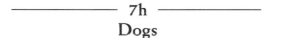

7h
Dogs

Simon stood in the rock chamber with a pistol in one hand and a flashlight in the other. He was biting his lips and moving the beam of the flashlight from face to face, figure to figure, trying to understand. But the light never seemed to illuminate enough. It was too sharp, too focused to illuminate the reasons and connections; it moved from one object to another, isolating each one. "219.291, 111.1," he said, and each digit of each number meant a feeling that was light-years away.

Martin Cohen was behind him, and with his right hand he was making patterns in the air. "It's all right, all right, all right," his fingers said. But his voice said something different: "Fuck, are you crazy? Put the gun away."

He was the crazy one. There were a dozen Aboriginals in that little space, and not one was protected by any shred of medication. One of them had already been hurt. It lay wounded at the demon's feet; the demon rose above it, free, unshackled, and gigantic, with a package in his hands. His long forehead, his enormous eyes, his cruel, sharp mouthless snout; he made some movement, some prestidigitation and the package disappeared, the natives cleared away. They pulled the wounded one away, and he was there alone, free, enormous, his bony fingers trembling in the air. He was looking at Katharine, bending his alien face to her; he was naked now. Simon let the flashlight beam move down over his ribs, his waist, and his protruding hips; he let the beam sink lower down the outside of his gigantic thigh, and then flicked it inside so that he could catch a glimpse of the long narrow penis. No wider than a finger, it hung down past his knees, and it was twitching and jiggling obscenely. Simon snatched the light away.

"Fuck, he must have run from Drywater," said Martin Cohen. "He took his sister's death and ate it. Be careful now he's strong."

The demon stepped forward and held out his hands. Simon let the light play on Katharine's face. Her eyes were almost closed. She was swaying slightly on her feet, and there was something in her face that looked like pure surrender, that looked like the moment when a virgin welcomes her first man, welcomes him in; he couldn't stand it. She stood there swaying on her feet. The demon stepped toward her. He loomed up above her with his hands held out, and they said something. Just a little movement, just a sympathetic twitch, perhaps, with his coercive mind. It was something about love.

Simon shot him in the shoulder. The gun didn't fire at first. Then it went off. It made a big noise in that enclosed space.

"Fuck you asshole," said Martin Cohen. And he said a lot more, a chattering under his breath, only Simon couldn't hear. The gunshot rang in his ears. It didn't seem to have much effect on the demon. He turned toward Simon and put his hand to his shoulder. But the Aboriginals were starting to move; they started to surge toward him, hesitant, unsure. He switched the light from face to face and held the gun out. Martin Cohen had disappeared down the tunnel. He was gone. Katharine was falling backward, as if the mental string which held her upright had suddenly snapped. He stepped forward to hold her and he dropped his flashlight. Oh, he thought. There was a small light from the oilstone fire. But it helped not to see clearly, not to see the demon's face, not to see the Aboriginals as they moved toward him; he held the gun out. Katharine subsided into his arms, but she could still walk. He pulled her back toward the tunnel mouth. And then he turned her around and slipped his arm under her armpits, across her breasts. He pushed her through the not quite completely opaque darkness with his gun held out, his back to the demon, and he could hear the Abos snuffling behind him all the way. But they didn't try anything, and by the time he got to the first chamber he was feeling less frightened. Katharine could stand up by herself. So he took the time to retrieve the water jug. It lay on its side where Martin Cohen had abandoned it.

Katharine was trembling and rocking in the middle of the floor. This first chamber was empty now. Weak moonlight filtered through the entrance. Indecipherable noises drifted through the tunnels. The important thing, thought Simon, is not to show you are afraid. The important thing is to accept what has to be. He knew the van was gone. And so he took his time. He filled the water jug at the pipe, three-quarters full. Then he carried it out into the moonlight, leading Katharine by the hand.

He could see the van's taillights a mile away, heading downhill, back toward Drywater.

Nothing stirred behind him in the tunnel.

He dragged the water jug across the open space, across the circle of tire tracks toward the road. The .22 felt heavy in his pocket. I should have kept the keys, he thought. Yet it was better to trust people; right now he felt powerful and exhilarated under the rising moon. No one was following them. He was standing with Katharine under the rising moon with the jug three-quarters full, and Drywater was less than thirty miles away.

It was cold, and there was a cold wind. He had gotten Katharine a jacket from the NLC supply room, a good, lined, heavy, hooded, canvas jacket. It was lying on the ground near where the van had been; now he retrieved it for her and helped her put it on. He zipped it up. He found her gloves in the pockets. She stood with her arms out. Shivering, she looked up at the moon. The light fell on her face.

He moved on for a while and she followed him. He stopped to listen and look back, and to let her catch up; he looked back often for the first few hundred yards and then less frequently. But when they reached the crest of the road itself he stopped again. Katharine stood beside him, and when he was reassured that no one had come after them, he reached out and touched her cheekbone. He felt a small sensation, a small comfort like a mouthful of food. A little bit of sustenance came out of her. "This is all there is," he said. "This is what makes us strong."

"This is what heals us," she said, and he felt a sudden happiness. She had heard him; she had spoken to him, and even with all the disturbances between them there was still a link that wouldn't let go, and it was stronger than the demon link, after all. Here she was. With him. Talking. That was the proof.

"Nothing else matters," he said, and she looked doubtful. He thought perhaps he'd gone too far, made too categorical a statement, not been sensitive enough to whatever she might possibly be thinking. "We'll find a way," he said, to reassure her.

"We'll find a way."

The hills were quiet. They stood in the middle of the road, looking east, down over the plain. The lights of the van were gone now. It didn't matter, at least for that moment. Simon picked up the water jug. It was too heavy, and so they drank a lot, and washed their faces and their hands. The water was astringent and harsh, cleansing, it seemed. It prickled on their skin.

He put another bullet into the chamber of the gun, and put it back into his pocket. When her hands were dry, he helped her with her gloves. Then he picked up the jug and they started walking downhill, back toward Drywater, toward Shreveport, back the way they'd come.

7i
Sex (iii)

She felt no fear. She walked beside him and said things. They came from a place outside herself and not from any process of thinking or deciding.

She said: "I feel happy," and it was so. She had a voice speaking in her mind. THIS PAIN IS NOTHING, it said. LOOK AT THE WORLD AND FIND ME IN THE WORLD.

The dark world spread away in front of her and the road ran through it. The moon was back behind her head. The past lay behind her, bloated and exhausted, for it had just given birth. This world had been pulled out of it just as the child had been torn out of its parent's throat. And maybe it was unformed and plastic like the child. Maybe it consisted of potential only, free from the past, and the cord had been cut. For one brief moment it was under her control. The pressure of necessity had not yet pushed it out of shape. The virus of other people's perception had not yet infected it with truth or lies.

Now in the cold, dark open air she could feel the thinking part of her subside. Here in the cold air with the patterned stars above her, the ratcatcher and the dragon and the crab.

As she watched, these patterns dissolved, and all the dark places in the sky were filled in with the stars she knew were there, until she could perceive above her a net without a center or circumference. A net of stars joined by fragile threads, and there was no pattern, no design, for these things were formed out of perception, out of individual creation, which had no place in this new sky. Human beings had it backward with their world of facts, their heaven of hypotheses. They were struggling and blind, and at that moment she felt an access of sympathy even for the dog man beside her. She took hold of his hand to guide him.

The soul's clarity. Its permanence. The infinite net of fragile threads that linked all creatures except humankind. Those threads that spread out from her were weak, almost impalpable, but they were gaining strength. Her body ached, but it was the pain that comes from moving muscles atrophied from long disuse, and she didn't mind it. The twin blades of human truth and human lies no longer had the strength or sharpness to cut these nets, sever these links.

She felt the people in the hills behind her. She felt the violent love that they passed to one another, that coursed through their bodies like food. A web with no center, and each knot held a stone that was clear and permanent, and each stone was equidistant from all others. It didn't matter

where you were, or if you went or stayed. Only human beings were restless. Only human beings did things, wanted
things. Changed the real world with their hands, not with
their minds. It was the mark of their incompleteness, their
isolation, their loss.

She squeezed Simon's hand, and he responded. See? she
thought. Even you can feel something. In front of them the
world was plastic, dark, unformed. Incipient in it were the
dream world, the ghost world, the world of the ominous
voice. Implied in it were the dead world, the number world,
the past world, the future world, the world of nineteen
clouds, and all the others. It was hers to make. "I feel," she
said. "I feel good," she said, and behind her head the moon
started to change color, and the long vowels in *feel* and *good*
were like long beams of light that spread over the landscape.
Silver changed to gold, and the gold light was more insistent, more penetrating, and it burnt the diamonds on the
plain with a fire that grew hotter and redder as she watched.

The dog man said something, but it made no difference.
How could it? She squeezed his hand to reassure him and to
cut him off. His words were wasted in this landscape. "How
warm it is," she said, and a hot wind blew out of the moon.

He was carrying a plastic jug on his shoulder. He said
something about the jacket, or at least he used that word. But
she turned her face to feel the warm breeze on her cheek.
"Don't look back," he said, and she heard him clearly, but she
didn't understand him.

"Don't?" she asked, trying to breathe some meaning into
him for sympathy's sake, for the sake of the warmth and
power that flowed through her from the hill and from the
moon and from everything behind her, that flowed down
each strand of the great net, and flowed through her and
blew down the road into the world.

"It's all right; don't worry," he said, and these words were like three little stones and two little chips of ice that rolled down from his lips and scattered in the mud. They had no significance in a landscape that was just coming to life. In front of her the red light flowed downhill and flowed into the desert plain, transforming all it touched. The ground softened under her feet. The cold mud softened, and the sound of her footsteps changed, descended a small scale. Above her a line of clouds unrolled from the east, a thin gauze of clouds that hid the stars but let the moonlight flow down unimpeded, and enriched, and purified, and strained.

The dog man said something about the weather, and she squeezed his hand. They were walking down the middle of the road. "Yes," she whispered, and the word slid out of her, a disk-shaped sound that spun away downhill, that curved away in an arc when the wind caught it and forced it to the ground. It hit a slope of mud and burrowed into it with a loud smack; the dog man turned his head to listen. "I. Feel. So. Happy," she said, the words spinning away downhill. "Happy," especially, with its big belly and the odd truncated tail formed by its second syllable, traveled in a long, erratic, high trajectory. When it hit the ground it cartwheeled along it, opening up a fissure in the dirt. More light seeped out of the ground. An army of creatures clambered out of the hole as if they had been waiting in the darkness for the liberating word. A flood of insects puddled out onto the ground, each with its iridescent carapace. Some of them lost their balance and they rolled and tumbled down the incline.

The dog man said something, and she squeezed his hand to spare him the futility of talking. It was difficult to look at his dark hairy cheeks, his lips pulled back into what was doubtless meant to be a soft expression. The moonlight glinted on his heavy teeth, and they were sharp and clean and white and good for one thing only, and she turned away from him and felt better. A bird flew overhead.

"Finally there's love," she said, and the land rose up to meet them. She was looking at the bird. It seemed to her an expression of love, one of a big defenseless species that had been extinct since humans came. It had a wide wingspan, and it floated slowly under the moon and moved slowly through the air as if always encountering some small resistance.

The moon had ignited a rosy color on its wings and on its belly. As the bird flew unsteadily down into the desert, this color seemed to drip from it as if it had been wounded by a shaft of moonlight and its blood was dripping down. It flew over the desert, and Katharine could see movement down there, new watercourses that had been dry in human time. There were towns of her people down on the new banks, and she could see the glimmering fires, and she was unsure whether she was looking out into the past or at the future. The gods made fire when the humans came. Because they fought the humans in the real world. Fire was an early gift, and like all gifts it was unnecessary and dangerous. Yet still she liked to see the fires spread over the plain, and she could smell the smoke as it wafted back. She unzipped her coat. The dog man was saying something about love, too, but he hadn't seen the bird. How could he have seen it? She turned to him and put her fingers to his lips to shut him up, because it was meaningless what he was saying. She made him put the jug down. He was shivering with cold. His lips were pulled back from his teeth.

She put her arms around him. Because she could not stand to look at him, she kissed him, and kissed his mouth closed. She felt that she could kiss his dangerousness away and seal it up inside him, and the more she touched him the colder and stiffer he got, while all around him the world grew warm. She could freeze him with her touch, and seal up the danger and the cold in him, and suck all the human coldness out of the world and let it flow back into him. "God," he said, "your hands are burning." She let her jacket slide off of her shoulders. They were standing on the road to Drywater, looking out over the changing landscape: the hills that rose and then subsided, the clouds that roiled above their heads. And everything that had gone wrong, the human spirit that had frozen the world and made it changeless, was passing through her body into his cold chest. "I knew it," he said. "I knew I could be sure of you," and she was passing her hands over his body and down over his pants; he was stiff there too. "It will be all right. I know it now," he said, and she reached up to seal his mouth shut so that the words stayed in his mouth. She forced the words back into his mouth and then she watched his throat knot as he swallowed them. They were like little pills that would explode in him. His medication. "God, your body's warm," he said, sucking on her fingers.

"Talk to me," he said. "What are you feeling?"

"This," she said, and she had hold of him now, and she was rubbing up against him, astonished that she had ever allowed this cold human part of him to penetrate her. Fascinated also by its shape and texture, its cold stiffness. And this stuff in him, this human grease that made his axles turn, she wanted to pull it out of him once more and make him waste it, and what began as idle fascination turned more urgent as he tried to pull away. "Oh, Katie," he said, "it's not the time. Wait for us to get home."

"Home?" They were in the land. The rocks and water. She let go of him and wiped her fingers on her shirt. Then she turned and ran down the road, letting him drag the jug behind her. She couldn't lose him. When she stopped, he was there.

He put his hand on her shoulder and she shrugged it off.

"What's wrong?" he asked. "I didn't mean . . ." He was the dog man, and the reason she had stopped was that she could see the other one come back from far away, and she could see the headlights of the white van coming up the road.

The van caught them in the light. It slowed to a stop. The Kiyungu priest was driving. He rolled down the window. "Get in," he said.

She didn't want to. But the dog man had his hand on her shoulder. He slid open the door.

"I couldn't leave you," said the priest. "I'm sorry."

She stepped into the back, and the door closed behind her. She lay down against the water jug and her damp jacket, and she closed her eyes. She heard the front door open and then shut. She heard talking. And in the same way that the two dogs had conflated under the demon's hand, now when she opened her eyes only one man was there, half white, half black, half ugly and half beautiful. Half strong and half weak. Half pimpled and half smooth. He was talking and listening, driving and resting, talking to himself: "I couldn't leave you back there even after what you did."

Silence. Then: "Let's not discuss it."

Then: "Turn around."

"No we can't."

"What do you mean? We'll drive straight through to Shreveport. Where's the radio? I'm not going on. This is absurd."

"No we can't because there're Aboriginals at Drywater like I told you. They're all over the road. The militia's come through Ludlow and they've pushed them back all through the fringes. That's my guess. I was still five miles away when I saw the fires and I had to turn around. They had motor vehicles, and the fact is they're not more than fifteen miles behind us down this road."

Silence. "That's why you came back."

A laugh. "Yes, whatever. I was right before. We'll get into Shackleton tomorrow and you'll see."

Silence. "Damn, it's cold."

"This is nothing." They were going uphill. They passed the open turnoff to the caves. Katharine stared out of the window.

The road came over a crest between the hills, and then it zigzagged down.

"How did you know it was them?"

"Who?"

"The Aboriginals. The rioters. It could be the police."

"You think I'm stupid? I could see them. They lit a fire and they had farm equipment from the Garner ranch. You know, a tractor."

"I don't know whether to believe you."

"You go fuck yourself. Believe me or not. Yes maybe I'm lying to you; I've done it before. You think this is something where you decide on a plan and it's the best plan and you do it? When has that ever happened to you, to anyone? Not this trip. That's the hallucination. No, we're just wandering around in circles lying to each other, trying to do whatever we can. Everyone knows a little part of the truth. It's always like that here. It's been like that from the beginning. Shit— what's that?"

He slowed down. Katharine was sitting against the sled. It was a peculiar sensation watching him drive. He was peering out toward an obstruction in the road. She could see the nub of his small ponytail against his white neck, and at the same time his dark face was looking back at her. He reached back toward her, pointing with his forefinger, smiling and frowning, but she didn't respond. There was something in her mind. It was like a little song:

BREAK HIM
SMASH HIM
WITH A ROCK OR
ELSE THAT PIPE

He turned back toward the windscreen. Katharine looked for the toolbox. It was open, but the hammer was gone.

"There's a stone in the road," he said.

The grade had leveled off again for thirty feet or so, and there was an open space on the right side of the road below a small embankment. Naked people clustered there, and one was carrying a length of pipe.

There was a boulder in the middle of the road, and Katharine could see that there might be just enough space on the left side to skirt around it. The van slowed down. "Be careful," said the man, and the car tilted down the left embankment as he drove around the stone.

Then the Aboriginals were throwing rocks, and the rocks were smashing against the side of the van. One window cracked, but the glass held. Then someone with the pipe was standing in the road, and he smashed out one of the headlights as the van lurched forward, speeded up. There was a concussion off the right fender and a yelp of pain. They were through, and they sped forward as more stones clamored on the roof. "My God," said the man.

BREAK HIM BREAK HIM, but there was no rock or pipe. She fumbled in the tire well. Her fingers closed around the shank of a screwdriver.

"You'd better go back," he said. He had his gun out and was rolling down the window.

But he was driving fast. "You are such an asshole. Man, I should have left you there. Because I swear to you that this is serious shit. These demons, you don't know. You don't know anything; you're not from here. You know it ran from Drywater and it's got its people now. McElroy said it feeds on pain. It was barely grown and then its sister died. Now it runs thirty miles like nothing. I unlocked its legs. Run—it could barely walk, I swear to you. What do you think it will do now? You shot it. Look."

Once again he slowed down. Katharine, sitting up, could see what he was seeing in the light of the single headlamp: a line of footprints in the mud, just the toes as they came down, the marks ten feet apart.

She was holding on to the screwdriver. But the man was staring back at her with the gun in his hand. His eyes were round with fright. And there was something else in them that she had come to recognize: a doglike stubbornness.

7j
On the Black Ice

They drove on into the darkness. Again the road climbed upward, but it had straightened out onto a long, slow grade that would take them up onto the shield. On either side the mud rocks spread away.

After a few miles Martin Cohen stopped the van in the middle of the road. He set the parking brake and turned off the ignition. He took his flashlight and got out of the van to check for damage. He checked the fender but there was no mark. He looked at the footprints on the road in front of them. He knocked on the side door and slid it open.

"Let's rest here one last time," he said. "Higher up it might be too cold to turn the engine off."

He pulled out one of the five-gallon gas cans and started to fill up the tank. "Let's get something to eat," he said.

He looked up at the moon. Clouds twisted around it. Where they were, a warm breeze would come up for several minutes and then subside, or be replaced by a freezing one. It was a mix of temperatures common in these longitudes, at these altitudes. In time they would move up into clearer, quieter air. Though even on the ice pack they could expect to be buffeted sometimes by warm dangerous winds.

"We should be able to drive the whole way," he said. "Harriet had an idea that we would fight in Drywater and then retreat along this road. She thought we could capture the radio at Shackleton; that's why she put in these studded wheels and all the cold-weather supplies."

Mayaram had opened his door, but he still sat looking back at the girl. Her head had lolled back to the side; she was asleep or semiconscious or pretending. "I'm so tired," she said.

"Yes, you didn't sleep before. It's all right. We'll drive on ten miles or so and then we will be safe. There's a place where we can stretch out the bivouac bags and I can make some food."

He closed the doors and got back in. He drove slowly, looking for the demon up ahead. Eighteen miles farther he turned off the road. There was a level space, a flat sheet of rock.

He cooked some noodles Romanoff on the butane stove, and they stayed for about five hours. This was longer than he wanted, and he sat worried and irritated, smoking cigarettes in the front seat of the van while the others slept. In his lap he carried the windbreaker with the .22 in its pocket, even though he'd never fired a gun. He sat listening to the radio until he started worrying about the batteries. He listened to the weather report from Shackleton Station.

Mayaram had done nothing to help. He had sat with the girl's head across his lap, and he'd eaten two helpings of noodles. He had tried to feed her some, but she had refused it. When he had insisted, she had thrown it up. Later he had put out an air mattress and then climbed with her into a single bivouac bag.

Cohen thought maybe he should have loaded them in the back and kept on driving, but he wasn't sure. Just the idea of their touching embarrassed him, and he didn't want to disturb them or break in on them or look at them. And yet they shouldn't stay this long. He wasn't sure what was behind them. Soldiers were in Ludlow—he had heard the news brief. But they had not penetrated over the line.

He had no wish to meet the demon on the road.

He got out of the car and stood on the other side from where they lay. He could see a long way back. There were no lights.

He walked a half mile back, and then a quarter mile forward from the van, carrying the windbreaker like a bag. With his knees cracking, he squatted down to examine the road. Gradually as they climbed higher the mud and sand was giving out, replaced by shattered rock. But still occasionally there would be a stretch of softer ground that still could take the imprint of a foot.

Early pioneers had described demons running long distances at speeds approaching twenty-five miles an hour. They had hunted them from helicopters. At first they had let them go when they crossed over the line, but once the link was broken they had hunted them with searchlights up into the ice. Their blood beat so fast, the cold didn't bother them.

Martin Cohen rocked back on his heels. He smoked his unfiltered cigarette down to the stub, and then he dropped it down beside the three-toed mark. Ah God, he thought: a human love of darkness.

He started to undo the rubber band at the nape of his

neck, for it was pulling on his hair. But then there was a scream behind him and a voice crying out. He stood up fumbling for the gun; he ran back with the gun in his hand. The bivouac bag was full of motion, but then Mayaram's head appeared from it. His arm came out. He had something in his hand, a short piece of metal which he flung away into the dark.

Then the bag was still and Mayaram climbed out. The girl lay inert. He stood above her clutching his right shoulder. "She stabbed me," he said. "With a screwdriver. I was asleep."

"I told you."

They just stood there looking down. Cohen had the gun out, but then he put it away. "I was sleeping," said Mayaram, prodding at his shoulder, "I can't believe it."

His face was full of shock. Hers, by contrast, was completely empty. The edge of the sleeping bag had fallen from her face, and she stared up at the sky through empty eyes.

"Man, I told you. What did you expect?"

Mayaram did not reply. He stood nursing his shoulder, but he was all right; his shirt was barely ripped. "Now that you're up," said Cohen, "maybe we should get moving."

The clouds twisted around the moon. "Maybe we should keep her in the bag," he said.

Mayaram didn't reply. Martin Cohen lit a cigarette. "Here," he said, and slid open the door. He fished out his pocket knife. Holding the cigarette between his teeth, winking at the smoke, he cut a three-foot length of rope from the spool in back of the passenger's seat.

"It's to restrain her," he said. "So she doesn't hurt herself." He threw away the cigarette half smoked. Then he knelt down and unzipped the bag, and felt the warmth escape. Katharine Styreme lay inert, and it was easy enough to tie her hands together at the wrist. He pulled up the cuffs of her sweatshirt to make sure the rope wouldn't chafe against her skin.

Mayaram was useless. "She loves me," he said.

"Sure."

Martin Cohen zipped the bag closed, and together they lifted her up into the van. "You sit back with her," he said. He slid the door shut and climbed over to the driver's seat.

They started forward. "No, she said so."

"You are such a jerk." He peered out in front. The road ran straight uphill. Even with one headlamp it would be all right.

But in a while he started talking just to calm himself. "It thinks we're following it. That's our problem. It thinks we're hunting it."

"I should have killed it."

"Yes maybe. Maybe kill everything. What the hell."

And a little while later: "But I guess that's what we do. We kill gods. We hunt them down and kill them. Like we hunted down Jesus Christ and Geoffrey Kiyungu."

"They're not gods," said Mayaram.

"No? You think a human being could run this far?"

"No. She called it a devil once."

"Yes, maybe so. But maybe if they're devils who could tell the difference if there's only one kind and it's real? Maybe they're what passes for gods in this sorry place. Because they feed on themselves, because they eat their own suffering and ours, and it makes them strong. Jesus Christ was nothing till we tortured him to death."

From time to time he looked into the rearview mirror. Mayaram was sitting on the sledge with his hand on the girl's forehead.

"It was hurting them," he said. "Didn't you see? It was

controlling them with pain. I don't know what we interrupted, but it wasn't pleasant. The pioneers were right. We
were a liberation for these people."

"It was a birth," said Martin Cohen. He flicked the high
beam off and on.

Small cliffs lined the road for a few hundred yards. Then
they gave out, and the dreary rock flats stretched away. He
glanced back at the girl through the rearview mirror. "Of
course she was artificially inseminated. Born in Mercy Hospital and then aged in an incubator. I remember the an-
nouncement."

They drove on for hours. The van labored uphill, a long,
slow climb. After a while Cohen turned on the heat.

"You know what this is about?" he said. "People like to
run it to the edge. People like to see how far they can go. It's
getting cold now. Did you ever try to kill yourself?"

Quiet for a long time. "No."

"Then you don't know what I'm talking about."

Quiet. "I came here."

"Yes then you do know."

In time there were more cliffs as they came up into the
mountains. The road had been blasted and hacked out of the
rock, and they slowed down.

"I apologize," said Martin Cohen. "I needed to prove you
needed me. That you could trust me to help you out.

"That you could depend on me," he said.

"That I could be of use to you," he amended, finally.

Quiet. And they crept on mile after mile. They left the
straight grade behind and started a series of long switch-
backs. The land disappeared off to the east side of the road,
and on the other side a copper-colored cliff loomed above
them. Martin Cohen drove slowly, looking for ice, but the
roadbed was made of cinders and crushed rocks. Aboriginals

had crushed them, hammered them to pieces for their demon masters in the old days.

But in some places there were snowdrifts, and it cheered Cohen to see that the road had been plowed. Most supplies came to Shackleton by air, but the staff kept the road clean for emergencies. The metal guardrails looked new.

They crossed over a series of ice ravines. The ancient masonry had been reinforced, and in some places it had been replaced by steel suspension bridges alongside the old stone spans.

Everything was carefully maintained. Cohen was relieved, but in a small way he was regretful also that the journey was to be so easy, that they would be able to drive straight through to the station, that there would be no need for his ingenuity and courage. He wanted to be of service to undeserving fools; he wanted to risk his life. He had pictures in his mind of landslides and avalanches and blizzards.

So it was almost a relief to come out onto the ice and find it hazardous and terrifying. A chain-link suspension bridge stretched over a black abyss, and then they were on the shield. The ice was broken and unsure for many miles at the edge; they drove along a roadway made of metal plates which rang under the studded wheels.

After turning through the mountains they went straight now, intermittently suspended above frozen waterfalls, black narrow chasms, and outcroppings of rock. Pinnacles of rock loomed to the west. But in time the feeble headlight no longer touched anything but ice. It was yellow and rotten, and in many places it had fallen away from underneath the metal road.

They drove past steel pilings that sunk down out of sight. The car was buffeted by sudden currents of wind. And they could hear the icefall: groans and distant crashes, be-

cause the glacier was always moving here, always spreading
and grinding and contracting. Sometimes the roadway lay
over the ice itself, but more often a dozen or so feet above it.
Then, blurred by the small distance and the insufficient
light, it seemed a stretch of angry water, yellow waves that
had slowed and hardened, changed in time but not in sub-
stance. The wind picked up noises off the ice that seemed
slow versions of ocean noises, ocean rhythms. And because
time seemed slow and the ridged, steel-plated roadway
seemed to run forever, the ocean's terrible relentlessness
seemed augmented here, in the same way that the movement
of a machine seems more relentless and unstoppable the
slower it grinds. It was as if the world were hardening and
the machine ran always slower as the ice hardened beneath
them, and all sense of randomness in the wind or the strange
crashes gradually decreased, and all the noises also became
part of a slow pattern. The ringing whir of the wheel studs
on the metal plates decreased also as the van slowed, and the
pattern of noise as the studs passed over the flexible joints
between the plates became more distinct.

The ice was hardening underneath them. It was changing color, too. The edge of the shield was always mixing
with a rubble of moraine and rock debris, and the ice was a
dirty froth. They passed over dirty stripes of white and yellow and gray and brown, and after thirty miles or so they too
seemed to be part of a pattern that was slowly darkening as
the ice hardened and purified and grew deeper, as the land
fell away underneath it. By the time they saw the lights of
Shackleton Station, high on Mount Erebus, twenty miles
away, the black ice had come up to meet them and the roadway ran on top of it, anchored now by massive rivets in the
surface of the shield.

"Look," said Martin Cohen.

The moon was low behind them now. The stars shone bright and ominous out of the side window. The ice, perfectly flat now, stretched away on all sides.

In front of them the roadway had been broken.

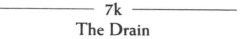

7k

The Drain

Simon was with Katharine in the back of the van, and from time to time he would rub the sweat out of her eyes. From time to time he would check the rope around her wrists to see if it was hurting her. She lay asleep, her eyes half closed.

Part of him was there with her. Another part was in the upstairs room in Goldstone Lodge. He saw Natasha Goldstone, naked from the waist down, standing by the window. When the door opened she turned, her face contorted—no. The van stopped, and Katharine lay under his hand. He couldn't look at her. He left her in the bag and climbed into the front seat.

There was a break in the roadway up ahead. The joints were broken, the rivets had been torn out. A gap of seventy feet or so had opened up between the plates; one had flipped back on itself. One had slid off to the left, all its anchors broken except one. The bare ice was uncovered. There was no mark on it, no path.

Cohen turned the headlight off but left the engine running. To the right of them rose up a mountain, its simple contour black against a red and purple sky. In front of them over the bulge of the ice, the colors were even more intense: a shifting curtain of magenta streaked with gold.

"Wow," said Cohen over the heater's roar. He took a cigarette out of his pocket, but he didn't light it. "Wait till we get up over that bulge and you can really see the drain."

"You've been here?"

"No."

There was a communications beacon on the mountaintop, a needle of red dots which lit up intermittently. Other lights, too. "Shackleton Station," said Cohen, smelling his unlit cigarette. As they watched, a helicopter swung around the mountain from the other side. A yellow searchlight poked down from its belly. It sank lower and then disappeared.

Cohen switched the headlight on again. The radio was in the glove compartment. He reached for it. He turned it on and left it grumbling with the volume down; there wasn't anything but static.

"Well," he said, "we'd better go and take a look. Put on the suit though. The X-rays should be terrible about now."

Simon climbed back again and fished out the survival gear. "This must be yours," he said, unwrapping a green suit with a white cross stitched onto its breast.

Cohen laughed. "No, it's the hospital corps. I've got mine here."

It was difficult to put them on in that cramped space. Once zipped up, they looked like lizards or insects or scuba divers. The orange masks were especially ridiculous and claustrophobic, with their breathing grills and plastic screens. Looking at Cohen, Simon felt absurd, in costume for a play. He pulled the windbreaker on over his suit to break up the effect.

They slipped out of the van as quickly as they could, opening the doors as gingerly as if they had been air locks. And it was cold outside, below zero Fahrenheit, perhaps. Certainly their breath made a thick smoke. Thick smoke poured out of the tailpipe of the van.

Cohen stepped out onto the ice, and Simon followed him. Their boots were studded like the wheels. Simon was surprised to feel so secure. The ice was soft. The boots dug in without effort.

He had a flashlight, but he didn't need it. In a little while he slipped it into the pocket of his jacket with the tinsnips and the gun. The ice was pure and black except for a stripe of yellow perhaps two-thirds of the way across the break in the road. It was a crack as thin as a hair, yet moisture bled from it. A rivulet of moisture ran down from it and then quickly disappeared, leaving a pattern of small ridges on the ice.

Nearby, Cohen knelt down to run his gloved forefinger over a three-toed mark. Then he stood up and stamped his foot over the crack. "This is all right," he said, his voice blurred by the grill.

Simon was looking toward the west. There was a fire in the sky, and golden flames of light reached for the zenith. Or it was as if the black sky were a curtain that had been torn apart, burned apart to reveal a universe of light. "We can walk from here."

"No chance. Not with her."

Simon was standing with his hands in his windbreaker pockets, looking at the light. His fingers closed around the muzzle of the .22, and it felt cold even through his glove. He heard the car door close behind him.

And then he turned around. The windscreen was steamed up, but it was clear enough for him to see Cohen stripping off his mask. To see him rolling down the window. "Tell me if you see a problem," he called out, and then he drove onto the ice, and he drove slowly forward. Simon walked beside the sliding door.

Then there was a crash, and the ice started to give. The van sank to its hubcaps on the driver's side. But Cohen didn't get out of the car. He gunned the engine, spun the wheels, and then all around them was a popping sound as the ice

broke. Simon yanked open the door and pulled out the bivouac bag with Katharine inside it. He slid it out along the
ice, which was sagging down all around them, which was
sinking down into a bowl with the van at the bottom; he
climbed up the side. It was still shallow, and he made progress up the grade, dragging the bag behind him as the van
settled down. Then there was an enormous crack like an explosion, and when he looked back the van had sunk down
farther still.

They were on the edge of the bowl. He dragged the bag
up over the black ice, where it had broken and split down.
Katharine was struggling inside the bag; he pulled it up onto
the unblemished ice before he turned around.

The end of the roadway sagged down over the edge of
the empty bowl for a few feet. He left Katharine in the bivouac bag, and ran back toward it and climbed out on it.
"Cohen," he said. The ice was white now where it had broken into polygons, and water or some other fluid seeped up
through the crack in the bottom where the van had sunk. He
could see a corner of its roof, part of its rear window as it
pointed down, part of its tailpipe belching mist until the engine stopped.

Katharine had gotten out of the bag. She stood on the
ice in just her sneakers and her sweatshirt and her jeans, and
behind her the sky had cracked apart. Angry coronas of red
light spread from the horizon, and she stood holding up her
wrists tied together and turned her face into the light. It
shone from her cheeks and her bare scalp.

"Oh, my God," he said. When he came running toward
her over the ice she turned away from him and fled away
over the bulge. He stooped to grab up the bivouac bag and
then he was after her, but she ran fast.

With every step they took the horizon grew brighter.

Perhaps clouds had obscured the magnitude of the view, and now they were drifting away. Even in the midst of this crisis that might kill him, that might kill her, he thought about it. He knew what he was looking at. It was not just light to him. He understood that he was looking down into the galaxy's fiery heart, into the destruction which circled round the drain, into the black hole at its center. The mind is treacherous, he thought even then. It cannot be contained.

As she climbed up the bulge, more and more came visible beyond her: the collision of whole stars. Fragments of stars, their centers leaking out a million miles behind them in long, blinding arcs. Flashes of intolerable brightness. The wreck of the universe behind her head; she turned her face back toward him over her shoulder as she ran, and there was such hate in her eyes, and such hate leaking from her mouth that he stopped. He thought: I'll never reach her. He thought: She is separate from me. He thought: I am alone. I will be alone.

Then the demon was there standing above her, farther up. Homo Celestis, appearing as if out of the sky, and he hadn't seen it come. Its hands were held out in a paradigm that Simon recognized: its forefinger held out, its seventh finger bent, its palm making an S-shaped curve and then repeating it, repeating it: KILL HIM KILL HIM.

71

Katharine (vii)

She turned back and the dog man was following her in his green suit, his orange helmet, and through the faceplate she could see his hairy snout. She stood on the ice with the storm crashing around her. Rain was falling, a steady rain

made not of water but of tiny particles that drummed against
her skin and fell into her mouth. The wind made patterns in
the rain. It made a whirlwind around her and snatched away
her words when she cried out. Flashes of lightning burst
against the faceplate of the dog man's helmet and illuminated his predatory teeth, his implacable eyes. She held
out her hands, joined together at the wrist, and she pointed
her hands back toward him. The storm and the wind and the
rain were passing though her from a place outside herself;
they swirled around him and confused him. She turned into
the lightning as it crashed across the sky, as it ignited purple
fires in the clouds, and she saw the creature on the black ice
above her—the animal, the demon, the changing devil, big
as the whole world with the storm behind him. He stood up
straight and naked and enormous, his clawed feet, his high
legs like pillars, his thin waist, his gigantic chest still laboring
from the long run, his pulse fluttering in his neck and throat.
His high head and his long skull. His changing face. His
hands held out, his fingers making patterns and repeating
them, and molding the storm so that it flowed through his
hands and into her and out of her again. She felt the pattern
of his hands growing inside of her and opening her up, as if
his hands themselves were pulling something out of her, giving something life. She felt him pull something out of her
and give it shape and strength, so that she could turn back to
confront the dog man. It was an anger. The demon gave it
birth and gave it shape. But it came out of her and it was hers
alone, a rage that flowed out through her joined hands, that
hit the dog man in the middle of the white cross on his chest,
that exploded against him and made him hesitate and stop.

The rage was new, plastic and new, and she felt her
mouth stretch wide to give utterance to it—a prolific thing
out of her sterile body. The dog man stood confused and

helpless, and she came down the ice slope toward him. Through the faceplate she could see his feral eyes. She could see he was afraid, afraid of this new thing that had come out of her. He hesitated, took a step backward, and then she was on him, battering his head with her hands tied together, kicking him as he stumbled and went down. He curled up and lay still.

She stood above him, waiting for him to move, but he did not. Then she turned her back to him and then the rage was gone. It disappeared into the whirlwind, leaving her empty and weak-kneed. She squatted down and bowed her head. In her mind the demon was speaking to her but she could not hear. The wind roared around her and buffeted her face, and the spray drenched her and stung her skin and stung her eyes. She closed her eyes. Now the particles were streaming through her body without touching her, and the storm softened and grew less. The wind died. The roaring in her ears and in her head died away, and once again the world was under her and in her hands. But because she had been purged, because she had been emptied, now she was ready to begin. She was ready to let the world fill her and transform her, so that she could make it into a new place for her unburdened self. A new world in which all these people and these things behind her would be dreams, objects in dreams, memories of nightmares.

She opened her eyes, held up her hands. Between her outstretched fingers she could see the creature on the ice above her summon his breath, inflate, and then his hot breath spewed over the ice. He was changing and she made him change. His body was changing as she watched, and as she moved her hands she slipped through all the different worlds with him. In each one he was a different part of her: the demon on the black hill, and he was gone. Her father standing at his desk in Shreveport in the dark, the light from the computer screen reflected in his glasses—he was gone. Jonathan Goldstone in the kitchen with his probing fingers—he was gone. Saint Teresa in the picture book at Ursuline, the corona flashing round her head, and she was gone. Katharine closed her eyes and opened them, and she was in the dream world and the ghost world and the dead world, and in every world the creature was there with her in a different shape. He was the basilisk, the beast that lives inside the mind and eats thoughts like food, and leaves a track of deadness in the tunnels of the brain. He was the word made flesh, and it was her word that made him. He was her thing and her creation. In the storm of abstracts he was the flat light that she shed upon the ground. In the sea of numbers he was her island of the one. She closed her eyes and the ice stretched away, and it was water, a hot sea of shallow water, and in the middle of it a stone pillar rising up, broken at its top. Birds nested there, sweet birds with long white wings, and they dove down into the spray, and one of them, the largest and the queen of all, flew up into a sky that became bluer as she rose, ever more blue as she spread her wings, and her white belly was defenseless, and the shot crashed out.

The dog man was crouching with a gun clutched in his hand. The bird pitched down into the sea. Three shots blew dust off the stone pillar, and she could see the three marks in a row. She opened her eyes and the demon was there, his hands pressed to his chest. And the storm was gone, and the wind didn't rush through her, didn't roar in her ears, and she could hear him in her mind, living in her mind, the wounded basilisk in pain, vomiting up her thoughts: KILL HIM KILL HIM.

She turned downhill. The dog man came toward her and she hit him again with her hands joined together, her fingers clasped. She hit him on his plastic suit and on his helmet. But this time it made no difference. Now he was invincible, so she turned away and ran back up the ice, stumbling, closing her eyes. There were still words in her mind, but she couldn't hear them until she bent down, bowed her head, and turned back inward to that place where the gift and the giver become one, where the maker and the object and the user become one, where the beast on the ice slope and its worshiper are joined, where each gives expression to the other. Turning inward, she felt him in her body, his voice soft and wounded, hard to make out until she moved into the world of symbols and beyond it to the border of the world of death itself. A flat wall to the horizon. A line of letters painted on it. And she stumbled down along the wall with her hand skimming the white surface: I IN MY COLD SPACE I AM ALONE AND I AM FINISHED HERE BUT THERE ARE WORLDS AND WORLDS AND WORLDS WHERE I WILL NEVER STOP BECAUSE I AM THE STICK THAT BEATS THE CLOUDS THE CLAPPER OF THE BELL THE PART OF YOU THAT'S FREE FOREVER.

The last words were faded, indistinct. There was a hole in the wall and she slipped through. She turned around, but she had lost her way. She was in the real world once again, where it made no difference who she was. Stars flickered on the desolate horizon, a cascade of light. It was the drain, and she had learned about it in tenth grade. Above her on the slope, crumpled in a pile of limbs, a dying Coelian. His dark blood on the ice. She had lost her coat and she was very, very cold.

VIII

⊠

Shackleton Station

They stood on the outside of the glass, looking in. She lay in a white bed in a white cubicle. The IV bottle hung above her pillow, and she was curled up on her side, almost asleep. Her hands were clasped under her cheek, and Simon could see the marks on her wrist where the rope had cut her.

Dr. LaTanya Watanab stood next to him. She was the director of the station. Dark and tall, she had been fifty when she left home.

"I'm sorry for your friend," she said. "We recovered the vehicle, but there was nothing we could do to save him."

Simon did not reply. He had come on crutches from his own bed just to look in through the glass.

"There was still Mellarin in her system," said Dr. Watanab. "Though we made adjustments, it is always easier when there's something to build on."

She was from Seattle, so they used English with each other. It was a language she spoke well, but with a small vocabulary and a clipped, peculiar accent: "She will be fine."

Simon had his hand against the glass, and she touched his wrist. He turned toward her and she smiled. "It will be fine," she said again. "But we had to rebuild everything. Her hair will have to wait."

He nodded and she touched his hand again. "I wanted to show you personally," she said, "because I must tell you how impressed I was when I heard about what you'd done. I'd never heard of that kind of heroism and selflessness. The road crew told me when they found you that you had taken off your own protection suit to give to her."

Awkward, he shrugged. The glass was double-paned. Katharine's face was small and gray.

"We lost everything when the car went down," he said, as if to explain. "Just the bag, and I wrapped it around my shoulders."

"Well, she's a lucky woman, and you saved her life. At considerable risk, I must explain to you. You had a long exposure. You would have done better to keep the suit and wrap her in the bag. She's better equipped to tolerate the ultraviolet. We're right on the edge of the irradiation zone. The hole in the layer can facilitate our observations, but it makes it fierce outside."

"I wasn't thinking."

"No. I only wanted to say that your devotion gave me hope. Especially considering what she is. For almost the first time since I've been here, it has given me some hope."

He had a hope of his own that she might be quiet soon. For an instant he thought that he might put his finger to her mouth, put his bandaged finger in her mouth itself, to stop what she was going to say. She said: "It's a new hope we can work together, every one of us. This last week has been discouraging. I mean, even though the loss of life was minimal, even after I heard the soldiers were finding no resistance in the Ludlow area, I was discouraged. I thought only the fact that it could happen at all shows a lack of understanding and cooperation, now after so long. So when I heard the two of you together had killed the creature that started all this, it was a relief to me. And that you had risked your life to save her. It was important to all of us, but especially to me."

There were no windows in the station, and the white corridors curved away on either side. They were lit with long fluorescent bulbs.

"We love each other," he said. He shifted the crutches underneath his armpits and looked down at his foot.

"Yes, I know. I'm saying it's beautiful and joyful. And so rare. You always hear what beasts men are, you know. That's what you learn. It's nice to see it's not true. It only makes me wish I'd met someone like you twenty years ago. Ms. Styreme is a lucky woman. No, please, I am embarrassing you."

She was handsome and gray-haired, and she smiled at him. On the other side of the glass, Katharine was lying curled up among the pillows of her white bed. Her eyes were almost closed